LAST
LIAR
STANDING

A NOVEL

DANIELLE M. WONG

Last Liar Standing
Red Adept Publishing, LLC
104 Bugenfield Court
Garner, NC 27529
https://RedAdeptPublishing.com/

---

1. http://StreetlightGraphics.com

For Brian—forever missed, forever loved

PROLOGUE

The average person has thirteen secrets right now. That's all I can think about as I step through the double doors of this run-down motel. Its lobby looks like something straight out of the 1960s, with faux-wood paneling and marmalade-orange armchairs. I clutch my bag tightly and cringe at the peeling shreds of outmoded wallpaper.

There is a uniformed woman crammed behind a cluttered desk—some sort of makeshift reception counter. She morphs her glossy red lips into a strained smile and flashes it in my direction, but the only thing I can focus on is her exhausted expression. She resumes sorting through a mess of documents before I attempt a weak grin in return.

A quick scan of the remaining area tells me that I am not alone. My shoulders creep up as I count the guests inside. Not just a few either. *Ten* others wait to check in. *Why is it so crowded?* My entrance garners more than a couple curious glances, and I immediately glue my eyes to the tiled floor.

Of the odd assortment of guests, many are seated in pleather swivel chairs scattered across the room. A fortysomething woman in a blue dress perches on the sole sofa as a conspicuously older gentleman snoozes beside her. *Are they together?* Sinking into the puffy upholstered fabric is tempting after the long drive here, but I decide to stand in line regardless.

I take my place behind a petite woman with two enormous Louis Vuitton suitcases. *She could probably fit inside her own luggage.* She

1

smacks her gum over the elevator music humming in the background. I stifle an eye roll and silently hope that the line starts moving soon.

When it finally does, the woman struggles with the handle of her larger bag. *It's jammed.* Just as I think about offering assistance, a middle-aged man in khaki pants and loafers jumps up to help. She thanks him in a chirpy voice and continues moving. He looks her up and down, adjusting the groin area of his Dockers before finally breaking a creepy stare. I don't even bother to suppress my eye roll this time.

Across the lobby, a young couple argues. Though their words are inaudible, their body language is unmistakable. It sends chills down my spine. He grabs her wrist, his knuckles turning bone white before she pries her arm from his grasp and whispers something in a hushed tone. I look away and try desperately to shake off the thought threatening to detonate my composure. When I glance back toward them, the woman is turned away, facing the window. Her skin glistens with tears and snot in the murky reflection.

Bark cloth curtains frame another window on the left side of the room. It was still dark outside when I parked, but a vivid sunrise is rapidly illuminating the sky. A flurry of color floods the horizon—wicked splashes of orange, yellow, and rose. I watch briefly before turning my attention back to the line in front of me. My heartbeat quickens when I realize that I am still at the end of it. *This is taking too long.*

I practice slow inhalations like Dr. Flynn taught me, but this place reeks of cigarette smoke. I inevitably fixate on an incessant clicking sound and find myself scouring the room for its source. My shoulders drop when I identify the noise—a teenager tapping his thumbs rhythmically against a bright phone screen. I wonder if he is composing a text message or playing a game. *Maybe he's stalking an ex on social media.*

We accidentally lock eyes, and I immediately look away. Letting my gaze linger for more than a moment feels too risky. I can't afford to be seen here, let alone recognized. I fish a pair of jet-black aviators out of my purse then throw them on like a mask.

The average person has thirteen secrets right now. This is what I think about while my anxious stare lands on the far wall. Aged photographs hang in mahogany frames, and a faded travel poster reads, "How to stay safe on your vacation!"

"Safe" is such a relative term. I have not felt safe in as long as I can remember. When someone else enters the lobby, my paranoia instantly swells. I try—and fail—to steady each breath. As I fidget with my car keys, I wonder if any of the other guests are harboring secrets as dark as mine. *Are they on the run too?* I wonder if they can see the fear leaching through my skin. *Do my shaky hands give me away?* Most of all, I wonder if anyone in this motel knows what I've done.

CHAPTER 1

The worst thing about paranoia is its relentless amplification. It gradually takes on a monstrous life of its own until the fear consumes every thought—dictates every action. Some might call it an obsession, but I detest the connotations of that word. This is no impassioned fixation or compulsion. The chaos in my head stems from veritable trauma.

This paranoia has become my own personal demon. It's the reason my heart has not stopped racing since I left home. It's the reason that I keep glancing over my shoulder as I check in to another no-name motel in this tiny Nevada town—about an hour south of the bustling boulevard known as the Strip. As the young front desk clerk bends down to fetch a pair of keys, I realize that we are finally the only two people left standing in this tiny lobby. No one else is here, and this is exactly what I need right now—to be off the grid.

To say that I feel exhausted would be the understatement of my hellish year. I have been driving for hours without so much as a quick bathroom break at some sketchy gas station. My T-shirt is stained with layers of sweat and smells vaguely of Swiss cheese. Once I pry open the door to my room, I spot a large spider crawling across the wall inside. Though I would normally bristle, I drop my bags and look the other way. I need a hot shower. And rest.

Physical discomfort has become my new normal. Even after a rinse in the disappointing stream of lukewarm water and a clean change of clothes, my skin crawls with inerasable remnants. Memories that cannot be washed off.

4

I lie in bed and try to recall what it feels like to crave sleep—to actually look forward to it instead of dreading it with every fiber of my being. It's nearly impossible to settle on a position. Comfort is out of the question, but I would give just about anything for a semblance of relief. I writhe around on the motel bed to no avail. Part of me wants to blame it on this cheap mattress, but the other part knows better.

I never exactly got a formal diagnosis. Understandably so, the doctor was hesitant to prescribe me too many medications during our initial appointment. I stole a glance at her pad as she stood up to get me a glass of water. *Insomniac, anxiety-prone, clinically depressed...* The list went on. I tried to do things above board, but it was far easier just to procure the pills myself.

I resisted taking them at first. I really did. The prospect of forming a dependency, of taking the wrong dosage paralyzed me. I had already witnessed the horrendous side effects of pill popping firsthand—friends falling prey to the addictive cycle, patients losing touch with the physical world. *Will I reduce myself to a cautionary tale?*

I decided it was best to refrain for the indefinite future. Until one vicious, gut-wrenching night. The kind that comes out of nowhere and shakes you to the core. It felt like my heart—beating and bloody—was being ripped straight from my chest. I could barely breathe or whisper. Air was inaccessible, and every word was locked inside my shivering chest.

I feel that familiar sense of unease tonight. It starts as a tiny bud, a mere inkling. But it will soon bloom into something bigger. A force that I won't be able to face alone. I sit up and fish anxiously through my cluttered bag until I find an orange plastic bottle. Seconds later, I dry swallow three pills and settle back into bed. But before I fall into an inevitable slumber, I swear I can hear people whispering on the other side of the door.

I AM ALREADY REVIEWING a mental list before my room comes back into focus the next morning. Just because I'm in a chemically induced haze doesn't mean I have forgotten why I came here. At this point, the plan is ingrained in my brain. All week, I have rehearsed like an actor memorizing lines. I can't afford to mess anything up.

As I strip off my night clothes, I catch an unwanted glimpse of myself in the bathroom mirror. Fortunately, my diverted glance garners little more than a pale spark of flesh and violet veins. I feel thick stubble in the hollow of armpits and realize it has been far too long since my last shave. *A razor*—I should add that to the list.

After tossing my cell phone on the sink's edge, I hop into the shower. The warm rush of water feels foreign at first. Other than the quick rinse last night, this is my first proper wash in four days. Such a bold transgression would have been unthinkable in my past life. Lately, though, personal hygiene has been the last thing on my frantic mind.

I twist open a plastic bottle of motel shampoo and glob it into my unruly mess of dark hair. The formula smells sickly sweet, like one of those cluttered perfume shops in the corner of a crowded mall. Those stores used to give me headaches—nasty ones that would linger for hours. I loathed the perky salespeople who would spritz customers with their best-selling scents without permission.

The water pressure is much stronger this time—a welcome change from the tepid trickle I encountered last night. I scrub every inch of skin until it turns raw. Then I let the hot water run over my shoulders, begging it to undo the knots burrowing in my neck. It fails to do the job.

I step out of the tub and pad across the strategically placed hand towel I MacGyvered into a bath mat. Leaving damp footprints in my wake, I bend over and start to towel dry my sopping strands. While

I'm distracted by several split ends, a surge of blood rushes to my brain.

A sudden tinny noise makes me whip around. My breathing quickens, though I feel utterly stupid when I realize what the sound is. My phone, vibrating against the ceramic sink. I give the text a read until it sends shivers down my spine, then I chuck my cell onto the bed.

This constant jumpiness started recently. Growing up, I was always the calm one in my shifting group of friends. My college roommates used to see it as a challenge. They would take turns trying to scare me shitless—jumping out from dark corners and grabbing my shoulders or slapping me on the back before I swallowed my food.

A subtle smile spreads across my lips, half cynical, half somber, as I think about the person I used to be. *A plucky child, a bright student, and a promising...* It doesn't matter anymore. *This* is who I have become.

CHAPTER 2

I stare through the peephole of my motel room door and wait. The curtains are drawn just as they were when I arrived, and the fluorescent lights are turned off. My fingers brush against the brass handle tentatively, gripping then quickly releasing.

I want so badly to throw the door open and launch myself into the desert rain. My bag is packed—not that it was ever otherwise—and ready to go. *Too bad I'm not.* In the parking lot, a young man takes his time climbing into his white F-150. I cannot move until he leaves.

Although my vantage point is limited, I try studying his figure to pass the time. He appears to be about twenty years of age. Dressed in worn jeans and a leather cowboy hat, he leans against his truck, sipping a bottle of beer with a dark label. The relentless rainwater makes it slip and peel. Once he sucks the bottle dry, he tosses it across the lot.

There's a tug on my conscience as he unlocks his car and climbs into the driver's seat. The guy probably isn't drunk, but he definitely should not be on the road with that beer—or more—in his system. I purse my lips and watch him drive away. The old me would have marched up to the man and told him off. I might have even called the police if he gave me a hard time. Things are different now, though. I will not risk exposing myself.

After he leaves, I grab my bag and unlock the door guard. My fingers curl around the knob before slowly twisting it to the right. Now all I have to do is pull it back—open the door a crack and let the air rush in.

Just do it. I screw my eyes shut and tug, an instant sliver of bright light burning through my closed lids. Once it's ajar, I run.

The clock starts now. At my car, I open the trunk and throw my bag inside. Fasten my seat belt, stick my key into the ignition, then step on the pedal. And just like that, I am gone as quickly as I came. It's almost like I was never really there at all.

THIS MALL REMINDS ME of the one where I spent all my teenage summers. It is arguably more updated, but the general ambiance is similar. Back then, my friends and I used to try on designer outfits we couldn't afford while pretending to be famous. We even staged photoshoots in the dressing rooms so we could remember what it felt like to wear something that special—that lavish. We would live entire lives before going back to our respective homes.

I smile sadly at the memory and step into a beauty surplus store. My basket fills quickly—hair dye, powder foundation, and a smoky eye shadow palette. I already have my usual mascara and liquid liner, and both products will go seamlessly with my new look. After paying in cash, I leave the shop.

The lure of a designer boutique tempts me for a moment. Money isn't really the issue. Places here have so few customers that the sales associates will remember me without a doubt—I will be one of the few commissions of their entire week. It is much safer to go somewhere I won't be remembered. *Next stop: a random department store.*

As I expected, the building is teeming with eager customers. *Anonymous shopping.* I pile several pieces—a pair of jeans, cardigans, some shoes, blazers, and sunglasses—into a cart then head to the front. There is no time to bother with dressing rooms right now. The long lines threaten to derail my perfect plan, but all I can do is wait.

After checking out, I confirm that I have everything necessary. Now it's high time to leave the store. Walking back through the mall leaves me feeling nostalgic once again, maybe more so. My simple childhood memories feel so far away, completely removed from the life I live now. So much has changed since then.

The moment I step out of the mall, I'm instantly thrown back into my tragic present. Maybe I should have seen it coming. But there were never any signs. Even with my background and extensive training, I didn't. No one ever expects betrayal.

Shaking off my thought, I start to cross the street. About halfway across, I realize that I left my keys in the store. A quick glance over my shoulder brings a white sedan into view. The other cars are slowing down for me, but this one seems to be picking up speed. Pure instinct makes me quicken my pace. My stomach drops when I realize that I am the only pedestrian still crossing.

There are intermittent honks and a few faint yells, but I hardly hear them. The sedan fills my peripheral vision as my heart thumps against my chest. Instead of slamming on their brakes, the driver just keeps going. My throat closes around a scream, but it's too late.

I don't even feel the impact.

❧

MY SENSES ARE DULLER than a blunt knife, soft from overuse. I roll my tongue along the roof of my mouth, tasting blood as I go. The sheer bitterness makes me gag. I start drawing a hand to my neck, but I do not make it very far. There may as well be ten-pound weights secured to each arm.

Although I am immobilized, my thoughts are whip fast. They dart around my brain like tiny ricocheting Ping-Pong balls, too quick to follow. I have the unnerving sensation that I am trapped, paralyzed in the midst of chaos and unable to process my surroundings. All I can see is a blurry haze of lights and colors.

My hearing comes back slowly, like the short hand circling a clock. Each and every sound is muffled. Eventually, I can detect pitch and volume—a woman's shrill tone and a man's husky timbre. I think I hear a child crying, calling for his papa between tears.

A strident series of beeps emanates from some unidentifiable place. When I try to turn my head, I realize that I am still frozen. My effort is entirely wasted as the sound amplifies, growing louder and stronger until it overcomes me. Something pulls me back under, dragging my consciousness into another dark void and swallowing me whole.

CHAPTER 3

When I open my eyes again, I am staring at a stark-white pop-corn ceiling. The blurred room finally settles into focus. Bright panels of fluorescent light weigh down my already heavy lids, and I have to fight to keep them open. A sterile scent—some sort of cleaning agent—makes my nose twitch. I am almost certain that this is a hospital room.

The chilling sensation that stifled me before comes rushing back. Temporary paralysis—that unmistakably vulnerable state—exactly like a nightmare I used to have. *Or was it a memory? A premonition?*

Relief washes over me as I wiggle my fingers and turn my head with ease, though my legs continue feeling like boulders. This is probably just a side effect of some heavy-duty medication. I release a breath and stretch my arms out slowly, relishing the return of a simple ability.

"You're awake," says a warm voice.

I turn my attention to the doorway and watch a middle-aged woman enter my room.

"I'm your afternoon nurse." She gestures to a white board I hadn't noticed before.

I nod, squinting briefly to make out the red block letters.

"My name is Cathy," she says before I can finish reading. Cathy enunciates every syllable and speaks in a deafening tone. She sounds like someone reading nursery rhymes to a group of preschoolers.

I open my mouth to respond but cannot find the words.

She approaches my bed. "How are you feeling?"

I shake my head and open my mouth again.

"Do you know what year it is?" she asks even more loudly. "Who is our president?"

Now I am irritated. "Puh-please just... give me a moment," I manage before she can hurl another question at me.

Cathy is taken aback. "Of course. Take your time."

"Thank you." I pause before answering. "Yes, I do know. The year... is 2013. And our president is Barack Obama."

Cathy looks down and purses her lips. "Okay," she says, a bit too quietly.

I can tell that something is wrong. "He was elected—" I am interrupted by two quick knocks on the door.

"Hello there, Dr. Parsons," Cathy says in her original tone. "I was just asking her a few questions."

I strain my neck to see a tall, slim woman hovering in the doorway. Her brown hair is pulled back neatly into a ponytail, and she's rubbing a clear gel—probably hand sanitizer—between her palms.

"Great. Thanks, Cathy." Dr. Parsons enters the room and smiles in my direction. She moves to the foot of my bed and pulls out a clipboard. "You can call me Amanda," she tells me.

"Hi." I try to prop myself upright. I'm still lying flat on the bed.

"Oh—here. Let's get you situated." Cathy locates a remote and begins to adjust my motorized bed. "That okay?" she asks once I'm in a seated position.

"Yes, thanks." I groan as sudden feeling floods the length of my body. Intense pain emanates from each limb.

Amanda turns to Cathy. "Can you up her meds?"

"What's going on? My legs... they hurt like—" I glance down at the thick white blankets covering my lower half. "They hurt like *hell*."

Amanda grimaces. "I'm so sorry. Cathy is going to get you some more medication to help with the pain."

The nurse leaves as Amanda moves closer to me.

"Aside from the leg pain, how are you feeling?" she asks softly.

I swallow another moan and focus on formulating an answer. "My head... feels fuzzy. It hurts, too—dull and achy."

Amanda nods, assuring me that the medicine will help before asking another question. "Can you tell me what year it is?"

"Two thousand thirteen."

"Okay. And can you tell me your name?"

"Veronica Kwan. But I go by Vonny."

"Great, Vonny." She makes a note as relief floods her face.

Cathy reenters the room with a bulging bag of clear liquid. She hangs it from a hook on the IV pole next to my bed and untangles a few different tubes. Then she stops, turning her attention to me.

"Let's put your hand here," she says while propping it up on a small pillow. I hadn't even noticed the cannula in my right hand. I frown, wondering how long it has been there.

"What happened?" I ask as she flushes my IV.

"Vonny," Amanda chimes in, "I'd just like to ask a few more questions, and—"

"What happened to me?"

Cathy finishes up quickly and defers to Amanda.

"You were in a bad accident," the doctor tells me. "Hit by a car about a week ago while you were crossing the street."

"A week?" I ask in disbelief. I'm sure I have only been here for a couple days at most.

"Unfortunately," Amanda continues, "you weren't carrying any possessions when you were found, save for some cash and a tattered shopping bag. Nothing useful, though—no wallet or phone. So we had no way of identifying you until—"

"Where am I?" I demand.

"You're at Desert Glen Hospital in Nevada."

"But I live in New York." *What am I doing in Nevada?*

"Now that we know your name, we'll be able to find out more details," Amanda says calmly. "Do you know how old you are?"

"Twenty-two. I just graduated from NYU—New York University."

Amanda looks at Cathy then makes another note on her clipboard.

"What happened to my legs?" I ask, remembering the intense pain from before.

Amanda lowers her voice so that it's barely a whisper. "I'm afraid that you were injured very badly." She leaves the statement hanging there, failing to answer my question.

"My legs."

"Both your legs are extremely bruised and beaten up." She hesitates before speaking again. "But you're very lucky that they're not broken."

"My..."

"I'm so sorry, Vonny." Her words sound slow, like taffy being pulled apart.

My entire body feels like it is sinking into the hospital mattress.

"You're probably getting drowsy." Amanda glances at her watch. "The medicine can do that. Let's try..."

Her next words are lost. The entire room goes black.

CHAPTER 4

I open my eyes again and immediately remember what Amanda told me. *The accident.* I was hit by a car. The sheer shock of that news is enough to unravel me, but I can't let it. There are plenty of appalling stories about people getting severely injured and struggling to survive. Or worse, fatalities. The latter reality hits especially hard for me.

I wince as an unwanted memory surfaces.

OUR ANNUAL CHINESE New Year party is just hours away, and I am up to my shoulders in supplies. I drove straight to the venue after school to set everything up. My trunk is still teeming with folded red napkins, streamer packs, and golden dessert trays, not to mention several precariously stacked platters of handmade dumplings.

I am in the midst of unloading decorations when I notice a discrepancy. My face falls as I recount the favors—some of them are missing. I must have forgotten the other box at home. I glance at the clock, realizing that I won't make it back in time to finish decorating.

My parents are meeting me here after work. Maybe they can make a quick stop on their way to the venue. I dial my mom's number, but she doesn't pick up. My dad doesn't answer either. I realize that they are most likely just stuck in traffic—an inevitable reality of living in the city.

Another hour passes before my phone rings, but it's not my parents calling. A man on the other end quickly introduces himself as a police officer. Although his words are muffled by spotty reception, each one hits me like a bullet.

"Your mother and father were hit by an oncoming vehicle."

NEITHER OF MY PARENTS survived the crash. Death on impact—that's what the officer told me when I arrived shortly after. *Death on impact.* The parallel between my current circumstances and their fatal accident makes my head spin.

My bruised legs are still hiding under a thick white blanket, but I refuse to even look at them. I prefer to imagine myself lying on the tiny blue sofa inside my Greenwich Village apartment. Like I've just gone for a long walk around the city and am simply resting my feet.

The visualization helps momentarily before my skin begins to sweat. Several hospital quilts are layered over me like thick, needlessly heavy coats of paint. I hurl them off at once until all I am left with is an airy sheet. Being careful to keep my legs covered, I peel it back, only to reveal a profuse amount of sweat staining my hospital gown. I place a clammy hand on my forehead and exhale.

A stubborn clump of damp hair is matted around my face. I finger comb it back and tuck the strands behind my ears. I have not seen a mirror since I woke up, but there isn't a fighting chance I look halfway decent. *Least of my worries.*

It suddenly occurs to me that I am not alone in this room. Cathy, clutching a dry erase marker, stands several feet from my bed. I eventually realize that she is updating a white board mounted to the far wall. I lean forward, squinting until the words come into focus.

Patient: Veronica Kwan, Age:

But my age is left blank. I am about to fill Cathy in when Amanda walks into the room.

"Hi, Vonny." She speaks in the same sweet voice as last time. "How are you feeling?"

"I'm all right," I tell her. "A little thirsty—could I have some water?"

"I'm on it," Cathy says before swiftly leaving the room. "I'll get your lunch tray too."

Amanda thanks her before turning back to me. "Are you able to answer a few more questions?"

"Sure." I prop myself up once again. "I'm ready."

"Great. Let's pick up where we left off last time. What year is it?"

"I've answered this question multiple times now," I say, trying to diffuse the irritation in my voice.

"I know. Please just try—"

"Two thousand thirteen!" I nearly shout.

Amanda glances into the hall and lets out a breath. Then she steps toward me and places a gentle hand on my arm.

"I'm sorry," I say quietly. "But you both keep asking me things that are so obvious, and I don't really understand why I'm still here. Can't I just leave?"

"Look, Vonny," Amanda says in a soft voice, "I'm going to be completely honest with you."

I peer up at her through dark lashes.

"You've had a serious accident. The car that hit you did a lot of damage to your body." She pauses briefly and gestures to my bruised legs. "But it also impacted your head. We're dealing with a traumatic brain injury here."

I shoot her a confused look as Cathy returns with a meal tray.

"Anyway," Amanda continues as I accept a water cup from Cathy, "the scans revealed significant swelling in your brain."

I gulp down a generous portion and furrow my brow. "I—I don't understand."

"We're hoping that there wasn't any permanent damage. I'm still very *hopeful*." The last word is awkwardly high-pitched.

"So... you're asking me questions to determine how much damage the accident caused?"

"Sort of. Sometimes, brain swelling goes down relatively quickly. But it can take a lot longer in other cases."

"Okay," I say between sips.

"You were wondering why I keep asking you what year it is."

I nod expectantly.

"Well, it's not 2013 anymore."

I nearly spit out my water then force it back down. "Wait, what?"

"The year is 2022."

My stomach drops. "Is this some kind of joke?"

"I assure you this is not a joke." Amanda pulls out her phone and taps her finger frantically across the screen. Then she holds it inches from my face.

I am staring at a *New York Times* article dated 2022. "B-But that's impossible." I squint at the screen in disbelief. "It's 2013."

"It's actually not," Amanda says calmly.

I feel like I have been punched in the gut.

"I know it's scary, but please try your best not to worry too much. This is completely normal. Sometimes, people come out of accidents not even remembering their own names."

Her words do little to soothe me.

"And Vonny," she continues, "it's a good sign that you remember significant aspects of your past—I did a quick Google search this morning and found you in the NYU alumni database. You were a student there until 2013."

I know that, I want to say. *I just graduated.*

"Like I said, we're very hopeful that more details will come back as your swelling goes down. You might even wake up tomorrow and remember everything about the past nine years..."

Amanda keeps speaking, but her voice has faded to an inaudible background noise. All I can think about is the shocking bomb she just detonated. I finally understand why she was hesitant to give me details—why she chose not to tell me any of this sooner. Amanda was trying to preserve my sanity. *Unfortunately, that ship has sailed.*

I AM NOT HUNGRY, BUT I force myself to eat a few bites of lunch. The tray Cathy brought in holds one soggy turkey sandwich, green apple slices, and a sad chocolate pudding cup. It feels like I am back in elementary school. I pick up the sandwich, bite into the soft bread, and chew.

Just as I am about to push my food away, something catches my eye. A tiny silver spoon is left untouched at the edge of my tray. I reach for it tentatively and grasp the handle. Then I hold it up to my face.

I flinch at the sight of it all—my sallow skin, the drastic swelling, and a trail of deep purple bruises. My cheeks are inflamed beyond measure. Cuts and gashes canvas my forehead. But what shocks me the most isn't the injuries.

Beneath them, I see someone I do not recognize. A stranger stares back at me—a much older woman reflected in my makeshift mirror. I slam down the spoon and look away. Then I pull my eyelids shut, wishing I was back in New York.

CHAPTER 5

The evening hours pass slower than molasses. Despite my best attempts at simple distraction, my eyes keep returning to a large clock across the room. *Five o'clock, five fifteen, five thirty.* Every increment is a reminder of the time I have lost—the time I am losing now.

Why can't I remember anything? Nine whole years of my life are missing, and I cannot do anything about it but *wait*. Wait for the swelling to go down, for my body to heal, and for someone to come looking for me.

I compile a mental list of loved ones, sorting through my deceased family members. Both sets of grandparents passed away years ago, and my parents were only children. I have no siblings, aunts, uncles, or cousins in tow.

Living without any relatives hits even harder now. I am anchorless, completely adrift. Then again, almost a decade has passed me by. I might be married by now. I could have a doting husband at home, children to take care of. Little ones who call me "Mom." I might have an entire family of my own and not even remember them.

That thought makes my stomach churn. But the reality is, a family would know I was missing. *So why hasn't anyone come for me?* I pry my hand from beneath a tangle of sheets and fidget with my wristband. The staff updated it to include my name: Veronica Jane Kwan. At least I know who I am. *Who I was.*

Yesterday, I thought I was twenty-two years old, a recent grad with the world at my feet. I remember NYU's commencement ceremony as if it really *was* yesterday. Crowds of people filing into Yankee Stadium, cap-and-gown-clad students buzzing around the sunny field, and my friends cheering each other on as we accepted our diplomas.

My friends. The realization dawns on me like a blaring horn. I have—*had*—a tight-knit group at NYU. There was Abby, June, and Spencer, but Abby was my absolute best friend. The last thing I remember is a drunken evening of celebration at our favorite local bar—drinks on me.

"CHEERS!" ABBY'S VOICE is barely audible over the deafening music.

We clink glasses and hover over the counter. "To us!" I shout. Rhythmic beats reverberate through me as I throw back my shot.

"Once more for the cheap seats in the back," Abby says after ordering another round.

"To us!" we yell in unison.

The song finally changes, the volume easing ever so slightly. Throngs of our peers revel in post-ceremony bliss. This bar is more packed than I've ever seen it.

"I can't believe this might be our last hurrah," I tell Abby. Her face immediately falls. "Do you think we'll—"

"Vonny." She throws an arm over my shoulder. "I don't want to cry tonight. We have the rest of our lives for that."

"Okay. No reminiscing. No past, no future. Only now."

"That's the spirit!" Abby's eyes flicker.

I laugh and buy us more drinks. We down them quickly, pretending like this isn't our last group outing before I leave New York.

"Now—" She grabs my hand and pulls me away from the counter. "Let's dance!"

THE MEMORY OF OUR CELEBRATION fades, pulling me back to reality. *Where is Abby now?* We supported each other through nasty breakups and stress-inducing finals. There is absolutely no way we would have ever lost touch. People always talk about life pulling friends in opposite directions, but not Abby and me. Not a chance. I fumble around for the call button and press it incessantly.

Cathy enters moments later with a frantic look on her face. "Is everything okay?"

"I remembered someone! My best friend—her name is Abby. Abigail Knowles, if you're looking her up."

Cathy nods as the corners of my mouth lift. It's the first time I have smiled in this hospital.

"She's from Denver. Well, she lived there before starting at NYU—we were roommates freshman year! She probably ended up staying in New York, though. That was always her plan."

"I'll look her up right away." Cathy leaves the room.

There's a pivotal shift, like everything might somehow work out after all. Abby can catch me up on everything I have missed—major life changes, significant events, and awful dates we probably wanted to forget in the first place. I will tell her not to gloss over any detail, no matter how minute. I want to hear it all.

I'M WATCHING AN EPISODE of *Friends* when Amanda walks in.

"That's a good one," she says with a wink. "Chandler at his finest."

I force a smile and mute the TV.

"So, Cathy informed me about your friend." She pauses and glances down at a Post-it note. "Abigail Knowles?"

"Yeah, Abby," I say, unable to hide my excitement. "We went to school together."

"We haven't been able to reach her yet, but Cathy left a message with her receptionist. Hopefully, we'll hear back soon."

"Her receptionist?"

"Yes. Apparently, she's a recruiter at a large firm in Manhattan."

I swallow my surprise. Abby was a dance major and always dreamed of signing with a company after graduation. She had the talent too. *So why is she working in the corporate world?*

"In the meantime," Amanda interrupts my train of thought, "can you think of anyone else we might try to call?"

I shake my head, certain that Abby is the best person to contact. She is—was—like a sister to me.

"Okay. Well, please let me know if you think of anyone. We're having a lot of trouble finding a... solution."

I know what she means. Since waking up, all I have been able to tell her is my name and a load of outdated information. I know my New York apartment address, favorite coffee shop, and cell phone number, but none of it is actually *mine* anymore. Cathy checked.

"You don't seem to have an Internet presence either," Amanda says gently. "No Facebook profile, LinkedIn account, blog. Nothing."

"Um, well. *Abby*. She'll call back. She has to." I'm not sure who I am trying to convince more—Amanda or myself.

"Of course she will." She forces a nod. "I'll keep you updated."

For the first time since I have been here, Amanda's face is shrouded with doubt. It is clear that she doesn't see Abby as a viable "solution." Even more obvious, though, is that she pities me. And that—even inflicted by a doctor—is the worst feeling of all.

CHAPTER 6

Today is day thirteen. Almost two weeks have passed with no progress to show for it. I still cannot remember anything useful, and Abby has yet to call back. My hope grows thin like yarn unraveling into thread. It is only a matter of time until I give up completely.

I am sick of lying in this hospital bed every day. My legs are slack, useless limbs dangling from my body. Amanda says they are still too bruised to move around much despite our collective attempts to ice and elevate them into submission. *Maybe a surgeon should just saw them off.* Currently, my legs' only function is to cause me pain.

Nurses come and go like clockwork. They draw blood, check my vitals, and deliver meal trays three times a day. I have met five of them so far. My favorite nurse is still Cathy, though. *By a landslide.* She sneaks me chocolate cookies from the downstairs café, so there is really no competition.

Amanda's footsteps rouse me from a light sleep. "Do you have a moment?" She hovers in the doorway, glasses resting on her narrow nose bridge.

"Of course."

She approaches the foot of my bed with a clipboard. "Your recent scans came back."

I prop myself up while she thumbs through a stack of pages.

"Given these results, we can move forward with a diagnosis."

My heart sinks as she elaborates. *Retrograde amnesia.* It takes nearly an hour for Amanda to explain the term. I tune her out after a while, choosing to focus on her body language rather than her actual words. Among other things, it is bizarre to watch someone deliver bad news. Sometimes, I think the person relaying it actually suffers more than the one hearing it.

I should probably be listening, but I don't really need to. After all, I was a psychology major. The condition is basically a loss of memory-access to events or things learned in the recent past. "Access" is the operative word. Retrograde amnesia does not necessarily mean that my memories are erased or gone completely. It just means that they are locked away while my brain searches for an elusive key.

For the time being, I am forced to take comfort in that simple fact. There is a chance I will be able to remember everything in a few days or weeks. The brain is a fascinating thing—three pounds of white and gray matter, packed with intricate blood vessels and billions of neurons. The organ has intrigued me ever since I was a little girl. It is the reason I wanted to study psychology in the first place.

CATHY KNOCKS TWICE before coming in. Her graying hair is pulled back loosely, and the bags under her eyes look particularly pronounced this evening.

"Calling it a day?" I ask as she glances at the monitor beside my bed.

"I wish. They've got me pulling extra hours for the rest of the week."

I hear a slight buzzing before Cathy reaches into her pants pocket.

"You know what?" she asks after reading the screen. "I really need to take this."

I don't even have time to respond before she rushes out of the room. No sooner do I finish adjusting my pillows than Cathy reappears in the doorway.

"I meant to ask you—" But her expression halts me midsentence. Sheer exhaustion has given way to something else entirely.

She pushes a chair to my bedside before taking a seat. "Abby finally called back. Says she got all the messages I left."

A smile spreads across my face. "I knew she would." Relief washes over me, especially since I have spent the last couple of days blabbing about our friendship. I was fast becoming the wing's delusional amnesiac.

"Listen, hon." Cathy sets a hand on my wrist. "She—she confirmed that you were indeed friends at NYU."

Of course she did. I don't understand Cathy's sullen demeanor.

"The thing is... Abby says you two haven't been in touch for years." She hesitates before continuing. "That you're not even friends anymore."

The words are a gut punch—a fusillade of shock and hurt.

"I'm sorry." Cathy purses her lips. "I know that you—"

"Just let me talk to Abby. There must be some sort of mistake."

"Hon, she doesn't want us to call back."

"I-I don't understand." *None of this makes sense.*

"She says..." Cathy lowers her voice to a whisper, as if a quieter volume will somehow soften the blow. "Abby says she never wants to hear from you again."

CHAPTER 7

Emotions come in waves—denial, shock, confusion. Only the grief refuses to pass. Misery joins in, drenching me with sheets of torrential rain. I succumb to extensive amounts of sleep and leave my meal trays untouched. Eventually, my thoughts give way to resentment.

I blame Abby first. *How could she be so cold—so bitter?* She is the nicest person I have ever known. The dissolution of our friendship just doesn't add up, no matter how many times I dwell on it. Then I realize that it must have been me.

I am the reason that we are no longer speaking. That our relationship deteriorated—collapsed into pieces. That she never wants to see me again. *What could I have done to make her hate me so much?* I still have yet to come up with an answer.

Time passes slowly again now that I literally have zero prospects. I wonder what the normal protocol is for a patient who can't remember the past nine years of her life. If nobody ever comes to get her. *What if nobody ever comes for me?*

I stare out the window and take in the limited view. My days are becoming monotonous, and the wealth of television programming only goes so far in terms of distraction. I have flipped through every single channel and memorized the *TV Guide* schedule. Ironically, my memory recall has always been a strong suit.

The desert sky is an inky-black expanse. Without even glancing at the clock, I know that it is sometime around midnight, give or take. The night nurse checked my vitals around ten o'clock, and it has probably been about two hours since then. There may as well be an atomic clock in the back of my head, counting each and every second despite my protestation.

The darkness and scattered stars remind me of pre-sunrise runs around Greenwich Village. I was in incredible shape back then—always training for another marathon. A glance at my undefined stomach suggests that I stopped working out a long time ago. My lanky limbs only confirm the suspicion.

I am definitely not the person I used to be. After all this time spent inside a hospital, the old me might be going stir-crazy. Old Vonny would have developed cabin fever after only a few days. The current me couldn't care less, though. While lying down so much is a foreign feeling, at least I have been able to get out of bed more frequently now that my wounds are healing.

I just need my mind to catch up to my body. The only thing that scares me more than never recovering my memory is the thought of leaving this hospital before I am ready. In here, I have Cathy, Amanda, and a whole host of staff looking out for me. *But if I were forced out—thrust back into the world with nothing but a diagnosis...* The thought alone makes me shudder.

Until something changes, this hospital is my safe place, my surrogate sanctuary.

THE DAWN CREEPS IN through a parted pair of curtains—vivid hues that remind me of sherbet and cotton candy. I open my eyes slowly, relishing the beauty just beyond my windowpane.

"You're awake," says a familiar voice.

I startle and flip around to see Cathy.

"Didn't mean to scare you, hon. Just surprised to find you up this early."

"I'm just a little jumpy, I guess." I try to shrug, but I am tangled up in a mess of starchy sheets.

"I have some news. Abby called last night."

"I thought she never wanted to hear from me again," I say under my breath.

Cathy ignores my cynical comment. "She left a voicemail."

"What did she say?"

"She actually apologized for... well, I'll just let you listen."

Cathy steps closer and hands me her phone, which looks just like Amanda's—flat, shiny, and large. It is definitely an iPhone, but looks nothing like what I remember. I take it from Cathy and press play.

"Hi there," says a warm voice that I recognize instantly. "It's Abigail Knowles from Interim Recruiting. You're probably surprised to hear from me. I, um... I just wanted to apologize for sounding so harsh the other day. Your call surprised me, that's all. I haven't heard from Vonny in years. We had a sort of falling out, and I never really—well, I just didn't expect to hear her name." Her tone is clipped now. "I mentioned your call to an old friend after we spoke, and she told me that Vonny married a man named John Lewis."

I grip Cathy's phone tighter as the message continues.

"Anyway, I just wanted to let you know. I hope that helps. And... I do hope she gets better."

I replay the last part just to hear Abby's voice again.

"And... I do hope she gets better."

Cathy reaches for her phone. "I know it might be shocking, hon, but I thought you'd want to listen."

"Thanks, Cathy," I whisper while staring at the linoleum floor.

She gently rubs my back. "I'm going to let Dr. Parsons know, and we'll look into contacting him."

I mumble a response as she leaves the room. Listening to Abby's message, just hearing her voice, makes everything feel normal again.

It is as if we are still best friends living together in New York. As if the first call was a cruel joke—Abby trying to play a prank on me.

But it wasn't a joke. The reality is that we had a falling out and have not spoken in *years*. As much as Abby's voice comforted me, it is a sharp reminder that I am living a life I cannot remember. I am married to a man I do not know.

CHAPTER 8

I am running along a sinuous trail, sweat dripping down both legs and mud caked around my ankles. Verdant trees tower overhead while birds chirp in the distance. Miles deep inside an upstate forest, I'm armed with nothing but the clothes on my back. Rainwater blurs my vision as I round a corner.

Each forefoot strike brings me closer to something I cannot see. *An answer.* I strain to reach the end of this path, but its flat surface morphs into a tiny mountain right before my eyes. I squint as beads of rain blind me once again. I have to keep moving.

My breathing grows ragged while I tackle a sodden hill, feet sinking in with each step. Every muscle burns from resistance and overuse. My body trembles, about to give out completely, and I'm forced to slow my pace until I am barely treading up the slope. Then I freeze. Someone is watching me.

I sit up with a jolt. *Just a bad nightmare.* The curtains are still drawn from yesterday, and harsh morning light pierces me with its bright shards of yellow. I bring a hand to my chest while my heart thuds uncontrollably—nearly enough to set off the monitor.

Initially, my dream seemed like a memory. I used to run all over New York, and the suburban trails start to blend together outside of the city. Though I lost my way a few times during upstate workouts, I never felt anything close to the panic I did during that nightmare. The fear—pure paranoia—was something else entirely.

I manage to steady my breathing before a nurse delivers my breakfast tray—French toast, scrambled eggs, and turkey bacon. My waning appetite returns with a vengeance this morning as I devour the spread in front of me. I drench the spongy bread in syrup before sinking my teeth in, relishing every bite.

The vast majority of food here is better than anything I could ever make myself. I wonder if my culinary skills have improved at all during the past nine years. *Maybe John Lewis does the household cooking.* The train of thought nauseates me before I derail it and finish my meal.

After a shower and short walk around the floor, I am back in bed, watching TV. Part of me feels guilty for staying here any longer. The bruises on my arms and legs have faded significantly, and my face has returned to a semi-normal state. *Normal for New Vonny.* A series of wrinkles, faint but indisputably present, still surprises me whenever I scrutinize my reflection.

Abby used to put Olay Regenerist on as a preventative measure—one I deemed frivolous. Perhaps I should have followed suit. *Abby.* I was so distracted by my strange nightmare that I have not thought about her since last night. *Until now.* One little reminder, and I am overcome by the same pain I felt when Cathy first broke the news.

I try to distract myself with a muted rerun, but Amanda knocks on my door before I make it past the show's opening.

"Hi there," she says. "How are you doing?"

I flip off the TV and turn toward her. "I'm feeling better."

"That's wonderful." Amanda doesn't stop to question my lie. She pulls out her phone. "I spoke with Cathy this morning. The voicemail was helpful. I'm sorry about your friend, though—that's a real bummer."

I nod, ignoring the slight sting of her words.

"Anyway..." Amanda waves her hand through the air as if she is shoving the tension away. "I looked you up and was actually able to find a wealth of information."

"Oh?" The half question fails to convey how curious I am.

She looks down at her cell and swipes a finger across its sizeable screen. "We kept searching for Veronica *Kwan*. But I'm Googling Veronica *Lewis* now that I know you're married."

The reminder hits me like a ton of bricks.

"Here we go," Amanda says triumphantly. "Social media accounts—Twitter and Facebook—and even a few articles you've written."

"Articles? From NYU?" I was on the student paper freshman year but quit after a boring semester of writing fluff pieces.

"Actually," Amanda says before holding her phone out for me, "these are from a medical journal." She sounds impressed.

I stare at the screen in disbelief. "Severe Mental Illness in International Prisons." Authored by Dr. Veronica Lewis.

She seems to sense my incredulity. "I double-checked your photo in the bio section. It's you. You're a psychiatrist, Vonny. Or should I say, Dr. Lewis?"

"I-I'm a psychiatrist?"

She nods spiritedly. "Looks like you earned your degree from the University of Washington."

I remember sending out applications to graduate programs, but I was still waiting to hear back from most of them.

"You must have gotten married after grad school," she adds, still scrolling around. "Your last name is Kwan on all of the UW results. Not sure why I didn't notice these links before."

There's that word again. *Married*. Knowing that I have a husband is somehow more terrifying than the thought of enduring this alone.

"Wow, Vonny. It looks like you recently completed your residency at the University of California, San Francisco. That's a very reputable program."

My eyebrows rise. That *is* a good program, and UCSF was one of my top choices.

"Who knew?" Amanda beams. "A certified psychiatrist!" Her enthusiasm is infectious.

I hear myself laugh, realizing that part of me is relieved. For a moment, it feels like I am talking to a friend.

"I'm really—" My face falls, but it's not because of Abby this time.

"What's wrong?" Amanda glances up quickly.

"I... I don't remember any of it. I finished my degree and completed my residency, but I don't remember anything I learned." My voice is a mere whisper. "I know *nothing*."

Amanda puts her phone away and sits down beside me. Sympathy washes over the length of her face.

"It was all for nothing."

"Vonny," she says calmly. "That's not true."

"I-I won't even be able to practice. My license will be suspended."

We sit in silence for a moment.

"Well," Amanda says with sudden resolve, "don't give up on yourself yet. There's still a chance that everything will come back."

I flash her a skeptical look.

"Sometimes memories are triggered unexpectedly. By people, places, things—you name it."

I consider this for a while.

"Maybe being around your husband will help. I know it'll be a little strange at first, but who knows what might happen? Getting back into your normal routine could end up doing wonders for your mind."

She has a fair point. Maybe seeing John Lewis will help me remember things I have forgotten—temporarily lost. He probably knows what went wrong with Abby.

"Thanks for the reassurance. I mean it."

"Of course. I'm here for you anytime."

I attempt a lame joke as she stands up to leave. "Are you sure *you're* not the therapist between us? Could have fooled me."

Amanda laughs, heading toward the door. Then she pauses. "I figure that you already know, but Cathy left a message on your husband's cell. We'll let you know as soon as he calls back."

"Okay."

Logically, I should be dying to know more details about my current life. I could even ask for computer access. Apparently, a plethora of information about me exists online—about *both* versions of myself. Veronica Kwan and Veronica Lewis.

I could read the articles I have written over the years and find out what I specialized in during graduate school. I could cyberstalk myself—go through each picture, post, and comment in every one of my social accounts. But for now, I prefer to remain in identity limbo. I choose to feign ignorance of this alleged life I have been living for the past nine years. *No degree. No residency. No marriage.*

For the rest of the day, I am not Dr. Veronica Lewis. I am just Vonny Kwan—NYU grad and happy New Yorker.

CHAPTER 9

The half-baked plan to trick myself into a state of blissful ignorance is quickly foiled. *Denial: detonated.* Between making small talk with the nurses and hearing more about my online presence from Amanda, I am constantly reminded that the year is no longer 2013. Then comes the biggest shock of all.

Around lunchtime, I receive my first visitor. Correction—visitors. I expect an old friend or family member, maybe even a forgotten acquaintance or a long-lost relative. My best guess is wrong. The surprise visitors are two strangers dressed in black suits.

The first man is stereotypically attractive—in shape, tan, and well over six feet tall. If I challenged him to, he could probably run a four-minute mile. The man's scrawnier counterpart hovers just a few feet behind. He is considerably younger with bad posture to boot.

The first man is not one for pleasantries. "Mrs. Lewis." He nods gravely. "My name is Christian Lee. I'm a detective in San Francisco."

Detectives? I don't have any idea what they might want with me, but Lee doesn't give me any time to think about it.

"I'm working on a case involving your husband, John Lewis." Lee pauses for good measure and glances around the room. "Your husband is dead."

I look past them at Cathy, who stands in the corner of my room, clutching a pencil so tightly that her fingers turn white.

"I'm sorry to inform you of this in your... current state," Lee adds solemnly.

I swallow hard. "I-I don't understand. What do you mean?"

"He was found dead about two weeks ago." His matter-of-fact demeanor makes my stomach tighten.

"Two weeks? Where?"

"In an alley."

Cathy looks like she's about to burst into tears. I glance at the other detective, but he quickly averts his eyes.

"It's an alley in San Francisco," Lee adds, as if briefly acknowledging the memory-loss aspect of my condition. "We think he was on his way home from work."

At this point, Cathy walks over and squeezes my hand. "I'm so sorry, hon," she whispers.

"I'm sorry for your loss." Lee's partner steps closer as well. "I know this is a lot."

Lee shoots him a begrudging look before turning back to me. I can't tell if Lee is irritated or simply uncomfortable with this show of compassion. "Detective Ryan will be conducting the investigation with me."

Ryan flashes an awkward smile in my direction. "Pleasure to meet you, Mrs. Lewis."

I notice Lee roll his eyes and find myself sizing him up once again. *What is his problem?* Despite the detective's chiseled physique and handsome cheekbones, he is devoid of all charm and sympathy. Ice cold. Detective Ryan might look like a walking skeleton, but at least his demeanor isn't offensive.

For me, it is easy to fixate on the detectives' personalities and physical features. Anyone else would feel bowled over by the news of their husband's untimely death. But I have no memory of the victim. I am just shocked.

Lee asks me a few questions, but I am not much help. I feel the recurring need to remind him that I have retrograde amnesia. Luckily, Amanda rushes into my room before he can continue his interrogation. She is panting, and tiny beads of sweat drip down her face. This is the first time I have seen her look panicked.

"Vonny, I just heard the news," she says between breaths. "I came as quickly as I could. I'm so, so sorry." She furrows her brow and squeezes my hand just as Cathy did moments earlier.

I appreciate her support, but sadness continues to elude me. My face must be blank, an empty canvas devoid of all expression. Perhaps this heavy news is lost on me, or maybe I am just not ready to accept it.

THE AIR IN MY ROOM is disturbingly still, rigid with tension. I stare through a tiny glass window into the hallway, wishing I was an expert lip-reader. Amanda exited to speak with the detectives about twenty minutes ago. My amateur interpretation of hand movement and body language will have to suffice.

Ryan crosses his arms, licks his lips between sentences, and continues to avoid eye contact. A veritable nervous Nellie. On the other hand, Lee appears much more relaxed around Amanda than he did with me. The lead detective's stance remains open while he gestures freely and smiles more than a few times.

Amanda glances at me before I manage to look away, hoping that my prolonged stare wasn't too obvious. Then she shakes the detectives' hands and walks back into my room. I sit up a little straighter, pretending to watch the muted TV.

"We're going to keep you here for one more night. I think that would be best—as long as it's all right with you."

"Okay."

"It'll give us a chance to do more tests and make sure you're stable before we discharge you."

"Sounds good." I don't sound very convincing.

"Well, I need to get started on some paperwork. I'll check on you one more time before I leave for the day," she adds with a smile.

I fight the urge to ask her what Lee and Ryan said in the hall. *Was it about my memory? Am I somehow a suspect?* I shake off the thought and watch Amanda leave my room. As of now, I am dreading everything about tomorrow.

In the morning, I will be discharged from the only place I feel a semblance of safety. In the afternoon, I will go home to an empty house. In the evening, I will try—and fail—to pretend like I don't have a dead husband. And at night, I will lie still, hoping to steal just one precious moment of sleep.

CHAPTER 10

I am back in the forest, jogging along that same winding trail. Majestic oaks shroud either side, giving me intense tunnel vision. All that matters is the path ahead. I run toward something I cannot see—something that I need to see.

My breathing is rhythmic, but the back of my throat burns with each inhalation. I am so used to the feeling that it barely fazes me. The elements threaten my perfect stride, though, as wind rushes against my body and bullets of rain obscure my vision. *Don't stop. Keep going.*

There's that hill again, looming up ahead. I tread toward it as more rain gushes into my eyes. Just as I approach the slope, something makes me slow my pace. It is pure feeling—a sense of danger. *Someone is behind me.*

Once again, I wake up panting, completely out of breath. My heart races uncontrollably as the monitor beside my bed blares in shrill beeps that make my heart pound even faster. I swear it is going to beat straight out of my chest.

A night nurse bursts through the doorway. His worried expression tells me one of two possibilities—he is new and inexperienced, or something is seriously wrong.

"Are you okay?" His voice sounds miles away.

I am still so panicked and disoriented that I can barely think straight. The air is dark and hot, and damp hair cakes the back of my neck.

"Veronica?" The nurse is at my bedside, hovering over me with a doubtful look. The detergent on his scrubs and the sanitizer on his hands fill my nostrils as I suck in air.

"You're all right," he says, attempting a gentler tone.

I flinch as his hand grazes my arm.

"I-I..." My senses are heightened—sight, smell, touch—and I cannot stop looking over my shoulder. "I-I'm not safe."

"You were just having a bad dream. A nightmare."

"I'm not safe." My voice is barely a whisper.

"Let's try taking some deep breaths to steady your heart rate. In... out... in... out. There we go. That's better."

Although my heartbeat slows considerably, the thoughts and fears in my head proliferate. *I am not safe.*

The night nurse leaves me alone with my mind racing as quickly as my heart was minutes before.

AS OF THIS AFTERNOON, I am deemed stable enough to be discharged. *Stable—yeah, right.*

"I'm sure you're anxious to get out of here," Amanda says from behind a large clipboard. She sits across from me, filling out a stack of forms. "Just a few more things I need to sign off on, and you're good to go."

I am perched on the edge of my bed, resisting the urge to tell her I would rather stay.

"I heard you had quite the morning. Patrick—the night nurse—told me that you woke up screaming."

"I don't remember screaming," I say honestly. "But yes, I had a really bad nightmare."

She frowns and continues signing paperwork.

"Another one," I add.

Amanda sets the clipboard on her lap and eyes me knowingly. "I realize that this is all a bit scary."

I nod and fidget with the belt loops on my jeans. Normal clothes seem foreign after lying in a hospital gown for so long.

"They just felt so real," I finally say, breaking the silence between us.

She pauses to look up again. "The nightmares?"

"Yes. So, so real."

"Nightmares generally do," she says gently. "That's what makes them so frightening."

"These were different—both of them."

"What happened?"

"I was running through a forest." I fill her with as much detail as I can remember. "There was no one else around."

Amanda raises an eyebrow.

"And then it changed. I could tell that something *was* wrong. Someone was behind me." I sense a familiar tightening in my chest.

"Well, that does sound pretty scary. I'm sorry that you had such a bad dream—bad *dreams*."

"I don't feel safe," I whisper.

"Look, there's a lot going on right now. The accident, your memory, the recent news..." She avoids mentioning my dead husband.

"Whoever killed him might still be out there."

Amanda frowns again and bites her lower lip.

"They might come for me."

"I think the nightmares are probably the result of your apprehension about all the changes going on in your life. Maybe the hill represents the obstacles you face as you adjust back to normalcy."

Amanda's attempt at decoding the symbolism in my dreams might not be far off.

"Then again," she continues, trying to lighten the mood, "you're the psychiatrist."

I throw her a bone in the form of a forced smile. Poor Amanda—she probably wants me to leave just as badly as I want to stay. "You're right. There are just so many unknowns."

She turns her attention back to the paperwork in her lap. "I'm sure that you'll get into a new routine, and the bad dreams will go away on their own."

"I hope so."

"Trust me," Amanda says with a wink, "if we kept you here any longer, you'd be having nightmares about *this* place."

CHAPTER 11

Despite the brevity of our relationship, Cathy and I share a surprisingly emotional goodbye.

"You call me anytime, hon." She wraps me in a tight hug. "Anytime at all."

"Thanks, Cathy." I smile and accept a note scribbled with her mobile and home numbers. It dawns on me that I do not even have a cell phone.

As if sensing this, Cathy adds, "I'm sure you'll get everything straightened out once you fly home. Maybe someone can help you sort through things—a friend or even a neighbor." She gives me an encouraging nod, but I can tell that she is choosing her words carefully. Neither of us wants to address my dead husband.

"Of course. I'm sure there'll be someone."

I step into the Desert Glen Hospital elevator. Its sterile smell reminds me of the room—and safety net—I am leaving behind. After pressing the lobby button, I peer out at the busy seventh floor one last time. The familiar scene of nurses buzzing around the hall narrows, disappearing as the doors close in front of me.

I glance down at the heeled leather boots encasing my feet. These shoes—along with the skinny jeans and coat I put on an hour ago—are painfully tight. This is the outfit they found me in. A plastic bag hanging around my hand cuts off the circulation in my fingers, temporarily turning them white. A nurse handed it to me shortly before I was discharged.

"These were your only belongings," she said with a shrug.

I opened the bag to find some money, personal items, and the clothes on my back. The latter are freshly laundered but full of an unmistakable hospital scent. My only other possessions are the coral tube of lip gloss, one sparkly diamond ring, and a tiny wad of cash.

The money is not enough to pay for cab fare and a plane ticket, but my travel arrangements are taken care of. The detectives booked me on a direct flight to San Francisco that leaves in three hours. Apparently, I will be billed once I can access my bank accounts again.

I crawl into the back of a bright-yellow taxi and pull the door shut. "Airport, please."

"Sure thing."

I settle into my seat and stare down at the clear bag dangling from my wrist. I have already counted every coiled bill, and the bright lip gloss does little to pique my interest. The ring shimmers brilliantly under a patch of sunlight and holds my attention. I leave it in the sealed bag, admiring its details through the plastic. A rose-gold band houses the large princess-cut diamond exquisitely. I do not know much about carats or clarity, but I would bet it is worth a fortune.

"You going on vacation or something?" The driver's voice shatters my jewelry-induced daze.

I look up from the bag and pause, turning my attention to the window. We are gliding past a long stretch of brick apartment buildings stacked neatly behind verdant lawns and dewy flowerbeds.

"Home," I finally respond. "I'm going home."

DETECTIVE RYAN MEETS me at the airport with an emergency ID. The pair of us breeze through security, and the process feels strange with such minimal possessions. Carrying only a plastic bag is embarrassing—borderline pathetic—at this point. I remove its meager contents and toss the bag in a nearby trash bin.

After putting the ring on my left hand, I tuck the lip gloss in my back pocket with the tight wad of twenties. This diamond is heavy on my finger as we walk to gate fifty. Somehow, Ryan looks even more uncomfortable than I feel.

"Would you like some coffee?" I ask him, breaking the silence. "There's a place over there."

"What? Oh—no. I'm okay, thanks."

I shrug and walk the short distance to a Starbucks kiosk. *They really are everywhere.* I slow my pace when I feel Ryan's gaze on me, pausing only to roll my eyes. Lee definitely instructed him to watch me like a hawk.

I shake off the thought and order an Americano. All I need to do right now is focus on getting home, someplace in San Francisco. *I don't even know my own address.* In fact, I barely possess any knowledge about the city. I visited briefly during college—a spontaneous trip with friends—but it was all sightseeing and tourist traps.

Maybe I live in one of those old Victorians near the Presidio, with a breathtaking view from my paned-glass windows. I would have breakfast in cute cafés and take long walks through the park. Or maybe I rent an apartment in one of those buildings off of Union Square—the ones with charming exteriors. I could shop on Market Street before eating my way through the Ferry Building.

"Tall Americano for Vonny?"

I grab my drink and step reluctantly back to Ryan, who still has his eyes glued to me. We spend another half hour forcing idle chitchat before boarding. For a second, I feel like we are old acquaintances catching up. Then I remember that he is investigating the murder of my late husband.

Other than a rough landing, our flight is uneventful. I instinctively head toward baggage claim before Ryan reminds me that I am traveling without luggage.

Right. As a chronic overpacker, I can say that this is truly a first. The last time I flew with solely a carry-on was probably during childhood.

I half expect the detective to accompany me home, but Ryan calls a car instead.

"Here's your address and house key." He hands me an envelope. "We secured a copy from your in-laws. Don't worry. The driver already knows where to take you."

I turn it over in my hands then step into a black sedan.

"Detective Lee and I will be in touch," he says before the driver pulls away. "Try to get some rest."

The ride back is bumpy and traffic-laden. I open my envelope to find an address printed neatly on a slip of white paper. The house number and street name do not mean much to me, so I pull out the key and examine its jagged edges.

Our trip consists mostly of freeways before we approach the tall buildings, cloudy skies, and hilly terrain that I remember from my vacation. San Francisco's sidewalks are decidedly more crowded than I recall.

Busy streets give way to residential lanes then private driveways and gated yards as the car climbs. The weather here is so overcast and misty. An array of striking, shingle-roofed homes peek through the heavy fog. I rub my bleary eyes and am instantly reminded of the giant ring on my finger.

I take it off then turn the band over, running my nails along its smooth rose-gold setting. This is most likely an engagement ring. *It has to be*. Or maybe it was an anniversary present—a gift from my doting husband.

As we enter another posh neighborhood, I am too distracted to read the street signs. Something else holds my tired gaze. I lift the ring close to my face and squint at the band's interior. There it is—an engraving in tiny cursive script. *Forever yours. Forever mine.* Those four words send a wave of dread through me.

I feel the car slow to a stop and hurriedly put my ring back on.

"Here we are," the driver says. "Home sweet home."

I peer out the window in disbelief.

"Here?"

"This is the address that gentleman gave me. Good old Pacific Heights."

"Th-this is where I live?"

"Yes, ma'am," he says with a chuckle. "Quite a place you've got there."

I fumble around for my envelope and double-check the address.

"Better hang onto this property," he adds. "She's a beauty."

My stomach drops. We are parked outside of an enormous, cream-colored house. I have never seen anything like it.

"Have a good one," the driver says as I shut the car door behind me.

"You too," I call back, but my gaze is fixed on the majestic building in front of me.

My possessions now include one tube of coral lip gloss, five wrinkled Jacksons, a shiny diamond ring, the clothes on my back, and what I can only assume is an outrageously expensive residence in Pacific Heights.

CHAPTER 12

The intricately designed brass doorknob is cool against my palm. My hand is still on it when a low hum emanates from inside my house, startling me. I was expecting complete silence. As I push the door open, a melody of chimes marks the top of an unknown hour. One of those grandfather clocks must be close by.

The entryway is nothing if not magnificent. My senses heighten as I attempt to take it all in—marble vases, mahogany floorboards, and exquisite vaulted ceilings with ornate details reminiscent of the Winter Palace. I stuff my key back into the envelope, tuck it in my front pocket, and shut the door behind me.

There are large paintings on each wall, staggered pristinely to frame a mesmerizing spiral staircase. My eyes widen as they trace the banister up to a large landing. Above, sunlight rushes through the type of arched stained-glass window often found in churches. Every block of color is marvelous. *What is this place?*

I might as well be a guest in someone else's home. This room is like a glossy picture torn out of an interior design magazine—the kind that Abby and I would flip through in college. We used to ear-mark pages just for the fun of it, laughing at the thought of owning such lavish pieces.

There are two long hallways stemming from the entryway. I slip off my shoes and choose the left one, tiptoeing across the polished floors. I intentionally avert my gaze from the walls as I go. If I look straight ahead, there is no chance of seeing photographs with people I cannot recognize. *That might send me over the edge.*

I continue until I reach the kitchen. This room is equally impressive, with state-of-the-art appliances and a large marble countertop that extends well beyond reason. There are several padded leather chairs tucked neatly underneath the bar. I wonder if I—*we*—used to entertain much. Then I notice something else.

There, perched perfectly at the edge of the stainless-steel sink, is a coffee mug. At first, it looks innocuous enough—just a dish waiting to be put away. Upon further examination, though, it is clear this is *his* mug. *My husband's mug.* I recoil as soon as I notice the untouched coffee inside.

My thoughts inevitably spiral. *Why didn't he drink it?* Maybe there was an early meeting at work, or perhaps he brewed the coffee but ran out of time. Maybe he simply forgot about it. Whatever happened, one thing is certain. This is the last coffee John Lewis made before his life ended.

My knees go weak. The room is not quite spinning but starting to warp at the edges. I draw a hand to my forehead and look for a stable surface. The counter is solid enough, but I have to escape this kitchen. I struggle into some sort of parlor, barely able to stand. *Everything is moving.* My vision blurs as I trip against a sofa. Then I collapse.

THE HOUSE IS DARK WHEN a shrill sound jolts me out of sleep. It takes me a moment to recognize the noise—an incoming phone call. I blink in the darkness and rub my eyes. *What time is it?* The ringing continues as I stand up and hurry toward the sound.

Of course. I—*we*—have a home phone, but I was not expecting any calls. The air is stiff and cool as I make my way out of the living room. While I pause in the hallway to search for a light, the ringing stops. My fingertips are clumsy against the textured wall, fumbling around until they find a switch. One flip, and the grand hall is illuminated.

The ringing resumes. I tread down the hallway, switching on more lights as I go. My feet carry me into a dining room—expectedly elaborate—but I continue down another hall instead. *This house is too massive for its own good*. Finally, I reach the kitchen, where I see a tiny flashing screen in the darkness. Luckily, I grab the phone on its last ring.

"Hello?" I sound winded.

"Mrs. Lewis?" It's Detective Lee's voice.

"Yes, hello. It's me."

"I apologize for calling this late, but I wanted to check in with you and follow up about a few things."

I glance at the oven clock. It's nine thirty.

"So." Lee clears his throat. "Did you arrive home safely?"

"Yes. I got here earlier this afternoon and have been... reacquainting myself with the house."

"Good."

I wonder why he is actually calling at this hour.

"Have you started going through possessions yet? Either your own or your husband's?"

"Not really. I'm pretty tired, but I might try tomorrow."

"I understand," he says coolly. "If you come across anything suspicious, please call Detective Ryan or me immediately."

"Suspicious?"

"In other words, anything that might provide insight into your husband's murder."

Lee does not mince words. I am still not used to hearing it all out loud, though. "Is there something in particular that I should be looking for?"

Lee pauses, calculating his next response. "Look, Mrs. Lewis—"

"Vonny."

"*Vonny*. Your husband's case has become a bit more intricate. When it comes to alleyway murders, we usually see armed robberies and muggings."

"Okay." I breathe into the phone, lamenting the fact that I did not turn on the kitchen light.

"Your husband was found with all of his possessions intact—ID, credit cards, keys, you name it. This makes the situation I mentioned far less likely."

I walk over to the opposite wall and flip on another switch.

"We now suspect that someone was targeting your husband for a very specific reason. The murderer likely had ill will against him."

My grip tightens on the phone.

"I know that this is a lot to process, but I want to keep you in the loop as much as I can."

"I appreciate that," I say honestly.

"The person who did this..." Lee lets the silence linger between us. "Their motive is still unclear."

What is he hinting at?

"There's no easy way to say this," the detective continues. "We want you to be careful—to keep an eye out. Not just for suspicious objects but people."

My stomach drops.

"Again, I apologize for calling so late. I realize that you're dealing with a lot right now."

"Do you really think that I..." My voice is faint. "That I might have a target on my back?"

"We're not jumping to any conclusions yet. The most important thing is to be aware of your surroundings during this investigation."

I swallow hard and try to steady my breath.

"Is there anything else you'd like to ask before I go?"

"I know this is probably a stupid question, but are you positive that it's really him? My husband, I mean. Are you completely sure?"

Lee clears his throat again. "We are. His parents identified the body earlier this week."

"His parents?" I forgot to ask about my in-laws earlier.

"Yes—Carol Ann and..." I hear Lee shuffling papers around and wonder if he is calling from home or is still at the office. "Charles Lewis."

"Where do they live?" It is definitely odd to be asking a detective details about my own mother- and father-in-law, but I still do not remember anything.

"Boston."

"Oh." I am not really sure what else to say.

"Detective Ryan and I informed them about your medical situation. I'm sure they'll be reaching out shortly if they haven't already."

"Okay." My voice wanes again.

"They're probably just overwhelmed with the news. Their son—your husband—" He stops. "These things are extremely hard on families."

For a moment, I sense a welcome strain of empathy in Lee's voice.

"Like I said before," he continues, "let me know if you find anything in the house. I should go. Goodbye, Mrs. Lewis."

"Before you do, I—"

Then he hangs up.

CHAPTER 13

I am walking down an empty street somewhere in my childhood hometown. The air is crisp, but an early winter breeze gives it a bitter edge. My boots crunch over frozen leaves as snowflakes cover the ground. All of the shop lights are turned off, and this block is completely deserted.

Where is everyone? I continue on, noting the vacancy in each store and restaurant. Up ahead, my favorite toy shop shines like a beacon—it's the same the one I used to spend hours in as a little girl. A smile spreads across my frosty lips as I peer through the vibrant windows.

Inside is the dollhouse that I always wanted but could never afford. It was the most expensive item in the store, painted baby blue with a wraparound front porch. Two robotic dogs—chocolate brown in color—sit beside the house. I look for a price tag before spotting the classic red wagon that my friends and I used to love. We would take turns sitting in it and pull each other around until our arms gave out.

Something interrupts my memory. There is a flicker in the window—a sudden movement that mars my reflection. *Someone is behind me.*

Before I can turn around, two large hands grab my neck. I kick and struggle to free myself, but the grip is too intense. Ten fingers dig into my throat as I gasp for air. I feel faint, losing consciousness by the second. The attacker squeezes tighter, crumpling my skin like a wad of newspaper. I try to yell, but the screech dies in my throat.

I wake up screaming with my own hands wrapped around my neck. *Choking or protecting?* It is impossible to know for sure. A thin layer of sweat glistens on each palm. Everything is blurry in the harsh morning light. I sit up and squint against the brightness, eventually mustering enough strength to stand. My legs are shaky, threatening to buckle beneath the rest of me.

I find my way down the hall and attempt to recall the night before. Overwhelmed by physical fatigue and mental exhaustion, I fell asleep before Lee called. *Didn't I?* Then we had that brutal conversation.

His words replay as I walk into the kitchen and run my fingers along the smooth marble countertop. Just thinking about his warning over "anything suspicious" makes me shudder.

The porcelain mug is still by the sink. *Panicking at the mere sight of a coffee cup. How pathetic.* It obviously took more than the mug to send me spiraling. The tipping point was my realization that my husband used it on the morning of his death.

He has touched everything in this household—sat at the dining table, cooked with these dishes, and read the novels lining each organized bookshelf. Then again, so have I. We probably engaged in most activities together. Shared meals might have punctuated our time, beginning and ending each day as a unit.

I wonder what kind of couple we were. *Was our marriage marked by affection or bickering? Did we engage in playful banter to keep the spark alive? Did it ever truly burn out?* For now, at least, our marriage will remain a mystery. I cannot furnish a single detail about John Lewis.

The idea that I am living inside *our* home—a place we created together—scares the hell out of me. I have been in this house for one day, but it feels like a tortuous eternity. Just staying here is too much to bear. *How am I going to get used to it all?*

This mansion is larger than any residence I have ever seen—much less lived in. There are so many rooms to explore, innumerable corners and crevices to familiarize myself with. Not to mention the entire upstairs level. I have troves of documents, photographs, and formerly sentimental coffee mugs to sort through. A familiar tightening begins to grip my chest.

I find a bathroom around the corner and splash cold water on my face. The porcelain sink console looks straight out of the 1920s, maybe '30s. The black-and-white geometric tiling is corrugated and cold beneath my thin socks. I turn off the faucet before noticing several sheets of busy floral wallpaper. I could be at a posh, art deco-themed hotel in the middle of Manhattan.

As far as I can tell, every space in this house is distinctly decorated. Each area seems to have a theme—the striking foyer, ultra-modern kitchen, and retro powder room. *Did we design our home together?* Before I turn off the light, I catch a glimpse of myself in the beveled mirror and stop in my tracks.

I have not seen my reflection since that day in the hospital. My tacit—and shortsighted—plan was to avoid all mirrors and photographs indefinitely. Looking at this face is still deeply unsettling. My former appearance was altered significantly during that missing decade. A face modified by time and inaccessible experience.

Laugh lines frame my mouth. *Are they the product of John's cheesy jokes or drunken game nights with friends?* Faint wrinkles reside between my brows. *The result of grad school exams or a stressful job?* I search the remaining inches of aging skin before settling on my own deep, dark, and unnerving gaze. These eyes have seen things I cannot recall. That fact, simple and definitive, terrifies me more than anything else.

I COME TO AFTER ANOTHER reluctant nap. A perilous concoction of lethargy and fear continues lingering in my bones, pulling me deeper into a sedentary state. Shreds of sunlight emanate from a narrow window on the far wall. My eyes scan the room until they land on an ebony frame, large and sleek, encasing a cream-colored document. After peeling myself off the sofa, I take a closer look.

My graduate diploma takes center stage, surrounded by a series of psychology certificates. Staring at the bold type is surreal. Here is tangible proof of my greatest achievements, my loftiest dreams coming to fruition. I am a psychiatrist.

I may not remember the past decade of my life, but the knowledge still dwells somewhere inside of me. Familiarizing myself with New Vonny's routine can only help. I try to switch into psychiatrist mode and analyze this situation methodically. *What would I recommend to a patient*? Pacing around the room, I mentally file through ideas.

The logical approach is to interrupt this cycle. Exploring these new surroundings—the set dressing of my former life—might help me regain access. Between my amnesia prognosis and ongoing nightmares, everything about this city feels daunting. *So does everything about this house.* I need to start somewhere, though.

I decide to break the task up into less intimidating chunks. My plan is to reacquaint myself with a different area each day, room by room, until I feel a sense of security within these walls. *My literal home base.* I can work my way up to venturing outside, going for a stroll around the block, and meeting my neighbors. Maybe I will even start running again.

I capitalize on my newfound bravery by starting this very second. My stomach dictates via audible hunger pangs that I begin in the kitchen. I have not eaten since yesterday morning—scrambled eggs, toast, and a pudding cup at the hospital.

There are several white cabinets lining the walls. I choose a floor-length one opposite the stove, pulling it open to reveal three well-stocked shelves. My appetite only increases as I eye the plethora of choices. Cereal boxes, cartons of organic chicken broth, and packaged rye crackers stare back at me.

A brief inventory of pantry items reveals that New Vonny is arguably more health-conscious than my college self. *A stark nutritional difference.* The opportunity to override my presiding college sweet tooth presents itself blatantly, but I turn it down. Instead, I opt for the most sugar-laden snack I can find—cinnamon maple granola.

I scour the other cabinets for a bowl before coming up empty. The closest vessel I can find is a scalloped casserole dish, so I resort to another one of my old habits. After prying open the cereal box, I grab a generous fistful of clustered oats, shove them in my mouth, then chew until my throat runs dry.

When I pull open the French door fridge, a rancid, overpowering smell is my only greeting. I slam the left door shut and plug my nose. After composing myself, I crack the fridge open again ever so slowly.

A rotten tub of yogurt sits menacingly on the second shelf. The container is ajar, its lid nowhere to be found. Dark-green mold climbs up around the edges, practically reaching the top rim. A groan escapes my lips as I tentatively extend an arm.

The sight and stench of the yogurt squelch my remaining appetite. Once I find some grocery bags—conveniently located under the sink—I seal the entire container and head for the automatic garbage bin against the wall. An equally displeasing odor overcomes me when I wave my hand to open it. Without looking, I drop the yogurt into the week's trash buildup of putrid food and who knows what else.

While I'm at it, I clean out the rest of the fridge. Bruised fruit, wilted vegetables, and an expired carton of milk land in my throw-away pile. I am pleasantly surprised to find plenty of unspoiled items hiding in the trenches, including a selection of unopened cheeses, one giant jug of orange juice, and two large pallets of eggs.

I open a window near the stove in an effort to air out this kitchen. The heavy morning fog hangs low, cloaking the backyard in shades of gray. If my college visit was indicative of anything, the weather will change in a few hours. I reach up and swipe a hand across the glass pane. Beads of condensation shift, but clouds still obscure my view.

After spotting a teakettle, I fish around for a box of English breakfast. My favorite kind is in short supply—only five bags left. Its place in the rotation comes as a promising sign, though. New Vonny still has good taste in tea.

I brew a steamy cup, wondering how long it will take to get used to this room. The sheer size reminds me of a restaurant-scale kitchen. It seems well equipped to cook dinner for a small army and large enough to seat all the troops. My childhood home had a tiny U-shaped nook that barely fit more than an oven. This space could easily house fifty people, maybe more.

I wonder if we hosted lavish parties or if we preferred intimate gatherings with close friends. *Did John and I have close friends?* Our social calendar is yet another artifact to be discovered over time.

I close my eyes, envisioning a soiree full of anonymous guests. Our private chef creates decadent spreads while uniformed waiters carry silver platters of hors d'oeuvres. I swim through the crowd, catching glimpses of each partygoer. Extravagant silk gowns with encrusted detailing and dapper black-as-night tuxedos abound.

A hand brushes mine as soft lips graze my cheek. *I found you.*

My eyes fly open. Measured breaths bring me back to the present moment—back to standing in an empty kitchen. *Who was that? Was it John?* Just like this morning, the line is blurred. It is impossible to distinguish dream from memory, nightmare from reality.

Maybe I will find my answer in another room. A myriad of secrets lurks between these walls. Bit by bit, I will uncover them and piece together remnants of the past decade until a clear picture presents itself. Maybe one day, this will really feel like a home again—my home. *Our home.*

CHAPTER 14

I spend the rest of my afternoon sorting through cabinets and cup-
boards. There are enough pantry items to stock a convenience
store. The only downside is a dearth of fresh fruits and vegetables.
Packaged snacks are fine for now, but I will eventually want something beyond canned soup and crackers.

My feet ache. I am still not used to moving around this much,
so brief breaks are proving necessary. Despite the residual soreness,
being upright is a much welcome change from lying in bed all day.
Gradually, retreating to the hospital is sounding less and less appeal-
ing.

I plan to finish the kitchen by this evening and start on the living
room tomorrow. A cursory stroll helps me map out the entire first
floor of this home. There are seven main areas on the lower level—the entryway, living room, hallways, parlor, dining room, library,
and a den that appears to be John's office. Despite a bud of curiosity,
I am avoiding the basement for now and will tackle the second level
once I finish up downstairs.

At some point, I will have to enter our bedroom, but sleeping
in the very bed I shared with a man I do not remember is still too
strange. Honestly, just thinking about it sends chills through me. I
am much better off on our couch for the time being.

Just as I return to the tap to refill my water, the doorbell rings.
I think about ignoring it but quickly realize that John's family—my
in-laws—might be stopping by.

I run a hand through my hair, cursing the fact that I have not showered in a couple days. There is zero chance of me looking presentable. I smooth my shirt with little to show for it and continue to the foyer. Thanks to the windows on either side of the front door—devoid of curtains—I can instantly see my guest. More importantly, she can see me.

Standing on my front step is a tall blonde who looks like she might double as an actress or a model. She may be wearing minimal makeup and a fitted pantsuit, but her figure and chiseled face could easily grace magazine covers and runways.

Maybe she has the wrong address. Perhaps she is looking for a different building—some director's mansion or a casting agency downtown. Her cheery wave says otherwise, though, so I decide to let the woman in. She could be a neighbor or coworker—someone I go to brunch and happy hour with. Her face lights up as I turn the door handle.

"Vonny," she says in a smooth British accent, "it's so good to see you!"

I flinch when she sticks her arms out for a hug.

"Right. Sorry about that."

This woman is obviously a friend, maybe even someone from John's family. I feel bad for her.

"You don't remember me, do you?" she asks as a rush of cold air wafts in.

I shake my head and peer outside. The sun is setting, and there is no car parked in the driveway. She must have walked or taken the bus.

"My name is Cheryl," she says softly. "May I come in?"

I chew on my bottom lip and wonder what to do. Despite wanting to trust her, I am justifiably suspicious of everyone I encounter at this point. Cheryl seems harmless enough, but appearances can be deceiving.

"I know that this is hard to believe, given the situation," she continues, "but you and I are best friends."

"I REALLY CAN'T APOLOGIZE enough," Cheryl says. "It breaks my heart that I wasn't able to visit you in the hospital."

We are both perched on the damask camelback sofa that happens to be my makeshift bed. I brewed us some tea, but Cheryl has yet to touch hers.

"Really," I repeat. "It's okay."

"I was in Tokyo for a business trip. When you weren't responding to my texts, I just figured that you were busy. But then I found out about what happened, and... God, V. I just feel so awful that you're going through all this." She opens her mouth to say something else but decides against it.

I nod, lost for words.

"The house looks lovely as usual." She flashes a broad smile. "You have always been such a genius when it comes to design."

Her attempt to cut the tension is heartening. *Poor Cheryl.* Two weeks ago, I was her confidant and best friend. But now I do not even recognize her. This realization softens me a bit, urging me to contribute to our waning conversation. The least I can do is talk to her.

"So... you said that we were—*are*—good friends?" The question sounds more awkward than I anticipated.

"Yes." She nods. "We met shortly after you moved to the city."

Cheryl's British accent adds a layer of sophistication to everything she says. Her impeccable style doesn't hurt either. I give myself an imaginary pat on the back for having such an elegant friend.

"Where did we meet?" I ask before taking another sip of oolong.

An infectious grin spreads across her crimson lips. "We were both at UCSF around the same time. Helped each other through it all."

"You're a psychiatrist too?"

"Pharmacist. We had similar schedules, though. You started your residency right as I was interviewing for mine."

Relief floods my face. "Grad school pals, then."

"Exactly—best mates. We've had so much fun together over the years." Cheryl's blue eyes sparkle at some unknown memory.

The sentiment makes me think of Abby, along with our mysterious falling out. I hide my hurt with a smile and offer Cheryl more tea. Her cup is still full, though.

"No, thanks. I should probably head out."

I am taken aback that she wants to leave so soon but quickly realize that it is already dark outside. "Oh. Of course," I murmur before we walk back to the foyer.

Cheryl bends down to slip on her Prada heels. For a moment, I truly wish she would stay.

"Listen, V—*Vonny*. I don't want to get in your way, but I am here if you need me."

"Thanks. I'm really glad you stopped by."

Something distant clouds Cheryl's eyes, but she blinks it off and gives me a quick hug.

"Maybe we could have lunch sometime soon?"

"I would love that. I'll call you to arrange a time." And with that, Cheryl steps outside into the darkness, looking impossibly chic as she goes.

I hover in the doorway, watching my best friend leave. She has such an intriguing presence—some intangible quality that makes me want to get to know her better. Cheryl is obviously drop-dead gorgeous, but there is something else too. Something trustworthy.

As I lock the door then walk back into the kitchen, I remember the forlorn look in Cheryl's eyes. It reminded me so much of my own—an odd fusion of sadness and nostalgia. But there was also a glimmer of hope in her eyes before she left.

I am her Abby. Cheryl's expression mirrored the exact feeling I had after hearing that painful voicemail message in the hospital. Thinking about it now makes my stomach churn. Abby, my former best friend, wants absolutely nothing to do with me.

I wonder if Cheryl felt that same way—or worse—when I first answered the door. Shared longing for our respective friendships makes me feel instantly closer to her. But Cheryl does not have to worry. *She won't lose me like I've lost Abby.*

CHAPTER 15

My dry eyes sting as I take in early morning light. The parlor is bathed in a ghostly whitish glow, and dawn has come far too quickly. Fatigue and emotional exhaustion still weigh my body down. I turn over, wincing at the crick in my neck before sharper pain ensues. It runs down the length of my spine, spiking as I move.

I sit up and gently massage my shoulder. Back in college, I could fall asleep on the floor and wake up completely refreshed the next day. Maybe my body cannot handle things like that anymore. Apparently, late nights and cramped positions take a larger toll with age.

On the bright side, my slumber was finally devoid of terrifying dreams. Perhaps seeing Cheryl had something to do with this new-found improvement. I definitely felt calmer after her unannounced visit.

I pull up my socks and pad into the kitchen. A bag of dark roast is sitting right where I left it by the sink. Minutes later, I am sitting at the marble counter, sipping from a red mug. I turn it over and read the white block letters: World's Best Husband.

This mug looks like the type of gift someone would buy in a pinch. A last-minute present for a forgotten occasion—merely an afterthought. It seems tacky compared to the pricier items in this house. *Maybe I bought it for John as a joke.* I wonder what kind of gifts we normally gave each other. *Silk pajamas? Spa certificates? Golf lessons?* After spending a few days in this house, I would be shocked if we didn't belong to at least one country club.

I finish my coffee and rinse out John's red mug. The kitchen window is gleaming—so spotless that I notice how clear it looks outside. Almost all of the fog has dissipated, giving way to a beautiful morning. Only a smattering of clouds remains in the bright blue sky.

For the first time since being here, I stare out into our expansive backyard. It is considerably nicer than any image I conjured up in my head. A manicured lawn verdantly stretches across most of the ground. Closer to the house is a cobblestone patio, with a fire pit surrounded by several red Adirondack chairs. An intricate gazebo canvassed in bright climbing flowers stands on the other side of the lawn. There are English roses, ivy arches, and delicate white trellises. Along with the other elements of this house, the entire yard looks like something straight out of a design magazine.

I tap my fingers against the edge of the sink and sigh. Unfortunately, I can no longer deny the fact that I need a shower. More than a few days have passed, and the stench emanating from my feet is impossible to ignore. I wanted to avoid the upper level of this house for as long as possible, but my plan will have to adapt.

The prospect of going upstairs makes my heart race. Our second story is another unknown—strange rooms and foreign spaces. There are too many possibilities crammed into one level. Attempting pragmatism, I shake my head and walk toward the foyer.

Our entryway is far less daunting in the sunlight. Everything appears cheerier somehow, like I am standing in a cozy home instead of an intimidating mansion. I take a deep breath and eye the staircase. Clutching the smooth banister, I ascend step-by-step.

Large frames in neat rows taunt my peripheral vision as I climb up to the landing. Crisp black-and-white photographs beg me to take a closer look. *Maybe just a quick glance.* I shake my head and press on, diverting my eyes from the wall as I go.

Deftly avoiding any and all pictures, I almost make it to the top. Then one photo quite literally stops me in my tracks. Unlike the others, there is some imperfection about it. In the top right-hand corner is a wrinkly bulge that my eyes latch onto.

I turn my head slowly until I am face-to-face with the image. The black-and-white photo depicts a narrow street of Parisian-style shops that I do not recognize. A travel shot, perhaps, housed by a blue mat in a thick black frame. My eyes dart back to that crumpled, bumpy area in the upper corner of the image. I hesitate for a moment, however brief, but ultimately cannot resist. My hands cautiously remove the black frame from the wall before turning it over. I undo five clasps then open the back in one fell swoop.

An aged picture practically falls out, but it is not the travel photo I first saw. I bring the small, colorful print to my face and examine it carefully. A tall figure stands at the forefront of the picture. *John.* Lee showed me a headshot of him at the hospital. His spectral blue eyes and subtle smile are instantly recognizable. Donning a tux and boutonniere, he stands before an altar. *Of course.* This is a photo from our wedding.

I lean in to take a closer look at the vibrant floral arrangements with baby's breath and cerulean bows. There are two stained-glass windows behind John. *Where am I?* Maybe this was taken at the beginning of our ceremony, mere moments before I walked down the aisle.

Just then, my fingers discover a crease. The picture is folded so neatly that I didn't even realize until now. I undo it with care, tentatively revealing the rest of the image. A gasp escapes my throat as I stumble backwards. Everything falls from my hands—the frame, a thin sheet of glass, and the mysterious photograph. I catch myself on the banister for support. The woman in the wedding dress is not me. It's Cheryl.

I get a hold of myself before proceeding. The frame I dropped along with its accompanying glass piece are intact, landing safely on the padded stairs. Exhaling, I bend down to pick them up. My fingers pluck the image from the snowy-white carpet, turning it over more cautiously than I did before.

My chest rises as I study the photo in its entirety. I run my fingers along the picture's edges, tracing its corners as my mind races. *When was this*? Nothing makes sense right now.

John and Cheryl make a gorgeous couple. Cheryl's ivory wedding dress further emphasizes her pristine figure. The lace bodice gives way to a voluminous tulle skirt, and the delicate collar detailing accentuates her slender neck. A cream-colored veil obscures part of her blond hair, which is gracefully pulled back in a tight chignon. I stare intently at Cheryl's face, scrutinizing every aspect of her angular bone structure. Her eyelids—dusted in mauve shadow—are swept shut while a demure smile plays across her lips. John looks at her through watery eyes, a loving gaze. *He looks happy*. They both do.

I have a million questions, but I don't know where to begin. *How did John and Cheryl meet? When were they married? Is she actually my friend?* Before I can figure out what to do next, the doorbell rings.

CHAPTER 16

Cheryl lifts a ceramic mug to her crimson lips. A pair of fitted gloves instantly reminds me how sophisticated she is. We are perched on the very camelback sofa that we sat on last night, sipping the same varieties of tea. She showed up shortly after I found the photograph, and thanks to the lack of curtains on my front windows, I think she saw the entire thing. *Impeccable timing.*

"What was all that? On the stairs, I mean." Her airy British voice wafts through the room.

I fidget beside Cheryl, unsure of what to say. I do not want to bend the truth, but I cannot bring myself to confront her yet. After all, I'm still processing what I just saw.

"Vonny?"

"I-I was just looking at all of the wall art." At least it's not a complete lie.

She nods, brushing back a strand of silky blond hair. "See anything interesting?"

"Not really." I sound unconvincing even to myself.

Cheryl raises an eyebrow, but remains silent.

"More tea?" I attempt to change the subject.

"I'm fine, thank you."

"Oh, okay." I shift uncomfortably in my seat, wishing that I could eliminate the palpable awkwardness. When I look at Cheryl's serene face, all I see is the woman in the wedding dress—a beautiful bride standing at the altar with my dead husband. "Actually..."

She turns toward me, face flooded with interest.

"Well, there was one thing."

She pushes her mug forward. "What is it?"

"I saw you, um, in a print on the wall." I look at Cheryl expectantly.

"I should hope so." She gives a short laugh. "I would be deeply offended if I didn't make the *famous* Lewis wall of photographs."

I am taken aback at Cheryl's sarcastic tone. She clearly doesn't know what I mean. "No. It was a wedding photo."

She stiffens.

"A photo of you and John."

Cheryl's striking blue eyes cloud over while she stares at me.

"I'm just confused. You both are standing in a church, and—"

"Can I see it?" Her tone is clipped.

"Sure."

The emotion in her eyes—intense and unreadable—scares me.

"One minute. Let me go and grab it." I walk back into the foyer and start to ascend the staircase. I lean down to pick up the photo when I hear something in the other room—a loud slam.

"Cheryl?" I call out. "Are you all right?"

There is no response as I pad back down each step and hurry through the hallway. The sofa is empty, and my friend is nowhere to be found. I look around the room, scouring it for any sign of her. *Nothing.*

The back door is slightly ajar, its sheer curtain rustling around the wooden frame. I immediately rush over and pull it wide open. My heart sinks when I see nothing but the empty yard. The Adirondack chairs, fire pit, and flower-laden gazebo are just where I last saw them. Cheryl is gone.

"THAT'S WHERE I WAS standing." I gesture to the ninth step. "And that's the frame that I found the photo in."

Lee regards me with an indecipherable expression while Ryan takes notes.

"It was hidden behind this picture." I hold up the black-and-white street print.

"And she just showed up at your front door," Lee says curtly. "Interesting."

I recount everything that happened since Cheryl came over yesterday. Her unexpected introduction, our brief conversation, and her surprise visit earlier this morning. After she left without any sort of warning, I called the detectives in a panic. Lee and Ryan arrived less than an hour later, and we have been rehashing details ever since.

"And you said that she introduced herself as your best friend?" Ryan asks from behind his notebook.

"Yes."

"Are you sure about that?" Lee asks in his signature pointed tone. "Semantics are very important here, Mrs. Lewis."

"I'm positive," I say coolly.

He starts walking toward the left hallway as Ryan and I follow closely behind. Although both men are dressed in suits, each detective exudes a drastically different energy. Lee is polished with a black button-down, slicked-back hair, and a clean shave. He oozes confidence while gliding into the parlor ahead of me. Ryan, on the other hand, looks just as gangly as the first time I met him. He is wearing the same baggy suit that he donned in the hospital. There are purplish bags under his sunken eyes, and I find myself pitying him rather than feeling intimidated by his presence.

"This is where she left from?" Lee points a tan finger at the back door.

"I'm pretty sure. I don't know where else she would have gone."

He opens the door and steps outside.

Ryan looks up from his copious notes. "You don't recognize her at all?"

"Not at all. She said that we met shortly after I moved to San Francisco."

Lee walks back in and glances at an end table. "Was that her drink?"

I eye the red mug and nod.

"Dump that and bag it," Lee tells Ryan.

Ryan puts on a pair of blue latex gloves and picks up the mug.

"We'll be taking this in for fingerprints," Lee says. "I'll also need the wedding photograph."

"Does that mean she's a suspect?"

Ryan defers to Lee, who purses his lips before responding. "Nothing is definite yet, Mrs. Lewis. A case becomes more complicated when additional people come into the picture." He sighs. "You were right to call us. We're interested in any sort of suspicious behavior, and that definitely includes unusual encounters like the one you had today."

I hand over the photo.

Lee gives me a hard look. "Before we go, is there anything else you'd like to tell us?"

"No." I shake my head for emphasis. "Not that I can think of."

"We'll be in touch, then. Remember to let us know if you come across anything else."

"I will." I follow the men back down the hall and into the foyer. "I really hope that we can figure this whole thing out. I just wish I could be of more help."

The detectives pause in the doorway.

"The truth always comes out," Lee says with a glimmer in his eye. "We're going to speak with your in-laws tomorrow."

CHAPTER 17

This time, I actually feel the fingers close around my throat. Jagged nails dig into my pale flesh as I choke. My limbs are wild beneath the attacker's relentless grip. I struggle, pulling and clawing to no avail. The energy leaves my body like sand in an hourglass, draining grain by grain until nothing is left.

I wake myself up with my gasps for air. The parlor comes back into focus as my eyes dart around the room, and I try to steady my breath. It was just a bad dream—an awful one. Pearly-gray light swathes the room in a nauseating fog.

The crick in my neck becomes notably more painful as I force myself up. A familiar soreness emanates from my lower back, and the stark lighting stings my bleary eyes. I massage each shoulder while taking a deep breath. *Why does this keep happening?* Once my heart rate returns to a normal pace, I walk into the kitchen to brew some coffee.

Before I reach for the canister, I see a drawer I haven't noticed before. Its discreet placement—completely flush with the cabinetry—make it almost undetectable. I initially assumed it was just another aesthetic choice. Unlike every other kitchen drawer, this one has no knob or handle. I probably would have passed it by again if I had been moving at a normal speed.

This time, I fiddle with its edges until I pry it loose. The drawer slides out with a screech to reveal a spiral notebook, two ballpoint pens, and a sleek laptop. Curiosity flickers through me as I reach for the computer and open it up. *Dead battery*. I check the drawer for a charger but have no such luck.

After twenty minutes of scouring the vicinity, I halt my search and resolve to look for a charger later. Preferably post-caffeination. While my coffee brews, I spot the phone that I have only used twice. Aside from utilizing my landline or venturing outside, I'm in a bubble.

Taking my first sip of sobering dark roast, I make a mental note to procure a working laptop, cell phone, and reasonable data plan. The hot liquid scalds my throat as I sip, wincing briefly at the burn, and swallow. Still, I appreciate its bracing effect and relish the feeling of my lethargy dissipating with every mouthful. I will do whatever it takes to keep myself awake at this point—anything to prolong the time before my next nightmare.

AT THREE IN THE AFTERNOON, just I am finishing a late lunch of canned soup, rye crackers, and sliced cheese, the phone rings. My stomach clenches as I hurry over to the receiver. I brace myself, assuming that one of the detectives is calling to ask me more questions.

"Hello?"

"Vonny? Oh, it's so good to hear your voice." I do not recognize the woman speaking, but her tone is somehow comforting. "It's Carol Ann. Your mother-in-law."

"Oh, um. Hi. Sorry, I don't really..."

"That's all right, dear. The detectives told us about what happened. I'm so sorry."

"Thank you." My impression is that John's mom truly means well.

"I would have called sooner," she says. "I would have hopped on a flight and visited you in the hospital—"

"That's okay. Please don't worry about it."

"It's just... well, we didn't hear from you or John for weeks. We didn't even know where you were, and then—" Her voice breaks softly.

I grip the phone tighter, struggling with what to say next. This poor woman just lost her son.

"And then we heard about John," she continues between sobs. "I-I still can't believe it."

"I'm so sorry," I say quietly. "I wish I could give you a hug."

"Oh, Vonny. You're so sweet—you've always been that way."

My lips lift into a sad smile.

Carol Ann sniffles. "I know we're both hurting, dear."

In this moment, I want to commiserate with her—to talk about John and what we miss most about him. But I can't. I still do not remember anything about my husband, much less about my mother-in-law. There is a long pause before she speaks again.

"I also wanted to talk to you about Cheryl. The detectives mentioned that you saw her?"

"Yes. She came by the house."

Another extended pause unsettles me.

"Dear," Carol Ann says firmly, "Cheryl is dead."

"*What?*"

"There was an accident. Cheryl was caught in a fire several years ago."

"She—she can't be dead."

"I know this is probably a lot to take in."

"But... she was just here."

Carol Ann is silent.

I suppress the urge to repeat that I *did* in fact see Cheryl—that I talked to her while we sipped tea and sat on the sofa.

"I'm sure that memory trauma can be very tricky," she finally says.

I know what my mother-in-law is implying, but my mind is not playing tricks on me. I need more information.

"Dear?"

"Did I know about Cheryl?" I ask her. "Before my accident, I mean."

"I think so. John and Cheryl had a complicated marriage to say the least. I assume he told you about it."

"Complicated?"

"Well..." She wavers for a moment. "Arguments, tension—things like that."

"Really?"

"Yes. Before they separated, Cheryl went on a trip to clear her head. That's when she—"

"Oh, God." *That's when Cheryl died.*

"John was so broken up about the whole thing. Couldn't ever quite forgive himself."

"That's awful."

"It was. But then he married you," Carol Ann says in a lighter tone. "You gave him the fresh start he was looking for."

I want to ask more questions, but my mind is still reeling from the news she just dropped.

"Anyway," she says sadly, "we weren't planning on having a formal memorial service. I think it would be too difficult right now given the circumstances."

"Of course." Part of me wonders if I should put something together. I wouldn't even know where to begin, though, or who to invite.

"Listen," Carol Ann says before we hang up. "Please let me know if you need anything—anything at all. We're in Boston, but the distance is no matter. We would gladly have you come stay at the house if that might make things—"

"Oh, thank you. I really appreciate that, but I should probably stay here for now. At least until the investigation ends."

"Of course. Well, please don't hesitate to call, dear."

"Thanks," I say in the kindest voice I can muster. "You too."

CHAPTER 18

Last night, I dreamt of Cheryl. It was not exactly nightmarish—more of a strange reverie. We were talking about John, discussing his funny habits and little quirks. Our conversation did not feel like one shared between people married to the same man at different times. We laughed like best friends, sipping wine while trading stories. The strangest part was that it felt more like a memory than a dream.

I sit up slowly and run my hand along the sofa where Cheryl sat just days before.

She was really here, wasn't she? The thought continues to ferment. I turn it over obsessively in my head, replaying our visit ad nauseam.

Carol Ann sounded so convincing on the phone, especially with her explanation of John's rocky first marriage. But Cheryl cannot be dead. *There's just no way, is there?* I mull over the possibility and glance at the sofa once more.

Although my makeshift bed is anything but comfortable, I have been trying to avoid the second level of this house at all costs. *Could it really be that bad?* At this point, I am just living in fear of my surroundings. I bring a finger to my lips and consider the prospect of venturing back up that staircase.

I finally decide to bite the bullet. If I don't do it now, I might never work up the courage. I owe it to myself—and John—to explore the remaining parts of our home. After downing a quick cup of coffee, I stand at the base of our grand staircase, staring up its polished banister.

I take a few tentative steps before looking to my right. An intimidating wall of photographs stares back at me. The wedding photo isn't among them, of course, but the memory of the discovery sends a shudder through me nonetheless. I shake myself off, ascending the remaining stairs.

Window light floods half of the hallway at the top in a whitish cast. The first door on the left is wide open, inviting me inside. I enter cautiously, noting the room's sumptuous textiles and luxurious details. It is even fancier than the rest of our house. I feel like I am touring an old Hollywood movie set. Deep-velvet throw pillows, silky curtains, and glints of silver and gold adorn what must be the master suite. This is it—*our* bedroom.

A large beveled mirror twinkles in the morning light. I inch toward my large vanity, admiring its chic display. Chanel perfume bottles have been arranged alongside fluffy brushes and golden lipstick cases. I am definitely not used to wearing such expensive makeup—or any makeup for that matter. College life did not call for Dior eye palettes or Armani silk foundation. Not mine, anyway.

I do my best to look past our sizeable bed and the frames hanging on our wall. Those are for another day. Instead, I move further inside the master suite's two closets—*his and hers.* I think about going into John's first but decide against it.

I flip on a silver switch, brightening my entire closet with an unmatched level of wattage. Three panels of glimmering lights illuminate every square inch. A crystal chandelier hangs proudly overhead, imbuing every article with unnecessary sparkle. Abby, a longtime *Vogue* devotee, would lose her mind over the impressive array of clothes, designer handbags, polished jewelry, and mile-high shoes. She always had an objectively impeccable sense of style.

Abby. I try to put her out of my mind and focus on the task at hand. There are embellished Balenciaga skirts, tailored Fendi suit separates, and beaded Givenchy evening gowns. Each garment is draped on a velvet hanger, complete with a photograph of me wearing the piece. All of the pictures are taken from the neck down. I count myself lucky, since seeing my current face so many times would be too overwhelming right now. There are literally hundreds of outfits.

A large trifold mirror stands squarely in front of me, highlighting my extensive wardrobe and showcasing my own reflection. I do my damnedest to ignore it. From what I can see, everything is kept in pristine condition, almost too flawless to touch. After a few more minutes of gawking, I turn off the lights and retreat back into the master suite.

From the elegant design of our room to its ornate embellishments, every last detail paints a picture of the person I apparently became. Given the ordinary home I grew up in, I have no clue how I managed to create such a sybaritic life with John. It all feels too indulgent. *How did I ever get used to this*? Maybe I never did.

All of this unfamiliarity makes me want to call Abby. She would know exactly what to say to make me feel better. Cathy's voice replays in my head: "Abby says she never wants to hear from you again." Maybe she would be willing to talk if I call her myself, though.

Capitalizing on my recent bravery, I decide to keep working. A spicy scent greets me as I step into John's closet and fumble around for a light switch. But instead of several flashy panels and a chandelier in my closet, there are only a few diffused golden beams. The lack of light makes my stomach tighten.

Ignoring the warning in my gut, I approach the lengthy rack of pressed suits to my left. Crisp button-downs and cashmere sweaters hang on the right side, framing me in a selection of my late husband's wardrobe. I pause to inhale more of that distinct aroma—perhaps cedar or sandalwood. I can't put my finger on it, but the scent is oddly familiar. *Of course it is.*

I run my hand along John's perfect line of suits. A herringbone jacket—slate gray and slouchy—stops me mid rack. Compared to the sleek, dark blazers around it, it stands out with its subtle creases and worn patches.

For some reason, the mere sight of it pulls me in. I reach out to touch it, only to stop short. My fingertips hover over the fabric. *What is it about this jacket?* When I finally close the gap, a strange thing happens.

It's only for a split second, but I see John. He's holding a bouquet of stargazer lilies. *My favorite flower.* I gasp and pry my hand away.

What was that? It felt like a vision or a memory. My heart picks up speed, and I screw my eyes shut, bringing my hand to my chest. This is the first real memory I have had since the accident. The details are fresh, foreign, and terrifying.

I try find a rhythm for my breathing. *I'm fine. Everything is okay.* I repeat these words out loud until I actually start to believe them. If nothing else, this memory shows that my brain is healing. The amnesia could be dissipating. I am finally making progress.

Amidst the spicy notes of John's cologne, I smell my own filth. A bar of soap and water from the downstairs sink obviously isn't cutting it. *I need a shower.*

Our grand bathroom is expectedly massive, with glistening marble and gold hardware. Avoiding yet another polished mirror, I undress, step into the glass shower, and crank the handle all the way. The scalding but sobering rush of water beats down my back, turning my skin red. Eradicating the buildup of grime that's accumulated since I left the hospital is a tiny but significant achievement. After enveloping myself in a fluffy white towel, I leave my dirty clothes crumpled in a pile on the floor—a bad college habit that drove Abby nuts—then walk back to my closet.

I select an outfit without giving it much thought. Everything in here is too fine for my tastes, anyway—my daily university uniform consisted mostly of denim, sneakers, and graphic tees. As I'm about to turn out the lights, I notice a set of clear drawers in the corner and let out a sigh of relief. The unit is filled with loads of basics—socks, underwear, and tank tops—that my college self would live in. I may not recognize any of the brands, but it doesn't matter. I choose a pair of navy-blue yoga pants and a striped boatneck top. Some running socks from the bottom drawer and a worn sweat jacket completes my less-than-chic ensemble.

Although I have no interest in wearing any of the designer gowns lining my closet, a sequined crimson gown catches my eye. With a fitted bodice and the sleekest silhouette I have ever seen, it is the epitome of elegance. Without warning, I feel the same familiar pull that overcame me in John's closet.

I extend an arm, stretching until my fingers are mere centimeters away from the richly hued sequins. They sparkle like rubies as I inch even closer. When I run my nails lightly over them, I am instantly transported to another time and place.

John and I are swaying to an unknown song while a crowd dances around us in some kind of ballroom, perhaps at a gala. He holds me so close that I can feel the skin on his cheek, smell his spicy cologne. The music pulses through us as I bury my face in the nook of his shoulder.

When I pull my hand away from the line of sequins, I am standing in the closet again. While the flashback startles me momentarily, I feel more intrigued than anything else. Maybe the first one—a sudden image of John holding stargazer lilies—was only frightening because it was unexpected. My first *real* flashback.

I consider looking through more of our clothes to spark memories. Maybe sensory stimulation is the best strategy—using sights, sounds, and smells to recover my missing chunk of time. The idea leads to an unsettling one. For a moment, it seems like I am conducting research on myself. *Psychological tests*. The truth is, though, I feel more like an unwilling participant in someone else's peculiar experiment.

My urge to call Abby intensifies. Whatever happened between us, I still think of her as my confidante. Maybe if I apologize, she will explain our mysterious falling out. *She has to.*

Before I can talk myself out of it again, I head for the kitchen phone. My fingers dance across the keypad, dialing a series of digits I begged Cathy to write down before I left the hospital. The phone begins to ring—one, two, three times. *What if she doesn't answer?* I am about to hang up when Abby's voice comes through.

"Hello?"

"Abby?" A wave of relief washes over me as I breathe into the phone.

"I told you not to call." Apparently, Abby recognizes my voice too.

"Please. Please just hear me out."

Abby sighs on the other end. I wait for a response, wondering where she is, what she's doing. *In the midst of a crisis at work? Sitting in Central Park during her lunch break? Shopping for new shoes at Barney's?* I have no idea who she is anymore, and that fact is more unnerving than anything else.

She starts again. "I..."

My transitory hope is met with instant dismay.

"I just can't."

I think I hear regret in her voice, but I cannot be certain. Snapshots of our college days—moments that feel so fresh to me—flicker through my mind. *I can't lose her.* Then again, I guess I already have.

"I have to go, Vonny."

I sense the pain in her words. *She's about to hang up.* I can only think of one thing that might sway Abby, so I make a last-ditch attempt to keep her on the line.

"Goodbye—"

"Falcon!" I practically shout into the phone. Our old—and surprisingly effective—code word for emergencies.

My interruption is met with silence. *She doesn't remember*. After all, it has been almost a decade.

"Okay," Abby finally says. "You have five minutes."

CHAPTER 19

After incessantly begging Abby to give me a chance to explain, I tell her about the accident. Hearing that my memory is basically on strike with no definitive end date softens her considerably.

"I didn't realize that it was so serious," she says.

"I just want to make things right. I still have no idea what happened between us."

"It's not that simple for me." There is so much pain in her voice. So much bitterness. It kills me to think I might be the source of it.

"Can we just talk about—"

"It's not a good time."

"Okay." My voice quiets. "Just let me know when."

She draws in an audible breath.

"Please, just *please* consider it. I miss you."

She exhales slowly.

"I need you, Abby."

"Okay." She pauses. "Look, I'm actually going to be there next week on business. I have a meeting in San Francisco."

Anticipation courses through me as she continues.

"I... I might be able to see you." Abby's tone confirms her uncertainty. "Maybe a quick lunch before my meeting."

"Okay!" I don't bother concealing my joy. "Yes—whatever works."

I realize that she is reluctant to see me, but I also hope that a little face time might help put things into perspective for both of us. I'm banking on it. Once we meet up, I will be able to find out what happened between us all those years ago. I can redeem myself for whatever I did—apologize for hurting her so badly. If all goes according to plan, I will earn my best friend back.

Minutes after jotting our lunch date down on a notepad, I find myself back upstairs. I want another glimpse of the master suite before looking elsewhere. Upon seeing it, though, I decide against sleeping in the bed. My eyes fall on the rumpled sheets where my late husband slept just days ago. The camelback sofa suddenly regains its waning appeal.

I flip off the light and try to shift my focus. My tired legs carry me out of our room, one uncertain footstep after another. In the hall, there are rooms on either side of me, but I am particularly drawn to one at the end. It is the only closed door I have seen so far. *Maybe it's shut for a reason.* I stretch out my fingers and grasp the brass handle, half expecting it to be locked. But when I turn the knob, the door creaks open.

I do not even need to glance around to realize what this room is. No particular sight, sound, or smell gives it away. There is only a feeling. I am immediately hit with a strong sense of familiarity—a visceral knowing—as I pause in the doorway. This is my office.

I step inside and am instantly immersed in another world. Unlike the rest of this extravagant residence, my office is modest. There's a sturdy desk, two armchairs, and not much else. My shoulders loosen a bit as I take in the scant furnishings. I approach my desk, examining the computer sitting on top, and touch its monitor. Inside the top drawer is a stack of legal pads and Moleskin notebooks. Some of them are blank, but most are laden with scratchy notes and ballpoint annotations. I select a random pad and begin reading:

Kevin Barry, 29. Crippling anxiety. Condition aggravated by familial disapproval—severity increases when Mother visits each month. Denies direct correlation.

The writing is messy, but it is definitely my own. Extensive notes fill the entire page and bleed into each margin. I flip through another pad, scanning additional patient profiles.

Shelly Kline, 43. Agoraphobia. Phone consult—lives in Spokane, WA. Intro call: discussed the most debilitating aspects of her condition.

Next, I open a nearby cabinet to find a series of manila folders, each containing printed forms and detailed patient information. Although I am barely scratching the surface of New Vonny's psychiatry practice, after digging through her highly organized archives and noting the attention given to each patient, I feel more connected to her than before. The office itself provides clues as well—there are a few frames, mostly diplomas and certificates, hanging on the far wall above a narrow bookcase. The wooden shelves house psychology manuals and several nonfiction titles I remember hearing about in college. I wonder if I have read all of them or even referenced the large majority of them over the years.

Looking through these possessions is like rediscovering myself via hard-earned relics. Staring at an expensive wardrobe is one thing, but reading notes in my own handwriting is decidedly stranger, more intimate. I reach for another folder when the doorbell makes me jump.

"MADAM! WHERE HAVE YOU been? I was so worried when I didn't hear from—" The man at the door stops at my confused expression.

"Madam?" His voice quivers. "I don't understand why you and—"

"I lost my memory. I-I have retrograde amnesia. I don't remember much about my current life. I'm not sure who you are."

The man's pale lips droop into a frown.

"I was in a car accident. I just returned from the hospital a few days ago."

"Oh, madam." Something registers in his watery eyes. "*Madam.* I am so sorry." He bows his head. "Please allow me to reintroduce myself, then. My name is Wesley Nathan."

I extend a tentative hand as he continues.

"I am your chief advisor. I manage finances and provide legal counsel in matters concerning you and Mr. Lew—"

I bite my bottom lip, realizing that he must know about John's passing. *Maybe that's why he stopped by.*

"The late Mr. Lewis," he adds solemnly with another bow of his head.

The respectful way he refers to John puts me at ease somewhat. Whether or not they were close, it's clear Wesley admired my husband a great deal. I invite him to sit with me in the dining room.

Wesley is wearing slim black loafers and a pinstripe suit, complete with a red bow tie and handlebar mustache. I stifle the urge to comment on his memorable ensemble. He reminds me of a taller, skinnier version of the Monopoly man.

"Please, make yourself comfortable. Tea?" I ask, creating a reasonable excuse to collect my thoughts in private. I hurry into the kitchen before he can respond. "Would you like cream or sugar?"

"No, thank you, madam," he calls back. "I prefer my tea black."

I eventually reemerge with two steaming cups—one English breakfast and one peppermint—and take the seat opposite him.

"Before we get started," Wesley says, "I would like to offer my sincerest condolences."

"Thank you," I reply between sips. "I appreciate that."

Wesley opens a black briefcase to reveal a stack of documents and manila envelopes. The selection instantly reminds me of my desk upstairs.

"If you don't mind my asking, what exactly is the purpose of this visit?"

Wesley looks up from an unknown page and blinks. "Yes, of course. I apologize for my abrupt timing."

I smile, reminding myself that he had no idea about my condition. He certainly wasn't expecting to have to explain basic procedures to me, let alone rehash everything from the past several years.

"Allow me to clarify," he begins. "Your husband initially employed my services to handle financial matters, such as bank accounts, long-term investments, and his generous property portfolio."

I nod and take another sip of piping-hot peppermint tea.

"I am also an attorney. Mr. Lewis performed a thorough background check before hiring me, during which he asked if I would consider managing his will. I later became his personal lawyer."

I nod again. He must have a wealth of information about us stored inside that leather briefcase.

"Is there anything I might be able to explain further?" he asks earnestly.

"How long have you been working for John?" I blurt a little too quickly.

"Oh, several years now. The two of you even honored me with a wedding invitation." He tilts his head, and a wistful look comes into his eyes. "Such a special day."

"I wish I could remember it."

"Well, that *is* a shame. But I speak on behalf of the entire staff when I say we were all so pleased when Mr. Lewis found love again."

Again? I nearly choke on my tea. "So you were working for John when he was married to Cheryl?"

"Yes, madam." He clears his throat and glances down at his files. "But back to business—the main purpose of my visit is to give you access to all of the accounts and answer any questions you might have about your financial situation." Wesley pushes his tea forward and extracts a lengthy document from the briefcase.

I consider asking him more about Cheryl but decide that I do not want to come on too strong. "All right, then," I say intently. "Let's start."

We spend the next hour going over bank statements, account passwords, and stock portfolios. Most of the information is predictable considering the state of this residence. We—I—have a lot of money. My eyes widen at each and every number, but I attempt to maintain my composure.

I find out some surprising things along the way, like the fact that I signed a prenuptial agreement before I married John. I guess it makes sense—most of the money was his to begin with. But I never pictured myself marrying someone that wealthy. It also dawns on me that I did not know his age until this visit. *John was forty*. I am thirty-one, so that puts our age gap at almost a decade.

Wesley goes over long-term investments next. We have a sizable amount of money tied up in stocks, mutual funds, and CDs. For now, I decide not to touch any of it. The truth is, I lack any valuable experience when it comes to investing. It's probably best to keep things status quo for the time being.

"I'll come back to your stock portfolio in a moment," Wesley says, making a note on the page in front of him.

My attention wanes as he moves on to the next topic. I swallow an oncoming yawn as discreetly as I can, stealing a glance at the wall clock between questions. It's been almost three and a half hours.

As if sensing my lethargy, he straightens. "Before I go, there are a few, shall we say, logistical items to discuss."

"Logistical items?"

"Just general information about your home."

"Oh—okay."

"Have you driven any of the vehicles yet?"

"Not yet." I am not sure how to tell him that there are still several areas of this house I have yet to explore, including the garage.

"Not a problem. I have extra copies of each key on hand. It's my understanding that Mr. Lewis was found with his keys when he..."

I look down at the table between us.

"Anyhow, is there any car in particular that you might prefer to drive? Perhaps the Lamborghini?"

My stomach flips. For the first time during our visit, Wesley smiles. He is probably amused at my lack of awareness regarding every asset.

"That would be fine," I say, attempting to give off an air of jaded coolness.

"Of course." He nods and fishes out a key from his briefcase.

"Thank you." I tuck it into my pocket.

"I assume you have already interacted with the home's state-of-the-art security system?"

"Uh, no. I actually didn't even realize that we had one."

"Not a problem. I can walk you through the entire system."

This man is a legitimate jack-of-all-trades. I silently wonder how much we pay him each year.

In the foyer, the late-afternoon light pours through the windows, filling the space in a hazy gray glow.

"This is where the controls are kept." Wesley gestures to a large Monet hanging at the bottom of the staircase.

I furrow my brow, positive that I misheard him.

"Just press here on the mat, beneath Monet's signature, and *voila*." Wesley taps the lower right-hand corner of the painting.

"But—"

Before I can object, the painting swings open like a cupboard door.

"There we go." He gestures to a panel of tiny screens and multi-colored buttons, all hidden behind a Monet.

My jaw almost drops.

"Interesting," Wesley says quietly.

"What is it?"

"The system appears to be deactivated."

"Is that an issue?"

"Not necessarily, but I find it to be rather odd. You and Mr. Lewis always kept it on. No matter what."

My stomach tightens. "Maybe he deactivated it before he left for work?"

"Perhaps." Wesley's gaze is fixed on the control panel. "Yes. That must be it."

I chew on my bottom lip. He does not sound convinced in the slightest.

"Would you like me to reactivate it, madam?"

"Yes. Definitely."

Wesley shows me how to activate and deactivate the system. I probably won't rely too heavily on it, but I understand the gist. He closes the painting before we walk back into the dining room.

"In terms of house staff," he says, "there's a maid, Linda, your personal chef, Thomas, and the driver, Albert."

Seriously?

"Your gardener works on a bimonthly basis," he adds.

"Um, no need for the maid or chef. At least not yet."

Wesley nods. "That's all I have for now. Do you have any additional questions?"

"You mentioned that I have a driver on call?" The question is foreign on my lips.

"Yes, madam. Albert knows the most efficient routes to all of your favorite destinations."

"Great." I breathe a sigh of relief. "Do you think he might be able to drive me to the grocery store tomorrow? I need to buy a few things."

CHAPTER 20

I spend the evening trying to process everything Wesley told me. Given what I've scrutinized, John controlled our entire financial situation—from daily spending to long-term investments. *Did he make every other decision too?* Thoughts of dependence plague me while I get ready for bed.

When I was younger, I craved autonomy and adventure. *Did I trade those dreams—everything I valued—for wealth and luxury? For ease?* The racks overflowing with fancy clothes, the expensive interior décor of our multimillion-dollar property, and a garage full of pricey cars all point to an answer I am reticent to accept.

Maybe everything changed once I fell in love with John. Then again, I went to grad school and became a psychiatrist. I followed through on attaining my previous ambitions. John's influence aside, my budding career does not exactly scream "trophy wife." I wonder what the dynamic of our relationship actually was.

SLEEP ELUDES ME. THE next morning, I roll off my sofa, feeling irritated and sluggish. But at least I did not wake up in a sweaty panic, screaming from another nightmare. That alone is something to celebrate.

I pull myself up the never-ending staircase and shower in our master suite. Frigid, stale air hits my body as I step across the marble. Tiny arm hairs stand up straight until I wrap a blue towel snugly around myself.

I exit the bathroom and pad over to my massive walk-in closet. Its size still takes me aback, along with every luxe item on display. Among rows of modish suit sets, a casual burgundy dress steals my attention. Its long sleeves and fitted waist appeal to me right away. I reach for it without hesitation, briefly stopping when my fingers touch the fabric. I half expect another flashback—something that will provide more insight into my life with John. Nothing happens, though.

I put on a pair of nude-colored stockings and slide into some black flats. When wet hair begins seeping into my dress, I hurry back into the bathroom to find a blow dryer. While the tool roars in my ears, I fish around a few drawers until I find one filled with beauty products—serums, creams, and cosmetics organized neatly into trays.

I was able to style my hair without the aid of a mirror, but makeup is another story. I have been dreading this moment for a while. My brain has conjured up reasons, valid and superfluous, to avoid it for as long as possible. I take a deep breath and finally look into the face that I hate. It serves as a constant reminder of all I have lost—my husband, my job, and nine precious years of my life. Two dark, overgrown brows frame an empty pair of almond-shaped eyes. My gaze is desolate. I slowly take in the sore sight of my skin, noting several rough patches I have neglected to moisturize since the accident.

Before I lose my nerve, I find a jar of Crème de la Mer and slather on two dollops. Then I select a flesh-toned foundation, along with some peachy liquid blush. The formulas breathe new life into my complexion. I instantly look less zombie, more human. Onyx mascara and pink lip color complete the look. I curl my lashes before dabbing on the gloss, watching a smile dance across my mouth.

I never wore much makeup in college, but I generally know what I am doing thanks to observing Abby. The thought reminds me of our impending lunch date. I was overjoyed when we first made plans, but I grow more nervous with each passing day. Maybe reality has finally set in. I am loath to accept that we will just be two estranged women eating together.

The doorbell interrupts my train of thought. I shut the drawers, tousle my hair, and run downstairs.

An older man waits at the door. He is slightly shorter than me—around five and a half feet tall in oxfords, pressed pants, and proper coattails. I turn the knob to greet him.

"Hello, madam," he says in a raspy voice.

I offer a smile. *Does everyone around here call me that?*

"Pleasure to see you again."

"Albert?" I ask tentatively, relaxing when he nods politely. I wonder if Wesley already filled him in on my amnesia.

"Shall we?"

"Let me just grab my house keys." I fetch them from the table and lock up behind us.

Albert opens the door of a jet-black Rolls Royce.

"Thank you." I climb inside and buckle my seatbelt.

"Shall we go to Mollie Stone's?" he asks, adjusting the rearview mirror.

"Um, sure. But Albert?"

"Yes?"

"I was hoping we could take the long route today. I would love to see some other neighborhoods on the way."

"Of course, madam."

During the drive, I make a few measly attempts at conversation, but Albert seems too focused on the road to engage. I smooth my dress and fiddle with the keys to pass time. Between the traffic and the variety of neighborhoods around, it feels like hours go by. Every house has its own distinct style. There are art deco homes, Spanish colonial buildings, and Queen Anne houses with turrets and bay windows.

Dense fog rolls by as we approach the Presidio, a former military post. I never came to this area on my college trip to San Francisco, but I remember reading about it in guidebooks. The entire neighborhood is expertly maintained. We drive down tranquil tree-lined roads, passing several elegant residences with stylish landscaping. A grouping of beautiful running trails gives me pangs of envy. As if sensing my awe, Albert narrates the last portion of our drive.

"Presidio Heights," he says in that distinct raspy voice of his. "This district is bordered by the lush Presidio National Park. The residential neighborhood is admired for its renowned architecture, rich history, and highly rated green spaces." Albert sounds like a bona fide tour guide.

The car finally slows to a stop in front of a large market.

"Here we are, madam. Shall I escort you inside?"

"Oh. No. I'll be fine. Thanks."

"All right. I'll be parked around the corner when you're finished."

The store is teeming with shoppers. I grab a cart and push it through the produce section, where people sniff fruit like their lives depend on it. I reach out for a container of blackberries when something rams into my heels.

"Sorry!" calls a young man as he rolls his cart away from me. "I'm kind of in a hurry, and you were in the way."

"It's fine," I say before grabbing a container of blackberries.

Something else brushes against my elbow and makes me jump. I turn to see an older woman putting apples into her basket. Exhaling, I glance across the store, trying to steady myself. This is the biggest crowd I have encountered since my accident. It is undeniably overwhelming, but I can handle this. I just need to keep moving.

I pile more fruit and vegetables into my cart before heading toward the deli.

A woman taps her pale finger against the fish case, pointing to a salmon fillet. "No! *That* one. The one underneath that piece in the back!"

There is no way I am going to stand in line behind that woman. She looks like she could eat me alive. Instead, I reach into the poultry case and select a pack of chicken breasts. I can pan-fry them with garlic and butter just like I used to. That simple dish is one of the few I have actually mastered.

I grab some pantry items—mainly crackers and potato chips—en route to the dairy case. Doing something routine like grocery shopping seems like an important milestone, albeit a tiny one. My confidence grows with each item I place into the cart. As I continue shopping, the mass of people bothers me less and less. Then I notice something in my peripheral vision.

A nagging feeling begins while I walk down the frozen foods aisle and intensifies as I make my way through the bakery. *Someone is watching me.* There is a man, face partially obscured by a cobalt-blue hat, that I have seen several times in different aisles. Although I did not think much of him at first, running into him so many times now strikes me as intentional.

I slow my pace to see if he lingers. It seems like every time I look over my shoulder, though, he is gone. Maybe I am just imagining things, turning a fluke into something more. My gut says otherwise, though.

I need to get out of here. I pile too many loaves of bread into my cart, which is now filled with an abundance of random food. But I am too preoccupied to care. My heart rate picks up as I hurry to the front of the store and accelerates further when I'm trapped in a lengthy checkout line. I pay as quickly as I can before rushing out to the car.

ALBERT DROPS ME OFF at home with several bulging bags of groceries. Cartons of milk, hunks of cheese, and a variety of fresh vegetables spill out onto the counter. I definitely went overboard shopping, but I was too distracted by the mysterious man I kept seeing. I need to know if he was following me.

After unloading the food, I venture back upstairs and change out of my dress. Leggings and a sweatshirt relax me a bit as I walk through my enormous closet, running my hand along a rack of extravagant gowns. What I need is another flashback. I am desperate for more information.

When my own garments fail to trigger one, I step into John's closet. His suits and sweaters feel stiffer than they did before. I open his sock and pajama drawers, combing through their contents to no avail. The doorbell rings before I can look any further. The number of unannounced guests I've received in the last few days is adding up.

I tread downstairs to find Wesley standing out front. He is wearing a suit similar to the one he donned yesterday, coattails and all. It is getting pretty late, so I wonder why he would stop by. I greet him with a smile as I open the door.

"Hello, madam. I have the items that you requested. May I come in?"

"Yes, of course." I barely remember what I asked him for.

He unloads a large paper bag. "One brand-new laptop and an iPhone with unlimited cellular data."

"Thank you so much. How much do I owe you?"

"Not to worry, madam. Mr. Lewis enlisted my services for life."

My mouth opens.

"His and *yours*," he clarifies quickly.

I am not exactly sure what that means, but obviously we can afford Wesley's fees. I make a mental note to check into the matter later.

"Would you like assistance in setting up the laptop?"

"No, thanks." I shake my head. "I'll manage." I have always been proficient when it comes to technology, and would honestly prefer to be alone right now.

"I'll be going, then," he says politely.

Suddenly, I remember that laptop I found in the kitchen drawer. "There is one thing, though."

"Yes?"

"I found an old laptop the other day, and I was wondering if you might be able to help me find a working charger for it."

"Of course."

"Thanks!" I jog down the hall and into the kitchen. Hopefully, searching my laptop will yield something useful—maybe information about John and Cheryl. I reach the drawer and pull it wide open.

"Everything all right?" Wesley calls from the foyer.

Silence is my only response. The drawer is empty. *It's gone.*

CHAPTER 21

I regain my composure and send Wesley home. Despite my better judgment, part of me believes that I moved the laptop and simply forgot about it. I check the kitchen, opening cabinets and peeking behind appliances. *Nothing.* My search starts out completely civilized and methodical but quickly devolves into a wild-goose chase around my own house.

Before long, I am tearing through shallow bookcases and rummaging through photo boxes—places where the laptop would not even fit. When I look up, the living room floor is strewn with novels, magazines, and pictures. It almost looks like someone broke in.

I should probably clean up this mess, but I am sure I saw the laptop inside that drawer. Almost certain. *I did find it there, didn't I?* Just like after my meeting with Cheryl, I obsess over the thought until I begin to question my own conviction. Doubt gnaws at my insides like a wild animal, refusing to stop at any cost.

Then I realize something. *The cameras.* I can check footage from our home security system. If someone did in fact steal that laptop, they would have definitely been caught on camera. I jog into the foyer and check behind the painting. My fingers run along the keypad, copying exactly what Wesley showed me the other day. Then I pull up the recordings and begin to watch.

What feels like two hours later, I still have yet to notice anything useful. Of course there is footage of Wesley coming to the door and Albert picking me up yesterday. I have video evidence of the ridiculous amount of food I brought home from grocery shopping but not much else. *No proof. No luck.*

The lack of findings leaves me more anxious than ever. If someone *did* steal the computer, they must have done it before Wesley helped me reactivate the security cameras. Or worse—the person who took it knows how to operate the system. I hold my breath while weighing my options.

I could do nothing. My brain is still healing, so maybe I did just misplace the laptop. But it would have turned up by now. I could set a trap. Something to protect myself and catch the hypothetical thief. *My God, a trap? I really am losing it.*

An arguably more rational idea takes hold—I could call Lee and Ryan. The detectives will know exactly what to do. Besides, it's probably smarter to keep them in the loop. There might be critical evidence on that computer.

Unfortunately, neither detective picks up. I manage to leave an informative voice mail on Lee's phone after calling Ryan. He will listen to my message in the morning. We can figure this out together. *Everything will be all right.* I close my eyes and inhale, repeating those words to myself.

I finally start to calm down when another thought pops into my head. All along, I have assumed that someone stole the laptop or that it might be hiding somewhere in this house. But an even worse option exists. I could have imagined myself finding the laptop. *What if it was never there in the first place?*

My heart beats faster as I look around the ransacked kitchen. I feel like a woman on the precipice of mental instability, approaching insanity. I hurry into the foyer and try to kill the thought. For the first time since being here, I feel safer sleeping on the second level. I want to stay in my own bedroom tonight.

Any motivation to clean the mess I made downstairs is wholly depleted. As I pull myself up the long staircase, my mind races with hypothetical situations—scenarios in which I end up hurt or worse. As I enter the huge master suite, I feel infinitesimal. Reality sets in that I am completely alone.

I avoid the closets and stumble into my bathroom. Patchy street-lamp light streams in from the tiny window. I cannot make out my own features in the mirror on the wall—my face is just a dark plane with sharp angles. I reach out and touch my shadowy reflection, pressing each finger against the glass's edge.

A soft click sounds, and the mirror opens. Much like with the Monet painting downstairs, there is a secret compartment concealed by this looking glass. A thrill races through me as I flip on the light. Stashed in the cabinet are several rows of pill bottles and prescriptions, all made out to me.

My brow furrows as I read through the medications. There is a prescription for everything from mild anxiety to severe depression. While I am justifiably caught off guard, my surprise quickly gives way to desire when I spot sleeping pills on the second shelf. After reading their label, I do not hesitate. My hands crack open the top of the container before I dry swallow two white tablets. They scratch my throat on the way down, giving me time to wonder if I really need them. I do.

I do not bother showering or removing my makeup tonight. Instead, I make my way over to the bed, peel back its covers, then crawl onto the left side of the mattress. My body sinks into the soft memory foam and the weighted comforter soothes me.

As I press my nose into the silk pillowcase, I pick up another subtle but familiar scent on the fabric. *John?* It's probably the smell of his shampoo or something.

In this moment, what might have unnerved me before fails to do so. I am completely at ease in this bed for two. Finally, the knots unwind in my shoulders, my muscles loosening under the sheets. A strong wave of sleep pulls me deeper and deeper into the mattress. Minutes later, it overcomes me.

I HEAR THE RAPPING before I open my eyes. There is a pounding sound, muted but jarring, coming from downstairs. *I should really get out of bed.* Instead, I bury my face in a warm pillow, and my body remains glued to the fitted sheet beneath me.

The noise continues, faster and harder. I think I even hear a man's voice, drowned out by space and doorways.

A lame attempt to sit up results in me sinking slowly back into the mattress. When I do finally open my eyes, shards of cruel light shoot in from a nearby window. I want to squeeze them shut again and pull the covers over my pounding head. A scratchy sound rumbles in my eardrums as rapping continues in the background. *What is that?*

When I finally locate my phone on the nightstand, I drag it across the wooden surface and pull it slowly toward my chest. The bright screen forces me to squint as I make out the numbers—it is one in the afternoon. This is the longest stretch I have slept since being back in my house. My brain slowly puzzles together the events of last night—realizing that the laptop was missing, searching for it, and finding those pills in the hidden medicine cabinet. I sit up straight when I remember calling the detectives.

The muffled voice I keep hearing is Lee's. He has been standing outside waiting for who knows how long, probably fearing the worst.

I pull a hand to my clammy forehead and swallow hard. This pill hangover is about a hundred times more intense than my freshman year blackouts. I push the comforter back, wondering what other side effects might appear with continued usage.

When the knocking grows louder, I use every ounce of energy to climb out of bed. Then I take a deep breath and begin to move. Leaning on both walls simultaneously, I fight dizziness as I make my way to the stairs then cling desperately to the railing. From the landing, I can make out Lee and Ryan on my doorstep.

Given my current state, they are the last people I want to see. Both detectives look up, and I practically feel their judgment seeping through the door, skyrocketing my current level of mortification. To say that Lee looks displeased would be a laughable understatement. He has dark circles under his eyes, and it seems like he didn't clock more than a few hours of sleep last night. That makes one of us.

I wrap my robe tighter around me and descend the remaining stairs. I need caffeine and potentially something stronger to combat the medication coursing through my system. I approach the entryway and unlock the deadbolt. Then I push open the door, which feels substantially heavier than usual. I squint into the afternoon sun and reluctantly welcome the detectives inside.

Lee speaks first. "Are you all right, Mrs. Lewis?"

"Y-yes, of course," I mumble. "Why?"

He and Ryan exchange disapproving glances.

"Is there somewhere we can talk?" Ryan asks hesitantly.

"Uh, yes." I gesturing down the hall. "Right this way."

The detectives follow me out of the foyer and into the hallway. I finger comb my hair and tie my robe tightly, hoping to exude a semblance of maturity. For all they know, I was up late reading novels or doing research. *Who are they to judge me*? The thought makes me stand a little taller as we approach the parlor.

I stop in my tracks. *The floor*. It is still covered in papers, knick-knacks, and open books. My heart sinks as I look around the room. Lee and Ryan stand silently behind me, no doubt wondering what on earth happened.

"Sorry for the mess," I say. "I was, um, doing some redecorating in here."

Neither detective responds as we move further into the room. There are some items on the end of the couch, but I push them aside and make room us all to sit.

"Did this happen before or after you called me?" Lee asks.

"Before," I tell him. "Well, before and after."

Ryan is visibly confused.

"I—uh. *Okay*. The truth is that I was half redecorating, half searching."

Lee regards me with raised eyebrows and an audible sigh. I should have given him a straight answer from the start. "The voice mail message. You mentioned that a laptop was stolen."

My mouth goes dry as I try to formulate a response.

"Mrs. Lewis? What happened?"

"Yes. The laptop—my laptop. Well, I'm not entirely sure actually. It might have been John's."

Lee does not break his stare. Clearly, he needs more of an explanation.

"I found it in the kitchen drawer. That was days ago. Then last night... well, I was looking for it, and it just wasn't there."

Ryan produces a scratch pad then jots down some notes.

"Okay," Lee says. "And you looked through this room when you were trying to find it?"

"Yes." I scan the vicinity and note how chaotic everything appears.

"Around what time did you realize that the laptop was missing?"

I start to swallow, but my mouth is cotton. *What time was that?* The details from last night are still so fuzzy.

"Just give me a ballpark," Lee says.

"I'm honestly not sure. Probably a few hours before I called you."

Ryan scribbles my answer on the pad and asks a question of his own. "Did you check the entire level, or just this room?"

"I mainly looked through the kitchen and this room."

"Did you—" Ryan stops mid-sentence when something steals his attention.

I turn to identify the culprit, but Lee figures it out first. Both detectives are staring at the new laptop that Wesley just procured for me, still sealed in its original packaging.

"And this is...?" Lee motions to the box.

"I just bought that one," I clarify. "Actually, I asked a staff member to purchase it."

The detectives resume asking questions, which I answer with shaky responses and half truths. I would rather not mention the pills.

"If it's all right with you," Lee says, "we'd like to do a thorough check of the house before searching elsewhere."

"Of course. That's fine."

"You scan down here," Lee says to Ryan. "I'll do a sweep of the upper level."

My stomach tightens as I watch him walk back into the foyer. *What if he looks around the medicine cabinet?* My pills were strewn about the counter last night, but I put them away before bed. At least, I think I did.

Forty minutes later, Lee returns to the parlor.

"Did you find it?" I ask hopefully from the sofa.

He shakes his head and takes the seat across from me. "No luck."

"Oh," I mutter between swigs of coffee.

"We did find these, though." Lee holds up my sleeping pills.

My stomach drops.

"The lid was ajar," he continues. "Pills scattered around your sink."

My brow creases as another wave of embarrassment washes over me.

"Are you having trouble sleeping?" Lee asks with a sudden shake of the bottle.

I nod. *No shit, Sherlock.*

He sets my pills on the table and waits for a verbal confirmation.

"I couldn't sleep last night. But I haven't taken them any other time."

Lee's face is cloaked in an unreadable expression.

"This entire investigation is the reason why I can't sleep."

He stares at me with inquisitive eyes.

"The circumstances, I mean. My husband is dead. I don't even *know* him, and I can't remember anything from the past several years."

Lee opens his mouth to speak but overrides his initial response with a nod.

"It's hard not to be scared in this house," I add.

"That's understandable. I'm sorry that you're, uh, dealing with this." He gestures to the general space between us. "Must be difficult."

This is probably the biggest show of sympathy I will ever get from Lee.

"So," I say. "How is the investigation going, anyway?"

Lee stiffens.

"Are there any updates on the case?"

"It's going fine," he finally says. "Unfortunately, I can't reveal much, but we're looking into some matters at Mr. Lewis's office."

"You have a new lead?"

"We can't disclose too many details," Lee repeats. "But I can tell you that we're talking to some of his coworkers."

Before I can react, Ryan enters the room. "Where did you say that you first saw the laptop?"

"It was in a kitchen drawer. Here, let me show you." I hop up from the sofa before Lee follows suit, with Ryan trailing behind.

In the kitchen, I point to the wooden drawer flush with the cabinet. "This one."

Ryan flashes Lee an odd look.

I ignore them both and fiddle with the drawer. My impatient hands tug on its hardware, jostling the drawer around until it slides open. I let out a breath, and then I freeze. The laptop is exactly where I first found it.

CHAPTER 22

Lee, Ryan, and I hover around the missing laptop. *This cannot be happening.* It was definitely not there when I searched the kitchen last night. I double—triple—checked this drawer. And now I look like a fool. Blood pounds in my eardrums until Lee finally breaks the silence.

"Is *this* the laptop you were referring to?" Smugness drips from his deep voice.

Incredulity is my only response.

"Well, I guess we're finished here." He and Ryan turn to leave.

"I-I'm sorry I wasted your time."

"Don't worry about it," Ryan says quietly. "Let us know if there's anything else we can do." The undertone of his offer sounds like irritation or pity, perhaps both.

"We'll be in touch!" Lee calls from the hall.

Only when the front door slams shut do I allow myself to collapse into a heap on the floor. The detectives just spent their entire afternoon searching for a laptop that was never even missing to begin with. Lee and Ryan must think I am a complete and utter idiot.

I eventually manage to peel myself off the polished hardwood. I am still lethargic from the sleeping pills, but hunger pangs drive me back to the coffee cupboard. While a batch of dark roast brews, I open a packet of ginger biscuits. Combined with the bold smell of the coffee, the snack provides a welcome dose of energy. I drain my mug, finish most of the pack, then tiptoe through the mess of items still on the floor and resolve to clean it up later. Right now, I want to resume my search of the upper level. The only way to understand my past is to keep going through this house. Maybe I will come across something useful or at least marginally interesting in my office.

My legs feel like lead as I climb each step. Cursing the pills under my breath, I finally reach the landing and pause to look down the hall. My office door is open. *I closed it last time, didn't I?* Then again, Lee just searched upstairs.

My heart picks up speed as I approach the doorway. Maybe I am just remembering it wrong, just like I did with the laptop. I force myself to take the final few steps and enter my office.

My shoulders relax as I glance around the room. Everything is exactly as I left it. There is a comforting stillness in the air that makes me feel safe, secure. Maybe the laptop debacle translates to an oversight on my part. Honestly, I was so exhausted last night that I probably saw it and simply forgot. After all, my memory is not the most reliable at the moment.

The situation is still unsettling, but I need to stop dwelling on it and focus on finding out more about my psychiatry practice. During one of my brain-trauma classes, I read an amnesia case study where I learned that resuming a familiar routine can aid in memory recollection. Maybe studying my own work will help bring other memories back.

Obviously, I will not be able to treat patients anytime soon, which sends me into another spiral about my wasted years of graduate school. But I cannot start feeling sorry for myself. If I do, I might never stop.

Before I know it, the student in me is engrossed by my own patient files and notes. As much as I want to keep reading, though, I focus on flipping through them as swiftly as possible. My eyes dart across lines of handwritten notes in an effort to trigger some sort of memory. Ultimately, I come up short. My curiosity amplifies before morphing into frustration.

I slam the stack of files against my desk and groan. This is clearly an impossible feat—a Sisyphean task. Just as I am about to give up completely, a scrap of paper on the floor catches my eye. It must have fallen out of one of the files. I lean down to pick it up and discover it is another psychiatrist's business card. *Dr. Paul Bertrand.*

According to the tiny print beneath his name, Dr. Bertrand specializes in cognitive behavioral therapy and owns a practice in Tacoma. I make a mental note and set his business card on top of the files. Maybe he was one of my colleagues—a coworker I kept in touch with.

After another glance around my office, I switch off both lights then make a point to close the door tightly behind me. Hoping to trigger another flashback, I beeline for my husband's wardrobe. Inside, I touch a few of his clothes, but nothing gives me the same feeling as before.

This is pointless. Sighing, I abandon John's closet for mine. I should've changed out of my robe and pajamas a while ago anyway. Once again, I am drawn to the impressive array of gowns and cocktail dresses. This time, one in particular catches my eye.

The emerald-green garment has a sleek design with a few crystal beads sewn around its collar. The aesthetic is understated elegance, like something designed for an anniversary party. Everything about this gown—its shape, adornments, and smooth velvet material—is familiar. I reach out and pull it off the rack without any hesitation.

Seconds later, I toss my pajamas onto the floor before slipping into the dress. Its fabric is cool, smooth, and sumptuous against my skin. The feeling is incredible. I start to zip up my dress, but it gets stuck halfway. I am so anxious to see how it looks that I run over to the full-length mirror at the end of my closet.

One glimpse is the only requirement for another flashback to take hold. Instead of a vision like I experienced before, there is only an intense sensation. A somatic knowing. Pressure at my back, followed by a hard push. Fear shoots through every limb and my stomach pitches as I plummet into some unknown darkness.

The memory ends as suddenly as it began when I catch myself on the closet wall, and my voice surfaces in the form of a guttural scream. In the spotless mirror, I see both my hands thrown up in defense. Makeshift protection against an invisible attacker. It takes a moment for me to stop screaming, to stop gasping for air. I am still not convinced that it's safe.

My first memories were so tender and comforting, almost like a dream. This one sends chills down my spine. I cannot stop shaking until I pull the dress off my body.

HOURS LATER, AS I LIE in bed, the memory still creeps around every corner of my mind. It will not stop haunting me until I figure out what or *who* pushed me. I fully acknowledge that I could have imagined the incident, conjured up a dark scene that never happened. *But it did.* I run my fingers through my hair. Everything felt so real.

Goosebumps dot my skin as I pull the comforter over my head. I try to bask in the feeling of my body sinking into the mattress, but it does little to soothe me. Then another realization hits, and I sit up straight. During the attack, I was standing in our house. I am sure of it.

Though I have felt paranoid about a lot of things lately, there is no doubt in my mind about this. If I was in this house when it happened, I'm closer to figuring out who pushed me. *Was it John?* My breathing shallows, and I can't help but stiffen. *Who else could it have been?*

THE ROOM IS BLURRED chaos. Waves of light warp, vibrate, and bounce off of dark smudges. I squeeze my eyes shut for a long time before attempting to look around again. When I do, all I see are dizzying bright spots and nebulous shadows. My surroundings finally come back into focus, settling into ugly shapes and pieces.

At first, I cannot figure out why everything is so hazy. *The pills.* I promised myself I would not touch them, but after yesterday's horrifying memory, I needed the help to sleep. I sat shaking in bed for the longest time, willing myself to calm down. I attempted happier thoughts and even meditated, focusing on the rhythmic pattern of my breathing.

Hours passed, but nothing quelled the increasing anxiety. My feelings inevitably morphed into an overwhelming mass of fear and hypothetical concerns that drove me back to the mysterious medicine cabinet. I stood there staring at the cluttered shelves, the brand names blending together in an incoherent mess. Eventually, I reached for the prescription I took the previous night and popped a single capsule into my mouth.

After the sheer embarrassment during my encounter with Lee and Ryan, I'm ashamed of my poor resolve. Two pills knocked me out hard. They rendered me nauseous, lethargic, and forgetful. I'd foolishly believed that cutting my dose in half would mitigate any side effects while preventing a sleepless night.

Twelve hours later, here I am, sitting in bed with the same fears darting around my head. *Who pushed me?* My scalp prickles as I feel the hands at my back and imagine them shoving me forward. The eerie sensation lingers as I sink farther into my mattress. I swat my palm through the air, wishing it were possible to physically swipe my worries away.

At least I have daylight. For now. Life is somehow less frightening during waking hours. Nighttime stirs up suspicions—suppressed and otherwise—with unease breeding in the shadows. Staying in bed all day won't help me shake off the anxious thoughts.

I hoist myself up. The first item on my agenda is to have a proper shower, mainly to wake myself up and ward off any pill-induced lethargy. Then I will go downstairs, drink a sobering cup of coffee, and tackle that mess I made the other night. I still have no idea what happened in the first place. *Was it ever really missing?*

On my way to the bathroom, I hurry past the closets, but my emerald gown is lying in plain sight. The piece of fabric that sent me reeling is crumpled into a hasty ball. Before I can relive the terror I felt trying it on, I rush into the bathroom then slam the door shut behind me.

Once I catch my breath, I take in the state of my countertop. A few open pill bottles line the edge, their contents spilling out in a colorful array of capsules and tablets. For a moment, I wonder if I accidentally mixed a few by mistake. I clearly have more products and prescriptions than I know what to do with. In addition to the pills crowding my sink, clusters of powder brushes and compacts wage a war with perfume bottles and fancy serums. John's area, on the other hand, is spotless, with nothing more than a shaving kit and some unopened cologne. The only similarity between our respective sides is a matching set of marble sinks. The symmetry of it all—two closets, monogrammed towels, his and hers sinks—is a sour reminder that my husband is dead.

Suddenly, something curdles deep inside my gut. My best effort to make it to the toilet falls short, and I grip the counter's edge until my knuckles turn white. Horrendous pain, sharp and churning, intensifies with no signs of stopping. I can do nothing to combat the mass of acid rising in my throat. Seconds later, I vomit into John's sink.

EVEN AFTER A SHOWER and a cup of tea to soothe my throat, my stomach still churns. I consider phoning Wesley for some Tums and Pepto-Bismol. Tempting as it is, I remind myself he's not some glorified butler. It is probably better not to bother him with this.

Near the phone, my scribbled note reminds me of my lunch date with Abby on Tuesday. *That's tomorrow.* The time really snuck up on me. The prospect of seeing her again lifts my mood a little. Bolstered, I finally get to work cleaning up the mess on my floor from the laptop search.

Picking up the papers goes fairly quickly. I place pages into little piles on the coffee table, resolving to sort through them later. Organizing the scattered books takes a bit longer. I scoop them up one by one and create neat stacks on the towering bookshelf.

My neck aches from bending down so much, and my head is still heavy from the medication. Standing too quickly makes me nauseous all over again. The sleeping pills *do* help me sleep, but dealing with additional side effects is not worth it. I make an aggressive mental note to avoid taking them tonight.

After splashing some cold water on my face, I swallow two ibuprofen liquid gels with my tea and pretzels. I don't want to tax my stomach more than necessary, but any reduction in pain—however minor—is worth it right now.

The laptop and phone that Wesley brought over remain untouched, still in their original packaging. I decide to start setting up my new cell phone first. I turn it on and begin downloading apps. My contacts tab is empty, and I do not have any information to input. I look for an address book or basic list of phone numbers. There has to be one around here somewhere, but I cannot find anything useful in the kitchen. I venture into the parlor and check our dining room. *Still nothing.* Before I can scour the rest of the lower level, a loud doorbell stymies my search.

From the foyer windows, I see a man on my doorstep, tall in stature with blond buzz cut and beady eyes. He looks sort of familiar—perhaps a friend or relative. I paste a smile onto my bare lips and open the door. A draft of cold air wafts in, bracing me before he speaks.

"Veronica Lewis?" the man asks sharply.

"Yes?" I notice the thick envelope in his hand.

"You've been served."

My jaw drops as he thrusts the packet toward me.

"These documents will explain—"

"What is this concerning?" I ask him. "Who sent you?"

The man steps back and clears his throat. "I'm here on behalf of Mr. Marshall Lewis."

"Marshall Lewis?"

"Yes." He regards me for a moment. "Mr. Lewis is the brother of your late husband."

"I-I don't understand. Why exactly is he suing me?"

"Mr. Lewis filed a lawsuit to claim his brother's estate."

"But..." I lose my train of thought. "John and I—"

"You can find more details in the envelope." With that, he makes a hasty exit.

John's brother is suing me? It's only after the man leaves that I realize who he is. *The guy from the grocery store—the one wearing a blue hat.* I remain frozen in place until the darkening sky startles me out of my daze. Time is wasting. I feel like I have just reentered my body, with the stiff limbs and sore neck to prove it.

As I shut the door, little beads of rain tap against the glass, pattering softly in a smooth rhythm. I sweep my eyelids shut, head back into the kitchen, then check the clock. It's been hours since the doorbell rang.

This used to happen when I was younger. Something would really bother me—usually a fight or tense conversation—and I would just sort of zone out. I cannot remember how old I was when it stopped completely, but the fugue states eventually faded away on their own.

I try not to worry too much, but letting things go has always been difficult for me. That strange encounter from this afternoon is still fresh in my head. I take a deep breath and brew more tea. My stomach grumbles for something more substantial, but I am too tired to cook. A handful of crackers and some cheese slices will have to do. As I wait for the water to heat, I think about the implications of the packet the man delivered.

I still have no idea what was in John's previous will. I assume that he left me the properties and most of his financial assets, but the possibility of a new document changes everything. *What if John really did leave the house to his brother*? I might have to move out immediately.

Wesley is our—*my*—financial advisor and lawyer. I feel bad about ringing him at this hour, but I don't know what else to do. Besides, this matter seems urgent enough to warrant an impromptu meeting.

WESLEY LOOKS CLEAN-shaven, refreshed, and wide-awake when I open the door. I am instantly reminded of my dirty clothes as he steps inside. I was too paranoid earlier to return to the closet after dashing out with my pajamas. Wearing his usual suit with coattails, Wesley carries the same leather briefcase he did before.

"The process server said there's a more current will," I tell him as we sit down at the dining room table. "I just can't believe John's brother is suing me."

Wesley opens his briefcase. "Not to worry, madam. We'll get this sorted out in no time."

I smile weakly at Wesley, grateful for his calm manner and reassuring tone.

"I have a copy of Mr. Lewis's notarized will here." He lays a document on the table and pats it.

I nod, straining to see it.

"At this point, the best course of action is for me to speak with Marshall Lewis's lawyer."

"His brother's? Are you sure?"

"Positive."

I bite my lower lip and tap a finger on the table.

Sensing my unease, Wesley chimes in again. "Trust me, madam. I will handle this matter with the utmost professionalism."

I look at the suited-up man across from me and succumb to a subtle grin. "I have no doubt that you will, Wesley."

We finish our conversation and walk back into the foyer.

"Sorry for the inconvenience," I say while he fetches his shoes. "We probably could have handled this over the phone."

"Not at all." He waves off my concern. "It is my job and honor to provide legal counsel."

I hand Wesley his coat and thank him again.

"Would you like any of the staff to stop by this week?" Wesley asks hopefully. "Perhaps your chef or the maid?"

I consider this briefly before deciding against it. "No, thanks. I'll manage."

"Are you certain, madam? Chef Thomas mentioned to me that he had some delicious vegan meals in mind. Of course, all of the ingredients are seasonal and locally sourced—"

"Am I a vegan?" I blurt before he can finish.

Wesley pauses before answering. "Why, yes. As far as I know."

"That's too bad," I say honestly. "Because I've really been craving a Big Mac."

Wesley regards me for a moment. *He probably doesn't even know what a Big Mac is.* My stomach finally breaks the silence between us, grumbling suddenly at the thought of a juicy cheeseburger.

"See?" I gesture to my core and smirk. "McDonald's cravings."

For the first time since I've met him, Wesley laughs. The sound is exactly what I expect—refined and concise.

"They still make those, don't they?"

"Oh, yes, madam. Special sauce and all."

I do not bother hiding my surprise at Wesley's comment. Instantly, his stuffy exterior melts. "Thank God for that."

A heartening smile spreads across his lips. Perhaps Wesley is more down-to-earth and relatable than I initially thought. Maybe I had only experienced his professional persona until now. For the next few moments, we stand there laughing, united by legal considerations and fast-food cravings.

CHAPTER 23

In college, I learned that the average person has about four to six dreams a night, but most of them are quickly forgotten upon waking. I always found that fascinating—the idea that we have these extraordinary experiences while we sleep, only to lose them the very next morning. But this morning, I remember one of them.

In my dream, Wesley asked about the missing laptop before he left last night. "Is the charger I procured satisfactory, madam?"

Of course I lied and told him that everything was working fine. I conveniently left out the part about said laptop going missing, in addition to the bit where I called Lee and Ryan in a panic.

As the dream went on, I sat downstairs, wearing a set of clothes I did not recognize. The laptop was perched on the counter in front of me, closed but fully charged. I opened it slowly to reveal a bright screen. Front and center was an article—some sort of news story. I looked more closely and realized that it was from the *San Francisco Chronicle*. The headline read: "Woman Found Guilty of Murder." I began reading until I noticed a tiny, pixilated photo near the top. Shock took hold of me as I stared at my own face.

Whether the dream was inspired by sheer guilt or simply my subconscious's way of processing the missing-laptop situation, I cannot say. Maybe it was my curiosity over what else the detectives might have found during their investigation. In any case, the dream feels like less of a nightmare and more like a cruel joke. Instead of waking up with a racing heart and erratic breathing, I feel only an odd sense of calm. The idea of me murdering John is so far-fetched that I am able to reject it outright. Besides, I have plenty of other things to worry about.

I venture into my closet and flip on the bright lights I am slowly becoming accustomed to. Everything hangs perfectly in place, save for a small clump on the floor. The sight of that green dress still makes my stomach churn. I consider moving it but ultimately decide not to. Part of me wonders if merely touching the garment might conjure another awful memory.

The possibility alone is enough to make me shudder. Although I was previously trying to trigger flashbacks, I cannot stand the thought of having any more. *Especially not right now.* Confronting my past is imperative—something I will eventually have to do. At the moment, though, I need to change into something presentable and morph into someone resembling a responsible adult.

Sweats and a T-shirt will absolutely not do. Not today—not for my lunch with Abby. After all, this occasion is a far cry from our pizza nights and scary-movie marathons. This is a mature conversation between two former best friends.

I try not to dwell on the "former" part of that statement. Instead, I distract myself with silk heels and leather handbags. *Too many options.*

Instead of focusing on footwear, I take one tentative step toward an impressive selection of denim. There are black midi skirts, white-washed skinny jeans, and darker distressed versions. I reach for a pair of indigo flares. Before I can touch the fabric, I nearly drop the hanger, afraid that any contact might unlock jarring memories. *How the hell am I supposed to get dressed*? I bite my bottom lip while mulling the question over.

This dilemma eats up valuable minutes. Then an idea pops into my head. *Here goes nothing.* I shut my eyes and reach out for the jeans. My fingers fumble around for a while, finally grabbing hold of the pair and bringing them toward me. I open my eyes ever so slightly, just wide enough to see the denim in my hands. Taking a breath, I pull the indigo flares onto my pale legs.

I have no clue why that worked, but I do not question it further. I am just relieved to be wearing clean clothes without reeling from a brutal memory. After putting on my black bra and tank top, I tiptoe over to a rack of sweaters and try the same technique with a lavender cardigan. *Another small victory.* To my relief, I am successfully dressed for lunch—flashback free.

I look down at my bare feet and realize that I still need shoes. My eyes rise, landing on the ballet flats. Walking through this city in heels is not worth the attempt. New Vonny might be able to prance around in stilettos, but I most certainly cannot. My gaze lingers on a glossy red boot for a few seconds. The shoe is undeniably familiar to me. Before I can remember anything, I snatch up a pair of dark pebbled leather flats and leave the closet.

As I step into my bathroom, I notice the clean countertop and give myself a mental high five. I felt so relaxed after Wesley left—much calmer than I did when I called him about the will—that I was able to be productive. After some chamomile tea, I managed to clean up the mess on my own and even fall asleep without any medication. The cabinet is probably crammed full of muscle relaxers and antidepressants, but I plan to avoid them for the time being, especially since I don't recognize many of the clinical names.

I stare at myself in the mirror, taking in all of my altered subtleties. The hollows of my cheekbones are too sunken in for a thirtysomething woman. My eyes appear dull, lifeless, and exhausted. *What happened to me?*

A quick application of powder and blush instantly renders me more awake. I swipe on some mascara to brighten my eyes and finish with a glossy pink lip color. Then I run a brush through my tangled hair, removing a fair number of knotted strands in the process.

After giving myself a nod of encouragement in the mirror, I leave the bathroom and gather my scant belongings into a tiny purse. Besides my phone, all I'm bringing is my ID, lip balm, keys, and a credit card that Wesley procured. I make a mental note to withdraw cash while I am downtown.

Post caffeine, my eyes flit around the foyer, eager for the first signs of Albert's arrival. When a dark Rolls Royce finally pulls into the drive, I grab my crossbody bag and slide my phone into its zippered pocket.

Our greetings and pleasantries fade to silence as we drive toward Market Street. Instead of forcing conversation or staring through the window like last time, I pull out my phone. There are a few pre-loaded apps, along with some that I downloaded like Twitter and Facebook. I do not recognize many of the other available ones. My fingers dart across the screen, trying to log into my existing social media accounts.

Facebook is first. I don't make it very far though, given my deficiency of password-related memories. I end up creating a new account just so I can search for Abby. *Pretending to be someone else is startlingly easy.* I spend the next several minutes scrolling through her profile, viewing a limited selection of public photos and status updates. My forefinger hovers over a picture when Albert's voice startles me.

"Is this all right, madam?"

I look up, suddenly aware that we are stuck in a row of static cars on some busy street. *This must be Market.*

"The Ferry Building is straight ahead." He gestures toward a structure in the distance. "Just a few blocks away."

I stick my phone back into my purse and tuck a strand of hair behind my ear.

"I apologize for not getting you closer," he continues, "but with this traffic jam, I'm afraid you'll be late to lunch."

"No worries. This is perfect. Thanks, Albert."

"Of course, madam. Just give me a ring when you're ready for a ride home."

"Sounds good." After taking the card with his phone number, I step out of his car and shut the door behind me.

A slew of oncoming traffic stuns me before I can get my bearings. I cross then hurry past a string of runners, moving farther onto the nearest sidewalk. Market Street is remarkably packed. Hybrid cars, commuter bikes, and brisk pedestrians rush by in a flurry.

It dawns on me that this is the most action I have seen in quite a long time. My near-solitary confinement—aka self-imposed isolation—in the hills fails to compare. Being surrounded by this abundance of energy is admittedly overwhelming. Nonetheless, downtown San Francisco makes for a welcome change of pace. The lonely house I currently inhabit feels worlds away.

Beating drums, flocking pigeons, and chatty tourists serenade me as I continue through the city. The cement is rough beneath these thin-soled flats. I slow my pace, peering into the cutesy windows of stationary stores and specialty bakeries, then meander through an outdoor craft market. There are displays of glass pendants and saturated canvases depicting the Golden Gate Bridge. I marvel at them, further intrigued by a series of bracelets made out of silver forks.

A smile takes hold when I spot the Ferry Building in the distance. Its exterior is partially shrouded by a parade of flags, clusters of cars, and crowds of people. After avoiding some skateboarders, I stare up at the grand entrance. The structure, covered in paint the color of the bay waters, stretches far in each direction, begging me to step inside and explore.

Inside, the market hall is filled with enticing sights, fragrant smells, and hungry shoppers eagerly mining each stall for food. It's hard not to get sucked in. Cases of artisanal chocolate truffles, bottles of organic wine, and barrels of fresh produce line the walls. My nose twitches when it detects an intoxicating scent that is spicy, savory, and sweet all at once.

I'm still searching for whatever might be causing the heavenly fusion of smells when I see her. *Abby*. There she is, walking through the building's far entrance.

My first instinct is to run across the aisle and envelop her in a gigantic bear hug. I fight it, knowing full well that said behavior would be significantly awkward. This meeting is already predestined to be tense. No embraces, extended or otherwise. Instead, I attempt a casual wave that looks more like someone hailing a cab.

Even from a distance, the first thing I notice is a ring on Abby's finger. The sparkler—a round diamond perched on a thin gold band—flashes as she removes her sunglasses. *She's married now*. This surprises me. Abby never wanted to be in a relationship, much less get married.

I move closer, noting her chic outfit and patent heels. She's dressed for her work meeting in a slim pencil skirt and tucked-in cobalt blouse. When we are mere inches from each other, I can't help myself and lean in for a half hug. *Rule officially broken*.

Abby stiffens slightly but forces a tight smile and obliges.

"It's so good to see you," I say as we break apart. "How are you?"

"I'm good." Her expression is unreadable.

Abby's face is slimmer than it was in college—far more chiseled and grown-up. She still has the same sweet look about her, though, with a pair of rosy cheeks that belie her current, more intense gaze.

"I thought we could get food from this place." She gestures to a tiny bakery-cafe. "They have gluten free stuff and some vegan options too."

I didn't realize that Abby followed a special diet, but I nod and follow her over to the counter. We both order sandwiches and drinks before finding a nearby bench to rest on. I wonder if we are having a quick lunch due to Abby's busy schedule or because she wants an out from spending too much time with me.

"You're married now," I say as we sit down. "Congratulations."

"Oh, right. Thanks." She glances at her shiny ring. "I actually got married a long time ago."

"What's his name?"

She takes a sip of her iced tea. "Nick." She runs a hand through her layered hair, which is darker and much longer than I remember.

"How did you two meet?"

"He did PR for the firm where I used to work." Abby looks like she wants to say something else but nibbles on her sandwich instead.

"So, you're a recruiter?" I ask between bites.

"Yeah—a legal recruiter. I kind of fell into it."

She tells me more about her job before changing the subject. "So, Vonny. What exactly happened?" It feels great to hear her use my nickname. "I know you tried to explain on the phone, but..." She shrugs. "I mean, you really don't remember anything?"

I swallow and set down my drink. "Nothing from the past several years."

"God. That's crazy."

"Our graduation day is the last thing I really remember," I say honestly.

I watch as my words wash over her.

"I can't believe you don't know what happened between us."

I shake my head and look down.

Abby chews slowly as a conflicted expression takes hold of her face.

"Will you tell me?" I ask gently.

"Um... I'm not sure. I just don't want to rehash everything and get into another fight, you know?"

"I don't. That's the thing. I have no idea what I did to damage our friendship so badly."

Abby eyes me intently.

"Please. Please tell me."

She sighs. "Okay."

I lean in closer, half curious, half worried about what I might find out.

"It all happened really quickly. We graduated and moved out of our old apartment."

I silently miss our shared place. It was bright and roomy, conveniently located between campus and my favorite park.

"I stayed in New York to start applying for jobs, and you were gearing up for grad school on the West Coast."

"University of Washington," I whisper, remembering Amanda's web search in the hospital.

"Yeah." Abby nods. "I helped you pack up your stuff and visited you after you moved."

Every bit of new information I gain makes me miss my absent memories even more—the good *and* the bad.

"I thought everything was going really well," Abby continues. "We got you all settled in Seattle. I spent a couple weeks there before flying back to New York."

"Did we keep in touch?"

"At first, yes. We talked on the phone constantly and had weekly video calls." She pauses for a minute and takes a long sip of iced tea. "But those conversations became less and less frequent."

"Why?"

"I could tell that you were being distant, and that went on for a few months. I figured it was probably just a period of adjustment—getting used to a new city and everything. But then you just *stopped*. Stopped calling. Stopped answering. I couldn't reach you at all."

I suddenly feel like we are talking about someone else, exchanging trivial gossip in between classes. "Then what happened?"

"When we finally did reconnect, you ended up hurting me badly." Her voice fades to a faint whisper.

"Oh, God. What did I say?"

Abby is obviously conflicted. "I really do think it's better not to dredge up the past. I don't want to argue right now, you know?"

I nod. "I understand, but I'd like to know what happened. It's killing me."

Abby sighs. "I missed our relationship so much, but I couldn't tell if you felt the same way. I thought about it for a while, and I decided to make one last-ditch effort. My parents threw me a huge twenty-fifth birthday party—rented out this amazing hotel and everything. There was live music and a ballroom-sized dance floor." She looks down at her feet. "And even though we hadn't spoken in ages, I decided to invite you. I thought it would give us a chance to catch up."

"Did I say yes?"

"You did... but you didn't show up to the party." Disappointment drips from Abby's words.

"What?" I can't hide my shock. "Really?"

She shakes her head. "I was just so upset. Maybe a little immature looking back, but the sadness gave way to anger. Then we had this horrible phone conversation. We both said some damaging things to each other that night. Things that neither of us could take back."

I consider pushing her for more details but choose not to.

"After that, I couldn't talk to you anymore," she adds. "It was too difficult."

I chew on my lower lip, wondering if she will say anything else.

"It was almost like you didn't care about our friendship anymore... like you stopped trying." Abby looks down. "So I stopped trying too."

I don't know what to say. *Why would I have missed her birthday?*

"More time passed. I assumed that you were busy with work and classes. Or that you made new friends in Washington." She shrugs. "And then I found out that you got married." The last word catches in her throat.

"In Washington?"

"I'm not sure. But I didn't even realize you were dating anyone in the first place." She frowns. "Then again, we hadn't talked for so long by that point. And that's that."

My mind is racing with theories and questions. That can't be all. *Why would I bail on my best friend and keep her in the dark for so long?* It doesn't make sense.

"Anyway," she says while crumpling her sandwich wrapper, "tell me about what's been going on with... you know."

"I will. But first, I want to apologize. Seriously. Abby, I am so very sorry. I honestly can't believe I ever hurt you like that." My voice trembles. "I wish I could take it back. I would do anything to salvage our friendship."

She doesn't say anything, but I sense a positive shift in her demeanor. Maybe an emotional weight has been lifted. With some of the heaviness gone, I feel significantly more at ease. Abby seems to take notice. She looks at me expectantly, waiting to hear about John.

This is an awkward transition, but I welcome the opportunity to confide in someone I am comfortable with. *Sure beats talking to Lee and Ryan.* I gather my thoughts before filling Abby in on my husband's death, sharing what I know about the investigation so far.

"I'm sorry you're going through that," she says sincerely. "I can't even imagine."

"The hardest part is not remembering anything about our marriage. I don't even know what John was like."

We sit in silence as I wonder if I should mention the flashbacks to Abby.

"You want to get some air?" she offers.

"Definitely." I stand up and follow her out of the Ferry Building.

The brisk temperature is a refreshing change from the stuffy space we were just in. A breeze passes by, rustling my hair as I pause in front of the pier. San Francisco looks stunning today. The city sky is bright, and the water glows a deep-blue hue.

"Do you think we can ever be friends again?" I ask.

She turns away, her gaze landing on the water. A ferry passes by as our conversation stalls. For a few long minutes, rolling waves and muffled background chatter are the only sounds between us.

"I'm not sure if things could ever be the same," she finally answers. "So much has changed."

My heart begins to sink, but she turns to face me again.

"*But* I'm willing to consider giving us another shot." She flashes me a tentative grin.

"You are?"

"Yeah." She nods once. "Let me know if you're ever in New York."

"Maybe I could even come visit sometime." I hope that I'm not pushing my luck. "I would love to meet Nick."

At this, Abby smiles broadly. The endearing expression I remember so well melts the years of hurt between us. "I would like that."

I am about to respond when someone catches my eye. I lose track of her for a second in the crowd, but then I see all six feet of her sleek silhouette, dressed in another tailored suit, her bright-blond curls bobbing. The woman who caused me so much frustration this past week, whose very existence made the detectives—and me—question my sanity, is across the street, moving swiftly away.

"Vonny, are you okay?" Abby's voice sounds from the background.

"It's her." An unknown force pulls my body away from the pier. Its grip tightens, dragging me into the crowd without my permission. This is not desire or longing. This is need—pure instinct. I am not

even fully conscious of what I'm doing, but I know that I have to follow her. I have to find Cheryl.

The woman's face is partially obscured. That *is* Cheryl, though.
I feel it in my bones. She moves further away while I try desperately
to catch up, pushing myself through clumps of sweaty bodies in
the process. Desperation overcomes me as I shove people to each
side—behavior that I would usually balk at. I am gaining on her, so
much so that I can almost touch those bouncy blond curls.

At last, I catch up to Cheryl. My fingers are inches away from
tapping her on the shoulder. She is drastically taller than me, made
even taller in heels. They click against the pavement as I try to match
her pace. "Cheryl!"

The woman turns, but when she does, she is not Cheryl. *No.*
Everything about her face is different—eye shape, bone structure,
and even her lip color. She shoots me a confused glance before resuming her route.

It doesn't make sense. The woman—everything about
her—screamed *Cheryl.*

"Cheryl!" I call after her until the word loses meaning. My
mouth goes dry, my throat tightens, and I grow dizzier with each
step. Pedestrians bump by, brushing my shoulders while I stagger
down the sidewalk. My stride slows, devolving into a weak amble as
my legs become jelly. The city starts to spin. Then everything turns
dark.

I HAVE NO IDEA HOW long I was out. My vision is blurred, and
both temples ache. I find myself sitting on a small wooden bench,
Abby at my side and the sun still shining overhead.

"You wandered off," she tells me. "I had to chase after you."

I open my mouth to respond, but my sandpaper tongue does not
comply.

"Here." She hands me a water bottle.

"Thanks." I take the longest swig possible.

She gives me a puzzled look. "It seemed like you were somewhere else completely. Your mind, I mean."

"I-I... it was her."

"What? Who?"

I look at her worried eyes and swallow hard. "No one. Nothing." The last thing I need is my only friend thinking I'm crazy.

Abby glances at her watch before a panicked expression floods her face. "This is such crappy timing, but I have to run to a meeting. The conference room is about ten minutes away."

"Of course. I understand."

"Do you have a good way to get home? I can call someone for you—"

"No need." I shake my head quickly, thankful for the concern in her voice. "I got it."

"I'm so sorry, Vonny. I wish I could stay."

"No—it's really okay. I'll be fine."

ALBERT APPEARS SLIGHTLY concerned when he drops me off at home. I see him peering through the car window, eyes nearly plastered to the glass as I fish around for my keys. Once I finally unlock the door, I flash the biggest smile I can muster and give him a little wave. I don't need Albert worrying about me and mentioning something to Wesley.

For the very first time, I feel a sense of relief while walking into this house. *I'm safe here.* Novel comfort envelops me like a warm blanket as I move through the kitchen. But once I start recounting events from this afternoon, the feeling fades as quickly as it arrived.

The evening is still young, but I want to crawl into bed and shut off the lights. My hunger was thoroughly quenched during lunch—probably because a sandwich and chips is the most substantial meal I have consumed since my hospital release. No dinner for me tonight. Besides, the thought of Cheryl is enough to obliterate any potential traces of appetite.

I felt so certain that it was her. My brain must have tricked me into seeing her—the mysterious woman who continues to haunt my dreams. I went after her so impulsively, thinking that I could get to the bottom of whatever really happened to John. But I chased after some random person like a maniac, shouting at the top of my lungs.

Maybe she really is dead. I might have conjured up a ghost based on memories alone—ones that I cannot access. John's death is already shrouded in so much complexity and secrecy. Here I am, though, complicating things even more.

While I lug my tired body upstairs, the possibility that Cheryl only exists in my head threatens to consume me. *Grief has strange effects on people. Maybe I did imagine everything.* The explanation is tempting, but there is still an obstinate part of me that refuses to swallow it.

Cheryl was here, in my house. She introduced herself as my friend, and I invited her inside. We sat on the sofa while drinking tea. We talked about how we met, laughing together between silences. She left. *I saw her.* I know it.

The memory swirls around my brain like a spinning top. I try to slow it down, to stop it completely. Every possibility—another variation of the truth—threatens to undo me. Eventually, hypothetical thinking exhausts what little energy I possess. My body drifts off into a slumber that is anything but sound.

CHAPTER 24

I am standing in our house, staring at the closed basement door. It's dark, almost midnight. My arms are clutching a box of something, but I can't quite tell what it is.

I reach out tentatively and turn the brass knob with my free hand. A shrill creak sounds, startling me as the door swings open. I take a deep breath before inching closer. My neck strains toward the staircase leading down to our basement. The space is cold, ominous, untouched.

As I take the first steps, a small but unmistakable sound comes from behind. I freeze, afraid of what I will find if I look over my shoulder. Then a pair of hands is at my back. Light pressure, followed by a firm push. The box falls from my grasp as someone hurls me into total darkness. The drop seems to happen in slow motion, but my scream comes rapid and piercing. I plummet headfirst down the lengthy staircase toward the hard floor.

Gasping, I sit up in bed and throw both hands my hands out. I reach for the lamp and quickly flip it on before scanning the room for my attacker. The empty room is bathed in a golden, almost ethereal glow, but my skin is drenched by a frigid layer of sweat. The tangle of sheets around my legs is damp, too, and I rip them off. I push a clump of matted hair away from my face, stiffening as I lean back against the headboard. *God. It's been weeks of this.* My mind is full of nightmares, and there's no end in sight.

As I take stock of them, I notice a common thread. At first, I always believe that I am alone. Then someone from behind attacks me.

This one was different, though. My terror was more than dreamt. *It was a memory.*

Burgeoning fear paralyzes me, and I ruminate on this in bed for the next couple of hours.

Tick, tick, tick. My bedside clock is louder than usual, more aggravating. I pull my pillow over my ears, but the ever-present sound is impossible to ignore.

Tick, tick, tick.

The noise multiplies in my eardrums until it feels like my entire skull is vibrating. When I cannot take it anymore, I grab the clock off of my nightstand then hurl it across the room.

A welcome silence follows the crash, allowing me to focus. After a while, I remember something else from the dream—a crucial element. But this latest bit leaves me wanting the clock to resume its ticking. Anything to drown out my revelation. Just before I was pushed, I heard a man's voice.

"Vonny."

The sound of my own name sends a shockwave through me. *That voice.* Something in my core tells me it belonged to John. The pieces are slowly falling into place, arranging themselves into a hideous puzzle. It all begins to make sense—the strange flashbacks in my closet and the eeriness of our home. Not to mention my recurring nightmares of being assaulted.

It was John. This chilling thought solidifies at the forefront of my mind. I don't know how badly he hurt me, or if it happened multiple times, but the memories and my feelings about this house leave no room for doubt. I have been so preoccupied by Cheryl and the detectives that I failed to see what was right in front of me.

Cringing, I bring my hand to my forehead. My situation's severity seems to swell by the minute. Yesterday, I conjured up Cheryl and chased after her in downtown San Francisco. And now, I just realized that my late husband was abusing me.

If my flashback in the emerald gown was accurate, John was violent on more than one occasion. Or maybe it was the same incident as the one from my nightmare. *Did aggression taint our entire relationship*? My consistent paranoia and trepidation seem to support and even confirm these suspicions.

I felt his hands against my back, shoving me down our staircase. I heard him just before falling. *Vonny*. My husband's voice. My name. But I cannot remember why. Maybe we had a bitter quarrel—an argument that turned physical. Or maybe he had anger issues. With John dead, I might never know.

Even though he's gone, I can't shake the fear that someone else might attack me. I cannot remember the last time I truly felt safe. As I start to uncover the truth, securing even a modicum of mental relief seems further and further out of reach. Things have gotten progressively worse since I woke up in that Nevada hospital weeks ago.

My thoughts continue to run wild, keeping me pinned to the bed and dragging me into a deeper and darker state of panic. John is gone, but that does not change the fact that I am a victim. Given my professional background, I know I need help. I am going to find a psychologist.

"HELLO?" DR. BERTRAND answers on the first ring.

"Hi." After finding his business card in my office, I was planning to leave a message. There is a long silence, and I assume he's waiting for me to continue. "Um, is this Dr. Bertrand?"

"This is he. How can I help you?"

"This is Veronica." I pause, giving him the chance to recognize me. "Veronica Kwan."

"Vonny?" The sudden uptick in his baritone pitch catches me off guard. "Is that really you?"

"Um, I'm sorry. I—"

"How are you? My God, it's been ages!"

I swallow hard. *Who is he to me?* We may be old classmates, former colleagues, friends, or complete strangers. Judging by his reaction, it sounds like we were close.

"A-are you still there?" His voice regains its deeper tone.

"Yes, I'm here." I move my phone to the opposite ear. "You'll have to forgive me. I, well, you see... I lost my memory."

"What?" He sounds genuinely shocked.

"I was in an accident. All of my memories from the past decade are gone." It still feels unbelievable to say out loud.

"You're kidding," he whispers into the phone.

"I wish I was."

"I-I'm sorry. I had no idea."

"That's all right. Not many people know."

"I understand."

"Anyway, I came across your business card when I was looking through my desk."

"Ah, yes." There is warmth in his voice. "You're probably wondering who the hell I am."

"Well... actually, yeah." I can't help but break into a little smile.

"You and me," he says gingerly, "we used to go out."

I dated another psychiatrist?

"Back when we were grad students," he adds.

"Oh... Dr. Bertrand, I—"

"Vonny, please. Call me Paul."

"Paul," I say slowly. "I just wanted to ask you a few questions." I hesitate for a moment, wondering if I should continue.

"Of course. Anything."

"I was actually looking for a recommendation. For a psychologist, I mean. The accident has really turned my world upside down, and I'd just like to see someone." I chew on my lower lip, deciding that it's better not to mention anything about John's death.

"That makes sense. One doctor comes to mind, but I'm not sure if she's accepting new patients this month. Let me double-check with her and I'll get back to you."

"That would be great." I let out a sigh of relief. "Thanks so much."

"Look, there are no hard feelings about what happened, you know." Before I can ask what he means, he says, "Why don't we meet sometime next week? I can explain everything in person, and I'm happy to catch you up on anything I can—details and whatnot."

I consider this before responding. "I'm not sure if that's a good idea. I really don't remember anything or anyone from that time period."

"I can only imagine," he says. "No worries, then."

"I'm sorry." I set his card neatly back down on the top folder.

"No need. With everything that's happened, I don't blame you."

His reply makes me stiffen. *What happened*?

"I'll let you know about that psychologist and be in touch," he says in a friendly tone. "Take care."

"Oh, and I live in San Francisco," I add before he hangs up. "I should have mentioned that before. I'd like to see someone who lives within driving distance if possible."

There's a long pause on the other end. "Of course."

"Thanks again," I say back. "I really appreciate it."

I end the call and stare at my cluttered desk. There are so many things that I cannot remember—facts, experiences, and people. Paul's words ring through my head: "And with everything that's happened, I don't blame you."

I try my best to ignore them. It will do me no good to dwell on Dr. Bertrand's—or any other ex-boyfriend's—sentiments.

I leave my office and head downstairs to make coffee. The late-morning light floods the foyer, with patchy shreds of sun peeking through a moody sky. The overcast weather reminds me of New

York. I roll my shoulders back, stretch out my neck, and walk into the kitchen.

My eyes are sore from a restless night of scattered sleep, and the light is even brighter in here. I glance at the large window above my sink before pulling the curtains shut. They aren't as opaque as I expect, sort of a gauzy material, but they help dim some of the brightness. My stomach grumbles, shifting my focus from daylight to breakfast.

I opt for chicken-apple sausage and black coffee. There are several packs of frozen links in the freezer, and I feel too lazy to cook anything on the stove right now. I pop two sausages into the microwave and inhale their greasy scent. New Vonny may be a vegan, but I am most definitely not.

The phone rings after I begin brewing some coffee. A few days ago, I would have rushed to the receiver. Any urge to answer eludes me right now. I let it ring until it rolls to voicemail, but my relaxed attitude quickly dissolves when I hear the recorded message.

"You've reached Veronica and John Lewis," my own voice chirps. It sounds unusually bubbly.

Then a man's voice says: "We're not here right now, so please leave a message at the beep."

John. My stomach drops.

"We'll get back to you." I giggle softly in the recording and whisper something to him.

Then John laughs, an a wholehearted, joyous, overwhelming sound fills the room.

"Thanks!" we both shout in unison.

The hum of us together stirs up a dizzying cocktail of emotions. We sound blissful, but my nightmare reminds me that it was probably forced enthusiasm.

Beeeeep.

My heart sinks a bit when the recording ends. This is the only way I will ever hear his voice until my memory comes back.

"Hello, madam." Wesley's ever-refined tone pulls me back to the present moment. "This is Wesley Nathan. I'm calling in regard to an item that we previously discussed. This is a rather important matter, so please give me a call at your earliest convenience. Thank you."

When the recording ends, I am left with a strange taste in my mouth. Tart and bitter. It's not the coffee, but I wash my caffeine down with a cold glass of milk just in case. I swallow hard as I think about the recording of John and me. It sounded so candid and carefree, unlike everything else in our life. It may have been the only imperfect thing about us.

I wash my dishes in the sink before phoning Wesley. Unsurprisingly, he answers on the first ring.

"Hello, madam."

"Um. Hi, Wesley." *He must have caller ID.*

"Thank you for returning my call so promptly."

"Of course."

"My message was regarding the will."

I feel a budding sigh of relief coming on. Wesley probably figured out that the will is fake and wanted to tell me not to worry. Everything is probably already taken care of.

"Unfortunately, there seems to be a complication."

I press the phone closer to my ear.

"I—well, you see..."

The feeling of peace scatters as he stumbles over his words. "What is it, Wesley?"

"Upon first glance, the new will seems to be legitimate. Marshall Lewis's lawyer sent me a copy. I have only taken a cursory look, but I wanted to let you know on the sooner side."

His words do not feel real, so I remain silent.

"It pains me to say this, but there is a possibility the will is legitimate. This document may actually be more recent than the will I have on file."

"What? I don't... Seriously? That just doesn't make any sense." My mind is spinning. "How is this even possible?"

"It shouldn't be, unless Mr. Lewis consulted with his brother's lawyer without my knowledge."

I inhale sharply as Wesley continues.

"I want to assure you that nothing is definite yet. *Nothing*, madam. Please don't worry more than need be. I—"

"I don't understand why John wouldn't have told you about this. Why wouldn't he have done that?"

"Truthfully, I don't understand it either. The shock is actually giving me hope that this will is a fraudulent document. Mr. Lewis *did* always tell me everything."

I swallow hard. This issue is definitely difficult for Wesley, too, but all I can think about is how I could lose everything before I recover the person I became and figure out what happened to John.

"I'm so sorry, madam. I can only imagine how daunting this must be."

Wesley goes on, but I can barely hear him anymore. Every word becomes background noise. The reality of this situation has fully set in, and my thoughts are racing as quickly as my heart.

CHAPTER 25

My panic increases as I pace around the kitchen. *Where will I go?* The question persists as I tune back in to my conversation with Wesley.

"Where does that leave me?" I ask him.

"What do you mean, madam?"

"I'm just wondering what to do. What happens next?"

He is silent. Perhaps he explained all of this while I was lost in my own thoughts.

"Am I supposed to call John's mother and let her know what's going on? Does she even know about this? She was so nice on the phone."

"I would not recommend that. Phoning your in-laws might escalate an already tense situation. Marshall is their son, after all."

"Oh." I don't understand all the details, but he makes a good point. I'm grateful he has my best interests at heart. "Well, what do you think I should do?"

"I suggest you prepare yourself."

My throat tightens.

"I am still hopeful that the new will is fraudulent, but while my team is working on this matter, I just want you to be prepared in case..."

"In case it's not fake."

"Precisely."

"What if they try to take the house while I'm still here?" My heart races as I consider the probability.

"That will not happen. But if it did come to that, I assure you that I would handle it. That's a promise, madam." His last sentence is solemn in tone. Wesley always sounds serious, but this is graver somehow.

It could be worse. At least I'm not going through this ordeal alone. I thank Wesley and hang up, but despite his support, I'm at a loss for where to start. Before I know it, I am stuck in a ceaseless loop of fretting, obsessing, and feeling helpless. I need to find a way to interrupt my futile thought pattern—something to take my mind off of in-laws and wills.

I wander over to one of the bookcases and stare up at the shelves. Each one is stocked full of hardbacks, from age-old classics to modern thrillers. Just as I am about to pick up *The Catcher in the Rye*—a personal favorite—something else steals my attention. I notice a shiny spine poking out from the top shelf and reach for it instantly. The deep-purple binding with a jacquard texture looks so familiar. As I remove it from the shelf, I realize it's not a book at all. The front cover reads: *Our Wedding Album.*

My stomach drops when I see a picture of John and me standing at the altar. It triggers the image of him and Cheryl that exacerbated this entire mess.

My better judgment tells me to put it away—to shove the album between Hemingway and Fitzgerald and never look back. It would be flawless symbolism, representative of their bitter rivalry. But my curiosity gets the best of me. I feel a familiar pull. A trance I cannot break free from. Soon, the desire overrides all reason.

I open the cover slowly, relishing the sticky sound of the seldom-touched pages. Inside is a maze of photographs and keepsakes. One portrait, two dried flowers, multiple copies of our vows.

In one photo, the officiant is perched between John and me at an ornate altar. I do not recognize our officiant at all. There I am, though, smiling jubilantly with my arm wrapped snugly around him.

The three of us share a similar expression as we gaze at what I assume to be hundreds of wedding guests. We look so at ease. I clutch my gown's pale skirt with a loose grip as the fabric flows from my fingers.

Like the flip of some unknown switch, a memory flashes before me. I am instantly jolted back to my wedding day. I smell arrangements of freshly cut flowers, feel the veil scratching at my neck, and taste the peppermint toothpaste I just brushed with. Every sense is heightened as my past becomes present.

John stands across from me, lips moving too quickly to follow.

"To have and to hold from this day forward."

My soon-to-be husband repeats the words after the officiant reads the vows.

"For better, for worse, for richer or for poorer."

John's palms rest firmly against mine.

"In sickness and in health, to love and to cherish."

His eyes glow before the final words depart his mouth. "Till death do us part."

I pause to peer out at the pews. Every face blurs together into one dizzying, indistinguishable mass. A flash of something flickers through my core. *Regret?* The officiant regains my attention and asks me to repeat after him. "I, Veronica Kwan, take..."

I lock eyes with John, his spectral blue irises meeting my own. The memory slows to a gentle pace. I am lost in a sea of emotion.

Then John leans forward, almost imperceptibly. The change is subtle, but his grip tightens in the process.

I adjust each hand in an effort to free my fingers. The further I shift, though, the more unyielding his grasp becomes. His stare intensifies while I speak.

"To have and to hold from this day forward..." My tongue is grainy as I recite each vow, growing drier with every line. A flood of conflicting desires courses through me more swiftly than I can possibly keep track of. I'm caught up in it, and the memory vanishes.

"...till death do us part," I repeat, but I am suddenly back in front of the bookshelf, the open album in my hands. My heart rate spikes before it settles back into a normal rhythm.

A hundred questions seem to surface at once. *Who all was at our wedding? Was I imagining John's intensity? Why did I feel so uncomfortable at the altar?* I roll my shoulders back, trying to refocus on the photographs in front of me. There are a few scattered shots—mostly blurred—of the ceremony.

Fuzzy figures loom in the background of one image, but cannot distinguish any particular features. *Are they our guests?* I glance at the unknown faces once more before turning the page. The people in these pictures might be strangers, but I am the one who feels like an outsider. Along with my foreign surroundings, this album only serves as a bitter reminder that I don't fit into John and New Vonny's world.

Abby remains the most accessible tether to my past life. Her absence in these photos and the memory makes me miss her all the more dearly. She should have been my maid of honor. She would have been an integral part of the ceremony, standing next to me on the most important day of my life. I want to call her or even just send a text about something mundane.

MY PHONE IS RIGHT WHERE I left it in the office after calling Paul Bertrand. Before I can text Abby, several notifications distract me. Two missed calls and a voicemail, all from Dr. Bertrand. I do not even bother listening to the message before calling him back.

"Hello?" The doctor's voice isn't nearly as cheerful as it was last time.

"This is Vonny again. I was just returning your call."

"Yes. I just wanted to tell you that my colleague is currently accepting new patients."

"That's great!"

"Yes, well," he says dryly.

I briefly wonder if our first phone call upset him. Maybe I should have been more gracious or agreed to meet up in person.

"Her name is Dr. Sarah Manning. I texted you the office phone number. Her practice is located in San Francisco."

"Oh—perfect. Thank you."

"Good luck with everything. I hope it all works out for you." His clipped tone reeks of sarcasm.

"Before you go, would you mind telling me what happened all those years ago?"

He is silent.

"You alluded to some sort of incident on the phone," I continue.

He waits another moment before responding. "I think it's probably best to leave the past in the past."

He sounds so different this time. *Borderline admonishing.* Dr. Bertrand was so willing before—he even wanted to meet up. Maybe he had more time to think about whatever it was that happened. Or maybe I really did upset him back in grad school.

"Is that all, Mrs. Lewis?"

The question catches me off guard. *Did he look me up online and realize that I got married?*

"Look, Dr. Ber—*Paul.* I need to know what happened."

I hear him tapping his fingers against the phone as my breathing quickens. *What isn't he telling me?*

"Please?"

He sighs. "All I can say is this—you and Professor Lewis had an *interesting* relationship. I think—"

"*Professor* Lewis? Who are you talking about?"

Another extended silence ensues.

"You really don't remember, do you?" he says faintly. "Well, maybe it's for the best."

"Please, just tell me what—"

"Goodbye, Veronica."

"Wait!"

The line goes dead.

For the next few moments, I hold the phone to my ear as if he might suddenly start talking again—telling me all about our fleeting romance and what I was like in grad school. *Yeah, right.* I finally set my cell down and start pacing around the room.

I need to think about the few things that Paul *did* say. There was really only one useful detail: "Professor" Lewis. *John was a professor?* The information fails to click until I stare at my framed degree on the far wall.

Not just any professor. *Mine.* I dated my professor. I married him.

BEADS OF RAIN TAP AGAINST our living room window, solidifying my desire to stay indoors. I am curled up on the couch, illuminated only by the glow of my laptop. It perches awkwardly on my legs as my knobby knees level like a balance scale at each tap of the keyboard.

I have no idea what I am actually looking for. My desktop is blank, save for a few folders at the bottom of the screen: *Class Notes, Assignments, Taxes.* All pretty standard.

So far, my desktop background is the most interesting item—an intricate, eerie, close-up photograph of the human brain. This entire laptop screams "psychology student." I wonder if I used it much after grad school, especially since most of the contents are college-related.

Tapping my nails on the edge of the computer, I glance at the darkening living room. *This could all be gone in a few days.* Taken from me and put into Marshall's possession. I really have no say in the matter. Despite the jarring memories, this house has become my physical and emotional sanctuary. The thought of losing it makes me sick.

I snap the laptop shut, close my eyes, and draw in a deep breath. *Hold for three seconds then exhale.* But instead of quieting my mind, the breathing exercise amplifies my racing thoughts. *Where else can I go? How can I possibly support myself until my memory comes back?*

With the new information from Dr. Bertrand, I am losing my already dwindling sense of security. But it's not about the fancy décor or the money—this is deeper than that. I feel a stinging in my eyes as the rain picks up outside.

The accident alone left me lost and disoriented, but John's death—and these subsequent legal proceedings—definitely added another dimension. Our house is where I lived and worked before I lost my memory. This is the last place I ever really felt like myself—New Vonny. If it gets taken away from me, I won't even know where to begin.

Reopening my laptop, I squint at the bright screen. Tears threaten, but I blink them back and launch an Internet browser. The least I can do is come up with a backup plan. I slowly type the words into Google: *Bay Area apartments for rent.*

I click on one of a plethora of results then scroll through pictures of a renovated condo in Oakland. After browsing a few more listings, though, I'm quickly overwhelmed and give up. Nothing is definite yet. Besides, if Marshall takes the house, a cheap hotel is probably my best bet for the time being. Some sort of low-stakes place to figure out my next move.

Before I shut the laptop entirely, I notice a tab of frequently visited websites and decide to click on one. *Facebook.* As the page loads, I realize that it's signed into my old account—the one I haven't had access to.

Filtered images and lengthy captions populate my news feed. While some posts are more entertaining than others, I refrain from

commenting on any of them. None of these names ring a bell. I wonder if any of my eight hundred plus Facebook friends could tell me
what I was like before my accident. But the people in these profile
pictures, just like everyone else from the past decade, might as well
be complete strangers.

CHAPTER 26

Dr. Manning looks like that stereotypical crazy aunt who only shows up at Thanksgiving. A thick mane of curly red hair sprouts from her scalp in all directions, and a pair of cat-eye reading glasses accentuates her large brown irises. She seems whimsical, if not a bit eccentric, but her office is all business and clean lines, decorated with the barest furniture—a minimalist armchair and tiny white sofa.

Dr. Manning speaks in a soothing voice that reminds me of Terry Gross's. I secretly pretend that I am her interviewee—a guest on NPR discussing my latest research instead of an amnesiac sitting in my first therapy appointment. Unfortunately, the similarity of their voices is so uncanny that it actually makes me more nervous. Dr. Manning runs through a laundry list of clinical questions before moving onto the purpose of our appointment.

"Tell me a little bit about yourself, Veronica," she says from behind a thick legal pad. "Why are you here?"

"It's Vonny, actually—just Vonny."

"Vonny." She makes a note.

"I've been having some, uh, memory issues." I should probably mention the accident, but she beats me to the punch.

"Why don't you tell me a little more about that? Was there a specific incident?"

"I was actually hit by a car recently. That's what caused everything."

"I'm so sorry." Her face knits into a concerned expression. "That sounds difficult to deal with."

I shift uncomfortably in my seat and glance around the office. It reminds me of a hospital room, with its pallid walls and scant furnishings. This setting contrasts heavily with Dr. Manning's warm demeanor.

"Vonny?"

"It is. Luckily, most of my physical injuries healed in the hospital. But the memory problem—retrograde amnesia—has been very debilitating."

Dr. Manning frowns with practiced empathy. "I have to be honest with you, Vonny. I've used some unconventional techniques to try to help patients regain memories in the past, but most of them were repressed memories."

I nod slowly as she continues.

"In other words, those patients didn't have memory issues due to an accident like the one you experienced."

My shoulders drop.

"You see, various types of trauma may cause memories to be repressed. This can happen at pretty much any age."

I read about repressed memories during college, but I probably learned a lot more in grad school. If I had access to those memories, though, I wouldn't be sitting here.

"There's a lot of controversy about memory repression," Dr. Manning explains. "Some of us believe in it, but there's a pretty big divide between researchers and clinicians. The validity of repressed memories is still hotly debated in this field."

"Interesting."

Dr. Manning seems to sense that I don't have much else to contribute and redirects our conversation. "I just want you to be aware of the fact that we may not be able to unlock the memories you're having trouble accessing."

"I understand. That's only part of the reason I'm here."

"Oh?"

"I'm missing about a decade. And as much as I would like to get all of that time back, there's something more specific that has been troubling me. I've been having these nightmares, then... well, flashbacks."

"Flashbacks?" She looks genuinely surprised.

"I'm not exactly sure how to describe them."

She smiles subtly. "Can you try?"

"Okay."

She resumes her note taking, pen flying across the page.

"They've all been a little different," I start. "The first one happened while I was walking through the closet—John's closet."

"Mmm." She nods encouragingly. "And John is your—"

"He's my late husband."

Dr. Manning cocks her head.

"Um. Actually, should we backtrack?"

"We can do that. Whatever you prefer."

Looking at my feet, I consider this for a moment. *I'd prefer not to talk about John at all.* That would be obtuse, though, given the fact that he's the very reason I am sitting here.

"I think that would probably be best," I finally decide.

"All right," she says in that smooth, Terry Gross-esque voice. "Whenever you're ready."

MY HEAD STILL ACHES from all the talking. Our appointment consisted mainly of me discussing my time in the hospital, John's death, and how empty our house feels. The whole thing felt like a one-sided conversation—a lengthy vent session.

Although we did not make any significant strides today, I booked another appointment in good faith. Given my experience and initial hesitation, I did not actually expect to have a major break-through during my first visit. It should take at least two or maybe more considering my circumstances.

After a ridiculously hot shower, I sink my teeth into a large bite of sponge cake. It sucks up every bead of moisture on my tongue. After a scalding but delicious sip of tea, I pop a pork dumpling into my mouth.

While soup and crackers have become my standby, I was craving something different this evening. Albert kindly agreed to stop at a restaurant in Chinatown on the way home from my appointment. It reminded me of a hole-in-the-wall place Abby and I used to frequent every weekend. We usually took turns buying a selection of favorites —*har gow, ham sui gok*, and *siu mai*. Tonight, my order consisted of more food than I could possibly eat, along with an extra almond cookie for Albert.

Apparently, my appetite is back with a vengeance. After polishing off my leftovers, I take a few sips of water while checking the landline's voicemail. There is a telemarketing message about installing new flooring, along with one urging me to upgrade our Internet plan. *Delete.* I am about to skip the last message when I hear Carol Ann's voice.

"Vonny," she says in a panicked tone, "I just found out what Marshall did. I can't believe his nerve. I'm so sorry, dear. Please call me back as soon as you can so I can explain. It's Carol Ann."

I save the message and dial her number.

She picks up right away. "Hello?"

"Hi, it's Vonny."

"Oh—good. Thanks for calling me back."

"Of course. I'm a little confused about your message."

"Let me explain. You're probably wondering what on earth Marshall is up to."

"Well, he's suing me for John's—*our*—estate."

"Yes." She sounds exasperated. "He feels entitled to some sort of... compensation. I guess he wants to be rewarded for being a lousy brother to John."

I feel even more confused than I was before, but I wait for Carol Ann to continue.

"I'm sorry, dear. Your memory loss. Let me back up."

"Please."

"Marshall and John were always competitive growing up. Two boys—go figure. Anyhow, they had a bad fight years ago. It was over something trivial that I can't quite recall. John tried to patch things up with his brother, but Marshall wouldn't have it."

I hold the phone snugly against my ear while she speaks.

"I love Marshall, but he was definitely our problem child. Always throwing tantrums in public, picking fights with other kids, and acting out at school."

"I see. And he never got along well with John?"

"There were moments. But overall? No." Carol Ann sighs. "The truth is, we haven't heard from Marshall in years. Not since he left home."

"Really?" I cannot hide my surprise. "That must have been a really long time."

"I made one last effort when we got the news about John's passing." At the mention of her son's death, she grows somber again. "Anyway, all I had was Marshall's old email address. I wasn't even sure he would get the message."

"But he responded?"

"That's the thing. He didn't. At least not until yesterday."

Given his estranged relationship with his parents, I wonder if I even knew about Marshall before my accident. *Did John ever tell me that he had a brother?*

"That's when I found out about this will nonsense."

"What did he say?"

"He told me that John promised to leave him the house and a large sum of money."

My stomach tightens.

"But I don't buy it. There's no way John would have done that—not with you to think of."

I want to take comfort in her words, but Wesley said that Marshall's document might very well be current.

"Dear?"

"It's just that I'm having our lawyer look into it, and he's not so sure that the will Marshall furnished is fake."

Carol Ann is silent.

"He says that I should be prepared for anything, and that I could potentially lose the house."

"Oh, God," she whispers. "There's no way."

"I really hope not." I nod.

"I'm so sorry that this is happening, Vonny. Your home is the last thing you should have to worry about right now."

I thank her before hanging up a few minutes later. The call leaves me with a strange feeling in my gut, perhaps resulting from the menacing reminder that I might lose this house. Or maybe my newfound knowledge of Marshall's volatile tendencies is the real culprit. I have a strong suspicion that it is a combination of both forces twisting and turning my insides. I feel like I might pass out.

CHAPTER 27

Dr. Manning is wearing the same woven poncho as before—vibrant in a bright purple shade. It cascades down the slopes of her pale shoulders. Instead of sporting cat-eye glasses, she has donned a pair of thick spectacles that magnify her pupils to gargantuan proportions. The doctor's curly hair is as wild as ever. Fiery red strands frame her head in an amorphous mass, vaguely reminiscent of a lion's mane.

The space around us feels more sterile than before. Initially, I was extremely hesitant about scheduling my sessions so close together. I saw Dr. Manning only a matter of days ago. She suggested making a follow-up appointment soon, though, since a higher frequency of visits can apparently aid in memory recall.

The possibility that these treatments could ultimately fail to produce results is not lost on me. But I do not have any other viable prospects at the moment. I am so desperate to reclaim my memories that I will try almost anything.

"Shall we begin?" Dr. Manning's soothing voice coaxes me out of my own head.

"Um, yes. I'm ready."

"How have you been feeling since our first session?"

"Honestly, I have been pretty stressed out."

"I'm sorry to hear that. Why do you think that is?"

I pause, pressing my lips together. This is the same impasse I hit last time. *Do I tell her everything?*

"Take your time. We're in no rush." Normally, I would interpret that phrase as sarcastic, but I can tell that she means every word.

"I..." After a few moments, I decide to bite the bullet. "I think my husband was hurting me."

She looks momentarily taken aback but her expression swiftly returns to its tranquil state.

"I can't be certain," I continue, "but I'm pretty sure that he was abusive."

"May I ask why you think that?"

"I was having these dreams. Horrible ones. Nightmares about random stuff—things like running on a trail or walking down the street. But they all ended with me getting attacked. In one, I was being choked."

"It's not uncommon for sufferers of high anxiety or PTSD to dream up such attacks. The body remembers even what the mind has locked away. Given what you've been through and the memory issues, your brain could be trying to process some unknown past trauma."

I nod methodically. My undergrad years taught me that much was true.

"But I'm getting ahead of myself." Dr. Manning picks her notes back up. "What was it about these dreams that made you suspect your late husband's involvement?"

Panic rises again, and I have to bite it back before I continue. "I had one that took place at home."

"The house you're living in now?"

"Yes—the place I shared with John. Anyway, I was about to go down to the basement, but someone came up behind me. They shoved me down the stairs. It was so sudden and aggressive. Like they were trying to kill me."

"Hmm. That sounds terrifying."

"It was. And I haven't had another one since."

After a thoughtful pause, she asks, "Is there something that makes you think John was the person who pushed you in this dream?"

"That's the other thing," I say quickly. "This wasn't just a nightmare. It was a memory."

"How do you know for sure?"

"I just do." I swallow hard. "Everything about it feels different... more visceral."

"Interesting. Very interesting." She scribbles something onto her pad. "Have you had any other memories since?"

"No, despite my best efforts."

"I see."

"So, about my nightmare—my memory. What do you think I should do? I want to know more, but I don't know how to proceed."

"It's a valid concern. I always advise my patients to take action immediately when it comes to abuse. However, this situation is a bit more complex."

"Because John is dead," I say.

"Exactly. And with your memory loss, it's impossible to be certain." She cocks her head. "That is, unless there's documented evidence of any kind. Perhaps a diary or a journal?"

"I haven't come across anything like that yet."

Dr. Manning takes a sip of water.

"I'll try to look when I get home," I add.

"The thing is, Vonny, our brains are complicated organs. They're always trying to protect us."

"Are you saying that it wasn't a memory?"

"Not necessarily. You just lost your husband. And while you don't remember him, you two shared a life together. There's a void now. Something is missing."

I wait for her to continue.

"Sometimes, our brains alter certain details to make things easier to digest."

I know what she's implying, and I don't like it. That I *want* to remember John as a bad guy so it'll be easier to accept that he's gone. I open my mouth to reply, but decide against it.

Dr. Manning glances at her notes. "Have there been any more flashbacks? I think you mentioned that they happened in your closet."

"Unfortunately, no. I've tried to look at things to cue my memory—photos, scrapbooks, and even social media. But nothing has worked."

"Well, trying to force yourself to remember can actually be counterproductive."

"What do you mean?"

"These things take time." She gives me a kind look. "You were in a bad accident. You sustained severe injuries—"

"I know that," I whisper. "But I *need* to remember."

She takes a deep breath and smiles sadly. "I can only imagine your frustration."

I feel my heart beating fast, pounding as I think about the situation at hand. "I mean, do you think I even have a chance, here? Is there a possibility that I'll actually get the past decade back? I-I'm really losing hope." My voice breaks as I hear the gravity of my own words.

Dr. Manning is quiet for a minute, clearly struggling with how to respond.

"Please be honest," I add quietly. The last thing I want is for her to lie in an attempt to protect my feelings.

"My honest guess is that if your memory *does* come back suddenly, it's going to be when you least expect it. It'll happen when you're not trying to remember anything at all."

AFTER THE SESSION, I glance at my phone and notice a voice mail from Wesley. I dial him back immediately.

"Thank you for getting back to me," he says. "I think you'll be very interested to know what I discovered."

"Is this about..." I pause, hoping that Wesley will continue speaking.

"Yes," he says in a hushed tone.

"What did you find out?"

Wesley is quiet for a moment before responding. "The document that Marshall Lewis presented is fraudulent. Much to my suspicion, it was not actually signed by John Lewis. *Nor* was the document notarized properly."

I hold my breath as he continues.

"The will is definitely a fake, madam. I believe that your brother-in-law forged Mr. Lewis's signature."

Relief floods my entire body. I really started to believe it—that everything would go to Marshall. I worried that I would have to vacate the residence in a matter of days. But *this* changes everything. *I'll be okay.* Even if nothing else works out, at least I'll have this home.

"Quite frankly," Wesley continues, "I'm appalled that he would do such a thing."

"Do I need to contact him? What if he tries something else?"

"Not to worry. I highly doubt that Marshall will push any further. I placed a call to his lawyer this morning, and everything will be straightened out soon."

"Thank you so much, Wesley. I-I honestly don't know what I would do without you."

"I'm just doing my job, madam. Think nothing of it."

I cannot help but smile. All this time, and I still haven't gotten used to his proper manner.

On the other end, Wesley is quiet. I think he starts to say something else, but I can't be sure.

CHAPTER 28

The vivid brain sprawling across my computer desktop is slightly off-putting, but my eyes fixate on every magnified nook and cranny. I can't help but wonder whose mind I am currently staring at.

A more pressing question eventually takes hold. *Who am I?* I need to learn more about New Vonny. Her likes and dislikes, what she does for fun, and what makes her tick. It feels like borderline stalking—diving deep into someone else's life. I am scraping the bottom of my idea barrel when it comes to unlocking the past decade.

Dr. Manning warned that trying too hard can backfire. Half of me believes her, but I also know that there is always a caveat. She even acknowledged that the memory recall process is different for everyone. So really, digging through my old files might actually work for me. Though my grad school documents don't look promising, there is bound to be some useful clue inside.

I click on a folder named Assignments. There are about thirty different word documents inside, but a quick scan of their file names reveals nothing interesting. Just midterm prep, interview transcripts, and various final project drafts.

Next, I try the Class Notes folder. At this point, I can't tell if I am looking out of curiosity or sheer boredom. A plethora of files pops up, each one dated in the same format. I choose *1/26* and watch as the document loads.

Topic: Ethics of Experimental Psychology
-Brief review on Milgram, Zimbardo, and Ebbinghaus
-ALWAYS follow guidelines and adhere to professional standards

-Cognitive Dissonance Assignment: Design experiment to conduct next Friday! (See handout)

-Pushing the boundaries of modern experiments—group discussion (Worth mentioning: Professor Lewis is as charismatic and funny as ever)

I cringe at my own commentary. Apparently, I was smitten enough to record my amorous feelings in class. John Lewis must have been charming enough to distract me, however briefly, from my copious note taking. *Guess that's part of the reason I married the guy.*

I shake my head. Instead of getting bogged down in files and Word documents, I should be looking online. In a new browser, I hover over the history tab. Recently visited sites only include Facebook and my recent visit to Apartments.com.

I click on the dropdown menu then select the tab I really need—Show Full History. To my surprise, a long chain of Google searches dominates the list. My fingers scroll down to the first few on display.

Nevada rest stops

Reno Motels

San Francisco to Reno route

These searches make sense, especially considering my car accident in Nevada. But the next ones cause my blood to run cold.

Surveillance Hacks

Handgun training in San Francisco

Covering your tracks

I bring a shaking hand to my temple. *Was I trying to hide something?*

An obnoxious buzzing makes me jump. I am so embroiled in my own search history that it takes me a moment to collect myself. I slam the laptop shut, walk tentatively to the foyer, then freeze when I see Lee and Ryan.

As I open the door, the detectives square off in front of me in dark suits and leather shoes. Lee's face is cloaked in an intensity I have come to recognize as normal, but Ryan's nervous eye twitch betrays him instantly.

I can feel the color leaving my face. "Is everything okay?"

Lee's voice booms into the foyer. "Veronica Lewis, you're under arrest."

"Wh-what?"

"Move." Lee pushes past Ryan and flashes a pair of shiny handcuffs as he goes.

I swallow hard as the detectives enter my house. Before I've even comprehended the necessity of handcuffs, I am pressed up against the wall by Lee, who shackles my wrists.

"Let's go," Lee says harshly.

I don't fight or even turn to look at them as I'm led toward the doorway. My heartbeat thunders in my ears as they talk quietly behind me. Outside, the otherwise peaceful street feels suddenly alien—the bright sky, landscaped lawns, and strangers passing by. I cannot even remember this neighborhood.

The sunlight pierces my eyes as reality overcomes me again. *I don't belong here.* I take a deep breath to steady myself, plant my feet, then turn toward the detectives. "What exactly is going on?"

Lee nods in my general direction but refuses to look me in the eye. "Please come with us, Mrs. Lewis."

"Why?" My voice rises several octaves. "I-I don't understand." Every word echoes through the foyer and up the grand spiral staircase.

"For the murder of John Lewis." His grip on me tightens. "Let's not make this any harder than it needs to be."

Everything after that feels like it is happening in slow motion. We leave the house, Lee ushers me into the back of his car, then Ryan drives us to the station. All of it blurs together. At some point, one of the detectives reads me my Miranda rights. The words are muffled and fuzzy—nebulous blobs of gibberish.

Someone gives me a glass of water. Another person says to fill out a stack of paperwork. They ask me questions in a tiny room, but I cannot speak. Someone else locks me in a holding cell. The guard, clad in thick-soled combat boots, wears an unmistakable grin as he slams the door. I am trapped.

THE HOLDING CELL IS different than I imagined. My mind pictured a stark, dim setup à la *Law and Order*. To describe this room as decorated might be a stretch or a flagrant lie, but at least there is a motivational quote plastered onto the textured wall: "Change your life today. Don't gamble on the future, act now, without delay." –Simone de Beauvoir.

Right about now, I *would* like to change my life. Being locked inside this cell is wholly unnerving. I sit on the farthest edge of the twin cot, tapping my fingers against its cold metal frame. Zero sound emanates from beyond the bars. No prisoners comparing sentences. No officers talking about last night's big game. Just me and absolute silence.

The jail allows me one call, and I use it as soon as possible. The guard walks me over to another long hallway and gestures to a phone on the wall. He stands behind me, watching as my shaky fingers dial Wesley's number. Those three rings are the longest of my entire life. *Answer. Please answer.*

"Hello?" He sounds different than usual. Surprised to hear from me, perhaps.

"Wesley!" I shout into the phone.

"Hello, madam. How can I—?"

"I'm in jail!" I shout again. Then I lower my voice. "They—they arrested me." I glance over my shoulder and notice the guard inching closer.

Wesley is silent.

"I just don't understand why I'm here. I didn't do anything." My mouth goes dry, voice becoming a strained whisper. "There's no way I could have done this, right, Wesley?"

"Hold tight, madam. I will sort this out."

I clutch the phone tighter. "What's going to happen to me? I can't—"

"I will handle it."

Before I can speak, I hear a quiet click on the other end. This is the first time Wesley has ever hung up on me.

"Time to go back," the guard tells me.

I comply, marching reluctantly back to my cell before he locks me in.

"Can I please have some water?"

The guard grumbles something before disappearing down the hall.

I think about my short phone call with Wesley, trying to analyze his reaction. *Does he really believe me?* Maybe he knows something I don't. His allegiance was to John first. Wesley could have suspected me from the very beginning. The idea leaves an unshakable fear in my gut.

I consider my web history, particularly the content of those last two incriminating searches. Still, I can't fathom being involved in my own husband's murder. Maybe I was just trying to protect myself—solely researching for self-defense. Or maybe his abuse pushed me over the edge. *There's no way, is there?*

I sink onto the end of the bed as I grasp at straws in the few memories I've regained. Those flashbacks of the attack sent me reeling with sheer terror. But as the panic subsided, there was something else too. More emotion swelling inside my body. Desperation. Bitter-ness. Rage.

Was I angry enough to kill John?

CHAPTER 29

Though I don't feel safe behind bars, my body is overcome by inevitable exhaustion. Scattered sleep finds me. Each time I wake, my mind hurts and my limbs ache, and the pain amplifies as I toss and turn. *I need to get out.* For most of the night, I straddle the elusive space between light slumber and complete alertness.

A clattering sound renders me fully awake around seven in the morning. I jolt upright as footsteps pad down the hall. It's the same guard who accompanied me on my phone call yesterday—young, short, and blond. He regards me with an amused expression before unlocking my cell door. A wave of excitement flutters through me as the hinges creak, but my hope dissipates when he wordlessly slides a breakfast tray inside. After slamming the door shut, he disappears down the hall again, leaving me feeling invisible, rejected. My heart sinks as I listen to his footsteps grow fainter.

Forcing myself to eat ultimately backfires. I vomit the runny scrambled eggs and soggy bacon into the cell's tiny metal toilet. I guzzle tap water to cut the acidic taste of my own puke then wipe the corners of my mouth with a paper napkin from the breakfast tray. The greasy scent of bacon lingering on it is enough to make me gag all over again. I push the tray to the farthest edge of my cell, suppress the urge to throw up a second time, then sink to the floor.

It must be another hour or so before the guard returns to collect my tray. He turns his nose up at the smell of vomit but remains silent. An extended clanking sound startles me, exacerbating my headache.

Waiting for the guard to close me in again, I stare up at the speckled ceiling and swallow my growing impulse to scream.

To my surprise, the guard leaves the cell door open. "Mrs. Lewis, come with me."

Squinting through damp lashes, I find him gesturing toward the hall.

I peel myself off the cement floor, wincing as my back muscles cry out. *How long have I been sitting like this?* I manage to stand and roll my shoulders back, dusting off my leggings and tunic as I go. Then I run a hand through my unwashed hair and pinch my pale cheeks.

The guard lets out an exasperated sigh as I head toward him. Apparently, I am taking too long. He shuts the cell door behind me and quickly points to the end of the hall. My mind races while I walk, wondering where he might be taking me. Perhaps Wesley stopped by.

The thought leaves an expectant smile on my face. *I'm going home.*

The guard escorts me to a tiny room on the far side of the building. I catch a glimpse of its interior, noting the bright overhead lights and suspiciously long mirror. I would know this setup anywhere. This is an interrogation room.

My chest tightens as the guard ushers me inside and shuts the door. I jump, bristling as the ensuing sound echoes around me. My breathing quickens. *I guess I'm not getting out of here today.*

This room looks like something out of one of those long-running crime shows Abby and I were obsessed with—mainly *CSI* and *Law and Order*. We used to watch episodes on lazy weekend afternoons, usually after doing laundry at the coin-op place across the street.

During commercial breaks, we would take guesses at the outcome of each episode, laughing at each other's crazy theories. We even bet nickels on who was guilty and which evidence would hold up in court. More often than not, Abby did her research. Plenty of websites were devoted to explaining interrogation tactics and techniques.

Abby and I read through many fanatical posts, some more unsettling than others. One article about observation in public and private spaces was penned by an indisputably paranoid man. His disturbing conclusion always stuck with me—that even after thoroughly checking your surroundings for signs of surveillance, you could never rule out the possibility that someone might be watching. Or listening. In other words, you should always assume that you are not alone.

An abrupt screech interrupts my train of thought. The door opens swiftly, revealing both detectives. Unsurprisingly, Lee walks in first. His strong presence has a way of smothering Ryan's gentler demeanor.

"Hello again, Mrs. Lewis." Lee takes the seat directly across from me.

Ryan sits in the other chair and sets down a thick folder that I assume to be my case file.

"Hi," I say dryly.

"Let's jump right in," Lee starts. "Tell me about your accident."

That takes me aback, and my face instantly betrays me.

"Something wrong?"

"Don't I need my lawyer?"

"This isn't an interrogation," Lee says with a wave of his hand. "We're just talking." His subtle grin is unsettling. I am understandably suspicious, but I have nothing else to say.

"I'd like to know more about your accident," he continues. "Enlighten me."

I look down at my fidgeting hands.

"Take your time," Ryan offers.

"Thanks," I say.

Lee sighs. "Why don't I be more specific? What landed you in the hospital?"

"Well, I was hit by a car."

"And where were you when this took place?"

"They told me I was in Nevada. That's where the hospital was located, anyway."

Ryan nods.

"I'm not exactly sure where the accident happened, but apparently it was somewhere near Reno or—"

"Right." Lee cuts me off. "Why were you there?"

"In the hospital?"

"No, Mrs. Lewis," he says sharply. "Why were you in Nevada in the first place?"

This, again? "I don't know."

"You really have no earthly idea what you were doing in Nevada?"

"I have no clue."

Lee doesn't let up. "Why don't you take a wild guess? Your *home* was in San Francisco. Your *job* was in San Francisco. Your *husband* was in San Francisco. So... why go to Nevada?"

I flash a confused glance at Ryan, but he immediately breaks eye contact.

"I really don't see the point in all of this," I say honestly. "I don't remember any of it, so how can I possibly guess?"

Lee massages his temples and opens my case file.

"We understand," Ryan says calmly. "It must be frustrating not to remember."

Lee shoots him a pointed look and stands up. "Detective Ryan, would you please give me a minute alone with Mrs. Lewis?"

I start to wonder if this is less of a good-cop, bad-cop routine and more of a tense disagreement about my potential role in John's death.

Ryan exhales before pushing out his chair then shutting the door tightly behind him. I am left with an extremely agitated Detective Lee. He remains standing, taking a few heavy steps toward me.

"Let's go back to the beginning," Lee says once he reaches his chosen position—only a few paces behind me.

I shift in my seat. Hearing his voice on its own is arguably far more intimidating. I can feel his enduring distrust, the stern expression on my back, and his rough demeanor.

"What do you mean?" I ask the empty space in front of me.

He doesn't answer right away. Instead, he gradually makes his way back to the other side of the room. The detective stops squarely in front of me so that our eyes have no choice but to meet.

I take a deep breath and wait for another question.

He smirks. "What I mean is, tell me a little bit about the early years—the time you first met John."

My shoulders relax a little. *Seriously*? "I don't *remember* meeting him. That's how amnesia works." *Why can't he understand that*?

He doesn't miss a beat. "Well, you've been back in the house for a couple of weeks now, in that grand home that you two shared together."

I furrow my brow. "And?"

"Has being there triggered any memories?"

I waver, hesitant to explain the confusing flashbacks I had in the closet.

He presses in harder. "Maybe seeing his possessions or looking at old photos reminded you of something."

"Um, well. There were these..."

"Go on."

I berate myself for succumbing to his tactics. I can't afford to say anything that might make me seem guilty. "Well, I had a strange experience when I was looking through some of our clothes."

A glimmer flickers in Lee's eye. "Tell me about them."

"I don't know if they were real or not. And it's difficult to explain."

The glimmer vanishes with a subtle eye roll. "I'd like you to try. This is the kind of stuff I want to know."

"Okay." I sigh inaudibly. "It felt more like a flashback. I was in John's closet, and one of his jackets stood out to me."

Lee cocks his head and offers an encouraging nod.

"Anyway, I went over to look at it. His jacket just seemed so familiar. And when I touched the fabric, I... I sort of *saw* him. I think maybe it was a snippet of a memory."

"And?" he asks expectantly.

"That's all it was." I shrug as my gaze falls back onto the table.

"Elaborate." He crosses his arms.

I shake my head. "That's it. That's all that happened."

"I need you to think harder."

I focus on the space between us. "I already told you. I don't remember *anything* from the past decade."

"That's not good enough. Think!"

My heart pounds in my chest, and each beat echoes in my ears. *Think.* My sweaty palms grip the sides of my chair as Lee's stare burns through me. *Think.* But it's all too much.

Lee swoops in and hammers his fist on the table. "C'mon!"

"I don't remember!"

There is a stiff silence before I start to cry—sporadic, piercing, ugly sobs that echo through the small room.

Lee parts his lips slightly before returning them to their pursed state. Without a word, he storms out then slams the door behind him. The jarring bang makes me jump.

THE SILENCE IN THIS holding cell accentuates my unremitting sobs. I keep trying to muffle the noise—*breathe through your nose, Vonny*—but it's no use. The tactic only serves to make me cry harder. It doesn't really matter, though, since nobody is listening. I have been weeping for the past few hours. My eyes throb, and both cheeks sting from the spread of salty tears.

I turn the interrogation over in my head. Ryan seemed somewhat sympathetic, but Lee made me completely fall apart. *How can someone be so cruel*? I probably gave him the exact reaction he was looking for and played right into his arrogant hands. The thought makes my eyes well up all over again. Moaning softly, I bury my face in both hands.

When I look up again, my vision is clouded with a slight blur, which I'm sure is from the strain of crying. The bars bleed together slowly, morphing into a thick iron wall.

Suddenly, fresh out of some unidentifiable void, it happens. All at once. It doesn't occur in pieces—nothing like putting together a jigsaw puzzle or building a tower of blocks. No, this is exceptionally different. It feels like a film playing in my head. The reel starts without warning and continues rolling without my consent. I have no choice but to watch. This is my life—the past nine years of missing time. I remember everything.

CHAPTER 30
NINE YEARS AGO

My apartment in Seattle smells like sulfur and moldy bread. I have tried everything I can think of—vanilla candles, peppermint oil, and good old-fashioned scrubbing—but nothing works. Yesterday morning, I went a little overboard with my bottle of air freshener. Now the sickly floral scent clings to everything inside this tiny studio.

I finish hanging a corkboard above my desk, pausing briefly to make sure it looks level enough. Then I get to work with the thumbtacks I found at a local flea market. They're brass ones with little red flowers adorning the tops, just like the set in my childhood room. I pin up a welcome-home card from the apartment manager then put the included set of building rules beside it.

After hanging a map of Seattle, the final touch is an old portrait of my parents. It is delicate, faded and torn along the edges, but it's the most recent photo I have of them. I run my finger along my dad's black hair and let my eyes linger on my mom's smile. Her blond curls frame her face beautifully, emphasizing those dimples I remember so well. I have them too.

My phone buzzes against my leg, and I reach down to slide it out of my pocket. A grin spreads across my lips when I see the text from Abby.

Just got off the plane. Waiting for bus. See you soon!

She is coming to help me finish unpacking. That's what we agreed on, anyway. We both know that the real purpose of her visit is to cheer me up. Since moving to the city a few weeks ago, I have been feeling a bit out of place. Barring my sweet octogenarian neighbors, I have yet to make any local friends.

The leasing agent told me that this development was a welcoming, tight-knit community, but I am currently unconvinced. My building feels like a ghost town, and the only sign of community I have seen is a poster advertising a local parents' club that reads, "We mainly vent about our children and sip wine."

Needless to say, Abby's visit is the only thing I have been looking forward to. I am meeting her at a nearby bus stop before we walk back to my place. A taxi from the airport would definitely make things easier, but both of us are broke. I'm just lucky that Abby could afford a round-trip flight across the country.

I grab my jacket before heading out the front door. Today is chilly and overcast, with high winds that send my hair billowing in every direction. *Figures.* A timid sun peeks through the clouds as I leave the complex's courtyard. On the way, I pass a verdant patch that reminds me of Central Park and instantly miss New York.

The neighborhood is eerily quiet, with barely any cars parked on the street. In an effort to distract myself, I pull out my green spiral notebook and read through my summer assignment guidelines as I walk. The project is essentially an extensive self-analysis.

Up until now, I have not made any significant progress, and I doubt I will. The fifteen-page essay requirement only grows more daunting with prolonged procrastination. I am supposed to observe everything that I do on a daily basis, from conversation patterns to fleeting thoughts that pop into my mind.

As I round another corner, I squint down at the instruction sheet. The tiny speck of sunshine above is getting brighter, evidenced by this paper's bright glare. The wind picks up, and I cling to the sheet with one hand and pull my jacket tighter around myself with the other. Just then, a group of screaming schoolchildren run by. The sudden burst is startling enough to make me lose my footing. At the same time, a rush of wind steals the page right out of my hand. It flies up into the air then across the sidewalk. I chase after it, but the current drags it along the pavement, just out of my reach.

I run for what feels like five minutes, sprinting until I am within striking distance. Just when I think I have it, my instruction sheet catches on a pair of worn black boots. Unfortunately, I have so much momentum that I can barely stop myself from colliding with the shoes' owner. At the last second, I split to the side.

"Is this yours?" The man's voice surprises me.

I unglue my eyes from the sidewalk and try to catch my breath. By the time I turn around to face the mysterious boot-wearer, he is already bending over.

"Let's see," he says while peeling the page off the ground. "It's a bit beaten up."

My heart is still racing when he stands back up. He's young, with tousled blond hair, broad shoulders, and dark eyes.

"Here you go." He extends the paper while taking a quick look at its contents. "Whoa, you're in the UW psych program?"

"Uh, yeah." I tuck a rogue strand of hair behind my ear. "I'm a new grad student."

A bright smile takes hold of his face. "Me too!"

"Awesome!" I say a little too eagerly. I accept the page from him and smile back. Our eyes meet for a brief moment, and I feel my cheeks flush.

"I'm Paul," he says warmly. "Paul Bertrand."

I inch a bit closer and shake his hand. "Vonny Kwan."

"Cool name—Vonny. I love that."

Paul is cute in a high-school-crush way, sort of resembling my boyfriend from sophomore year. They have the same messy hair and wide brown eyes.

"So, have you already finished the pre-class assignments?" he asks.

"Almost. I'm hung up on the self-eval one. It feels like a lot of pressure to analyze my every thought in a graded essay, especially before the program even starts."

"Ah—Professor Lewis's assignment." Paul lets out a quiet laugh. "I've been procrastinating about that essay for weeks."

"Well, I'm glad I'm not the only one."

"Lewis is supposed to be a hard-ass anyway. My friend said that was the hardest class he ever took. And he graduated with honors."

"But we're only first years." I frown. "I really hope that's not true."

"Eh, I'd rather get the tough ones out of the way on the sooner side." He shrugs as the words leave his mouth. "Leaves more time for fun at the end."

I feel an unmistakable rush when he looks at me. "Um, anyway... I have to go."

Paul isn't annoyed or taken aback as I would expect. He just stands there with a twinkle in his eye. "Okay, Vonny. I'll see you around."

"Yeah, definitely." I nod before turning to leave. "See ya."

He waves then strolls off in the other direction.

Twenty minutes later, I still can't help thinking about our fleeting encounter while I wait for Abby's bus. Paul comes across like a genuinely nice guy—a refreshing change from the duds I dated in the past. We only just met, though, so I could be jumping to conclusions. Maybe we'll be friends. *God knows I could use some.*

ABBY'S VISIT COMES and goes too quickly. We spend her last evening in Seattle curled up on the couch, relaxing after a busy day at Pike's Place Market.

"Can we break into that ice cream now?" she asks while *Seinfeld* reruns play on my tiny TV.

"You mean what's left of it?"

"Oh, right." She shrugs. "I forgot about the other night."

"I think that's why they call it a blackout."

"Yeah, yeah." Abby chuckles and taps my shoulder. "But in my defense..."

I muster a playful, mocking tone. "Happenings from the other night are *exactly* why you shouldn't touch tequila anymore."

"Well, what can I say? Margaritas are my weakness."

"Exactly."

"Hey. You may have amassed an unreasonably high tolerance, but you didn't make it through college scot-free." Abby moves closer, laying her head in my lap. "Cute boys are definitely your kryptonite."

"Point well made, counselor."

"Remember Jim?"

I cringe. "Let's not talk about *that* lovely chapter of undergrad."

Abby's eyes light up as she imitates my voice. "I just love his writing style, you know? Jimmy is such a romantic soul!"

"Oh, God. That was pretty bad, wasn't it?"

She wrinkles her nose. "Made worse when you dragged me to his outdoor poetry reading."

"I mean, none of the venues would let him perform—" I break into a laugh midsentence.

"Right!" Abby giggles. "You championed Jim's work like you were his agent."

"Ugh, don't remind me."

"I wonder what Jimmy-Boy is up to these days." Abby wears that telltale, devilish grin. "We could look him up and check—"

"So..." I need to redirect her. "Food?"

"Ooh!" Abby sits up. "How about that leftover Thai?"

"Now you're talking."

"I'll even let you have the *pad see ew*."

After peeling myself from the couch, I head into the kitchen to grab our remaining takeout boxes.

"You're the best," Abby says when I return.

I wink before handing her a container of curry. We dig in, munching on noodles while Jerry's comedy routine plays in the background.

I pout when the episode ends. "I don't want you to leave."

"I know." Abby frowns. "Me neither."

"How is it already Sunday?"

"Something about time flying by," she says between bites.

"Why can't you just move here too?"

"Believe me. I'm tempted."

"I wouldn't let you, though. That job is too good to pass up."

She smiles sadly before leaning in to hug me. "You really are the best, V."

"Love you," I whisper with damp lashes.

"Love you more."

These last few weeks with my best friend were exactly what I needed. We spent them exploring Seattle, laughing over midnight dinners, and raiding thrift stores for budget-friendly apartment décor. Abby brought a little piece of home with her—a magical warmth that I missed more than I realized. The comfort is already starting to dissipate, and it's about to leave for the foreseeable future—I have no clue how long it'll be until Abby's next visit.

The next morning brings another round of tears. While neither of us is surprised, we were not expecting our goodbye to be quite so difficult.

"This sucks," I say. We are standing at the same bus stop I met Abby at just weeks ago.

"I know." She gives my hand a squeeze.

I feel my stomach drop when a bus pulls up to the curb.

"Don't worry," Abby says without even looking at me. "It's the wrong one."

I nod, trying to feign composure.

"You're going to be okay," she tells me. "We both will." She forces a brave smile, but I know her too well to believe it.

We stand in silence beside Abby's rolling suitcase. She puts her arm around me snugly and takes a deep breath. That's how it's always been—Abby staying strong for both of us. But I need to be strong for her too.

"You're right," I finally say. "We'll be more than okay. And I'll come visit you too."

She smiles for real this time—a bright, toothy grin that lights up her entire face. "Promise?"

"Of course. We can trade off."

Abby nods. "I like that idea."

The correct bus pulls up seconds later. I give her another hug, reminding myself that this is only temporary.

Abby's eyes are watery. "Bye," she whispers before picking up her bag. "Love you."

"Love you more."

Abby has always been like a sister to me—the only person I ever truly connected with. *And now she's leaving.* The knot in my gut tightens as the bus pulls away. We both wave, refusing to stop until we can no longer see each other. This will be the longest time we have ever been apart. I don't know what I will do without her.

CHAPTER 31

C lass has not even started, but I am sweating bullets. Social Psychology is supposed to be the hardest course I will ever take. Not because of the subject matter but because of the person teaching it. Professor Lewis is a "hard-ass," as Paul so eloquently put it. This is more nervous than I have been in a very long time. I am attending UW on an academic scholarship, and I do not know what I will do if I fail my first class. I literally cannot afford to mess this up.

"You okay?" Paul asks from our seats in the back row.

"Yeah."

I think he believes me, but I cannot really tell. We have only been hanging out for the past week or so. I like Paul—I really do. He is simple and straightforward, albeit a little hard to read at times. But it's nice to have someone to talk to with Abby gone.

"Downtown Dan's tonight?" he asks casually.

The diner is close to my apartment, with great music, cushy booths, and saucer-sized burgers. We ate there shortly after running into each other again. I could not actually tell if Paul was asking me on a date, or if he simply wanted to hang out that day. Our chemistry is palpable—at least in my opinion. *Does he feel it too?*

"I'm in." I offer a playful smile.

Paul grins back. *Flirty? Impish?* Impossible to tell.

Other grad students chat quietly around us while everyone waits for Professor Lewis to arrive. There is only a minute left before our scheduled start time, and I am expecting the door to burst open any second. It doesn't. In fact, thirty more minutes pass without instruction. My anxiety begins to grow, but talking to Paul eases my nerves considerably.

"Back home, we had this teacher who would always show up late to class," he tells me. "Guy's name was Mr. Flycatcher—"

"Seriously?"

"No joke. Anyway, Flycatcher would mosey in toward the middle of second period with his mug of coffee. Didn't have a care in the world. He was rude to everyone too."

"Sounds weird."

"You bet. Anyway, at the end of the year, one of the girls in my class just couldn't take it anymore."

"What happened?"

"He was chewing this kid out one day—for being *late* of all things. So hypocritical, right? And this girl yelled at the teacher in front of everyone."

"Oh, geez."

Paul turns his nose up and raises his voice a few octaves. "Hey, Flycatcher! Didn't you know? You catch more flies with honey than—"

I burst into laughter before he can finish.

My reaction seems to entertain Paul, who has an amused grin plastered on his face. "Glad I could be of service."

Suddenly, the rest of the room falls silent. It feels like every eye is glued on me. My cheeks blaze. Apparently, I have already labeled myself as the class loudmouth. But when I finally look up, I realize that it is not my obnoxious laugh that stole everyone's attention. It is our instructor.

I was expecting a dowdy middle-aged woman or a hardened septuagenarian. But this woman is drop-dead gorgeous. In a black tailored suit with a silky white blouse peeking through her jacket, our professor strides across the wooden floor, heels clicking softly, until she reaches a large podium. The overhead lights emphasize her flawless bone structure and cast a glow around her mane of glossy blond hair. Everything about her is impossibly chic. My first impression is only solidified when she opens her mouth.

"Hello, everyone. Welcome to Social Psychology."

A British accent—posh and pristine. *Of course.*

"If you do happen to find yourself in the wrong section," she says with an arched brow, "now would be the moment to leave."

I glance around the room and notice that everyone else is just as captivated as I am, including Paul.

"My name is Cheryl Lewis, but you can call me Professor."

A few nervous laughs echo through the room.

"During the first part of this quarter, we will be focusing on prosocial and group behavior." She opens a folder with notes but never seems to reference the material. Professor Lewis makes constant eye contact without missing a beat.

I flip open my notebook and scribble down what she just said.

"First things first. Those of you who do well enough will have the option of taking the laboratory-based course I teach every few quarters. It *is* quite a magnificent opportunity to conduct valuable field research, so I highly recommend staying on top of your work this quarter. Make everything count." Professor Lewis taps her manicured nails against the podium as she says the last three words. They are painted in a bold red color, just like her crimson lips.

I glance at Paul, who seems enraptured by her every word.

"Let's begin with introductions, shall we?" She looks around the room until her blue eyes settle on someone in the front row. "Why don't you start us off?"

The first target is a tall guy, clad in jeans and a green sweater. He straightens up and clears his throat before responding. "Uh, hey," he says loudly. "I'm Mark. This is my first quarter in the grad program, and I'm pretty *psyched* to be here. No pun intended." Mark chuckles at his own awkward wordplay before sinking back into his seat. "Anyway, yeah. That's me."

Professor Lewis nods briefly at each introduction but offers no obvious reactions. The only movement she repeatedly makes is a subtle flick of her wrist while making notes on the sheet hidden behind the podium. I assume she is documenting something to remember each student by. Perhaps a physical characteristic—strawberry-blond hair—or a less obvious mannerism like overusing an upward inflection.

When it is finally my turn to speak, I stand up and roll my shoulders back. "Hello, everyone," I say while looking around the room. "My name is Veronica Kwan, but I go by Vonny. I want to study psychology because it's the only subject I have ever really connected with. I'm passionate about studying people to better comprehend their quirks and ticks."

Professor Lewis looks up from her notes. Although her expression barely changes, I think I detect something imperceptible flickering through her eyes.

"I believe that fundamentally understanding a person's deepest thoughts is the only way to ever truly help them," I continue. "It's necessary."

Professor Lewis holds her gaze on me while I take my seat. My cheeks burn from the entire class's attention, and I desperately hope she cannot tell from the front of the room. I am surprised to see her without a pen until the next person speaks.

There are several more introductions—some standing and others sitting. When the last student finishes, Professor Lewis dismisses us.

"You can hand in your summer assignments on the way out," she says before we leave.

It is not until class ends that I realize something odd. Professors usually give a brief presentation about themselves, mentioning their hometowns, amassed credentials, and current research topics. We revealed so much about ourselves during this first session—a whole lot more than I anticipated. But we learned almost nothing about our professor.

Cheryl Lewis is as mysterious to me now as she was before stepping through that door.

CHAPTER 32

I relish the warmth of Paul's hand as we walk through my apartment courtyard. His body heat is a welcome contrast to the chill of a September breeze. We just spent the entire evening at another local art show, where both of us imbibed more than a few glasses of wine. My face is flushed from drink and desire.

I unlock my door clumsily before Paul opens it for me. We walk inside and flip the light on, illuminating my cluttered entryway. I stumble over to the bed while struggling to unzip my expensive cocktail dress. The tags are still intact, so I can return it tomorrow.

"Come here," I say in my best flirty voice.

Paul leans against the doorway and smiles. "We should probably get you into bed."

"My thoughts exactly." I climb atop my twin-size mattress.

He walks over then gives me a long kiss on the cheek. I reach up to pull him closer, but he takes a step back before I can.

"Why not?"

He just shakes his head and grins.

"Fine."

He gently removes my heels. "Another time."

I am struck by how sincere he is. *Maybe too sincere for his own good*.

He pulls a fluffy duvet over my shoulders, rendering me sleepier by the second. Then he pauses before turning out the light. "Good night, Vonny."

The door clicks shut before I fall asleep. Even in my exhausted, tipsy state, I can appreciate what a good guy Paul is. He's my best friend in Seattle. My *only* friend.

"GOOD MORNING, EVERYONE." Professor Lewis enters the room carrying a Bankers Box full of files. Her voice is at once refined and authoritative. Her presence, an amalgamation of poise and wit, charm and power.

I have yet to see her in anything other than a tailored suit. Then again, I wonder if students would take her less seriously in a vibrant ruffled blouse and slim pencil skirt. *Doubtful.* This is our seventh class of the quarter. The others have flown by at a record speed—something that seems to have rattled my peers.

Most of our sessions have consisted of Professor Lewis lecturing while we frantically scribble down notes. A few students remain distracted, either by her exterior beauty or alluring accent, and are definitely falling behind. Eleven people have dropped the class so far, and I refuse to be the twelfth.

Professor Lewis unpacks the Bankers Box then spreads out multiple files on a large table. The faint sound of lead on paper catches my attention. A quick glance to my right tells me that someone is actually taking notes on this process, which makes me laugh. *Professor Lewis removes file folders at 10:15 a.m.*

Paul shoots a bemused look in my direction, and I gesture to the overly attentive student.

Our little joke is quickly forgotten when Professor Lewis starts the class.

"During our first class, I asked you to give me a brief introduction about yourself," Professor Lewis says from the front of the room. "Miss Kwan told us that in order to truly help a person, it's necessary to fundamentally understand them."

I am stunned to hear my name.

She looks up at me. "So, Miss Kwan, why don't you elaborate on that for us?"

Everyone turns toward the back of the room. My cheeks burn, flushing from the sudden and unforeseen attention. This is the first time our professor has singled anyone out.

"Why do you believe that?" she asks.

I take a deep breath, careful to steady my voice before speaking. "People are like puzzles. You need to know what the pieces are before trying to solve them."

A subtle smile dances across her lips as I wait for a verbal response. *Nothing*. Instead, she walks over to the files, runs her fingers across them, then selects one from the bottom of a small stack.

"Today, I thought we would take a slight detour from group behavioral studies."

The news of swaying from the curriculum sends a shockwave through the entire middle row. Some students scroll frantically through their laptop notes. Others flip though composition books at an otherworldly speed.

Professor Lewis's serene expression remains intact. "We will be discussing personality disorders during the next few classes. Of course, we don't have nearly enough time to cover all of them, so we will study a few in depth."

We are quickly divided into groups of three. Professor Lewis hands an unmarked folder to each group, instructing us to read through the enclosed documents. My group's file is all about borderline personality disorder. We are only given thirty minutes—no exceptions—to study the information before a class discussion ensues.

"WHO HAD NARCISSISTIC personality disorder?" Professor Lewis asks once we are all back in our seats.

"We did," a young woman in the front says.

"Tell me a few of the symptoms of this disorder."

I swallow hard. This is less of a class discussion, more of an oral pop quiz.

"Um, people suffering from it always want the best... and they tend to exaggerate their successes."

"What else?" Our professor is clearly unimpressed.

The young woman looks around fretfully at her group mates, but no one offers to help. "They, um—they need consistent praise?"

Professor Lewis raises an eyebrow. "Are you asking or telling?"

Everyone stiffens, including me.

"I-I'm sorry," the student says. "I don't remember."

The collective gaze shifts to the front of the room, eagerly awaiting our professor's reaction. She stands still, lips pursed and a hand stationed on her hip. After a moment, though, her entire demeanor changes.

"That's all right," she says softly. "Why don't you review the reference sheet, and I will come back to you?"

The student nods while exhaling in relief.

"Now, then." Professor Lewis taps a shiny nail to her lips. "Who read about borderline personality disorder?"

I peer at the two other members of my group, waiting for someone to volunteer. Nobody does.

"We did," I say reluctantly. My heart begins to race in anticipation of what's to come.

"What are the four types of this disorder?"

I take a deep breath. *Stay calm, Vonny. You know this.* "The four types of borderline personality disorder are discouraged, impulsive, petulant, and... self-destructive."

"Precisely." She nods.

I wait for another question, but she moves onto the next group. Tension melts from my shoulders once I realize I am off the hook.

Paul leans over from his group and grins. "Good job," he whispers in my ear.

A few more group representatives tackle Professor Lewis's questions one by one. Some of them do well, but others fumble like the first student.

When class is almost over, our professor clasps her hands together and glimpses around the room. "We are out of time, but I want you to read over your files before the next class. We're going to thoroughly examine these disorders and discuss a few specific case studies."

Paul lingers while I pack my bag, the rest of the students eagerly shuffling away on either side of us. We exchange a brief nod and walk toward the door together.

"Miss Kwan?" a distinct British voice calls after me.

I reel around to face Professor Lewis.

"Would you stay behind for a few minutes?"

"Um, sure." I shoot an uneasy glance at Paul, who offers a small wave before leaving.

Once the last student exits, I am left completely alone with her. This room is somehow larger and less comfortable without everyone else inside. There is nobody to share the intimidation with—no one to lean on if the pressure rises too high.

"Tell me," Professor Lewis says lightly as she approaches. "How are you enjoying classes so far?"

Forcing a smile, I consider how to best respond. "I like them. I'm excited to be exposed to a host of new topics."

"Such as?"

"Well, I didn't study mental illness as much as I wanted to at NYU. There are so many different conditions in existence, so much overlap to consider when diagnosing a new patient. I find it fascinating."

"Ah. Are you taking a class with Professor Dunne this term?"

"Yes." I nod. "One of his seminars."

"Wonderful. He is extremely well versed in the intricacies of mental illness. I'm sure you will learn a lot from him."

While I don't mind the conversation, I'm left wondering why she asked me to stay behind.

"Did you like New York?"

"Oh, yes," I tell her. "I absolutely loved it there."

"And Seattle?"

I open my mouth to answer, wavering for a second.

She lets out a small laugh. "Washington is not everyone's cup of tea. It's so bloody dreary here."

We both peek at the window as gray clouds swell overhead.

"Case in point." I shrug.

Professor Lewis seems amused. "You know, I read your summer essay the other night."

My stomach clenches. *Oh, no. I failed the assignment.*

As if detecting my dread, she waves a hand through the air. "No, no. It's nothing bad."

I look at her expectantly.

"I loved it."

Now I am stunned. My essay sucked—I'm sure of it.

"Your writing was... unflinchingly honest. The most refreshing essay I have read in a long time."

I wipe the surprise from my face and wait for her to go on.

"You see, most students try to impress me with fraudulent claims about their summer activities. They make themselves sound better than they actually are."

I silently congratulate myself for resisting the urge to lie in my essay.

"This all goes to say that I found your self-analysis captivating, Miss Kwan."

I don't bother editing my reaction this time.

"You're surprised?"

"Um, yes. A little bit."

Professor Lewis beams. "You shouldn't be. Honesty is rare these days, and it goes a long way with me."

Noting the message her last words impart, I match her smile.

"Every so often, my husband and I host dinners for standout students," she says. "We have them at our home in San Francisco."

"You live in California?"

"He does," she explains coolly. "I travel between San Francisco and Seattle. This term is easier since I am only teaching courses three days a week."

"That sounds exciting."

"Yes, well." She massages her left temple. "It isn't for the faint of heart."

I stare down at the wooden floor. *Have I overstepped*?

"Anyway, I was wondering if you might attend our next dinner."

"Really? I... wow. I would love to."

"Excellent." Her voice lifts noticeably. For a moment, she regards me with an unreadable expression. "I will send along details to your student email address."

"Sounds great. Thanks for inviting me." I hover in the doorway, wondering if I should mention that I can't possibly afford a ticket to San Francisco. I decide against it. This is important, and I will figure out a way to make it work.

CHAPTER 33
EIGHT YEARS AGO

Paul zips up my dress while I put on some dangly earrings. This pair is sparkly and gold—a birthday gift from Abby during our sophomore year at NYU. *I should really call her.* It has been way too long since we last spoke.

"You ready?" he asks, interrupting my train of thought.

"I think so. I can't believe it's finally happening."

We are staying at the Fairmont in San Francisco. This hotel is fancy and completely out of our price range, but Cheryl insisted. *Cheryl*—that's what she told me to call her. My professor extended an invitation to me for one of her student dinner parties last year, but I was unable to make it. I initially wondered if I had upset her, given the lack of response and invitations for the remainder of the year. My stomach was knotted up for months on end.

When I broached the subject one day after class, Cheryl was warm and pleasant, saying that she hadn't hosted anything in a while. Apparently, I am still in good standing with her—a veritable relief, because I earned an A minus in her course. *And an invitation to boot.* Now that she is no longer my professor, it feels a bit peculiar to be attending one of these events. But I am excited nonetheless.

"Wish I was coming with you tonight," Paul says quietly.

I turn and give him a tight hug. "Me too." I am still surprised that he was not invited, especially since Cheryl included Paul's name on the hotel reservation. While these circumstances are a bit odd, I try to shake off any concern.

"You look beautiful," he says sweetly as I apply my lipstick.

"Thanks, babe." My cheeks warm. "I'll see you later tonight."

"Good luck." He gives me a quick kiss. "You'll do great."

CHERYL'S HOUSE, WHICH is more of a mansion, looks stunning. I attempt to wipe the astonishment off my face while stepping through the large doorway. *Who lives like this?* I am instantly swept into a large group of people who I assume to be students and am escorted down a long hallway lined with flickering candles. Music hums softly from somewhere above.

Suited-up waiters pass through with trays of canapés and champagne. There are about twenty of us, and the drinks disappear rapidly. *Still no sign of Cheryl.* We are left to mingle amongst ourselves while we wait. I abhor small talk of any kind, so the first thirty minutes of this evening are nothing short of tense.

"Are you enjoying your second year at UW?" asks the first-year guy I have been talking to.

"Um, yeah. It's great." I'm still scouring the party for our hostess.

"Well, I'm loving all of my third-quarter classes..." His voice fades to the background as I pick up the faint sound of heels.

Finally, Cheryl floats down the low-lit hallway, blond hair glowing in the candlelight. The other students notice her too. Conversations fall silent, and champagne glasses stop midsip. The collective attention is rapt, unwavering.

Cheryl dances through the crowd like a ballerina—delicate, swift, and graceful. She is at once demure and commanding, brazen and mysterious. Instead of her usual suits, a crimson gown emphasizes her slim figure, and silver heels sparkle as she walks.

"Welcome, students." She flashes a dazzling smile. "Please, don't let my late arrival interrupt your conversations. I look forward to speaking with each and every one of you tonight."

Tentative chatter sounds while Cheryl scans the crowd. When her gaze falls upon me, I immediately stiffen. She nods in my general direction and approaches.

"Miss Kwan," she says genially. "I am very glad you could join us."

"Me too. I'm so happy to be here."

"How do you like the Fairmont?"

"Oh, I absolutely love it. Thank you so much for letting us stay there! It was so generous of you—too generous."

"No such thing," she says with a wave of her hand. She lifts two flutes from a passing waiter's tray then hands one to me. "Here. Better drink up. It's going to be a long night."

I laugh then take a lengthy sip, champagne bubbles burning my throat as I swallow. Cheryl finishes only part of her glass before placing it on an empty tray.

"I'll chat more with you later," she tells me before leaving to greet a small group of students standing in the corner.

When their eyes widen slightly at the sight of her up close, I wonder if this is their first dinner party too. It is easy to get caught up in Cheryl's overwhelming beauty. The woman could pass for anyone—a prominent actress, a famous runway model, or an esteemed designer's muse. For a brief moment, I almost forget that she is my professor. *Former* professor.

We move into the sizeable dining room for a lavish three-course meal. There are several separate tables inside, with cream-colored place cards in front of each setting. My seat is near a few students I have seen around campus. Jason, Nora, and Lee are all nice enough—perhaps a bit shy—as we discuss our classes during dinner. Everyone is noticeably distracted, if not disengaged entirely. We are all too busy stealing glimpses of Cheryl between servings and eaves-dropping on her every conversation.

The same waiters bring us golden plates of Caesar salad, roast duck, and tiramisu for dessert. Every dish is incredibly delicious—a welcome change from the takeout I have started relying on at night. By the time they serve us coffee and tea, I am absolutely stuffed.

At one point, Cheryl steps away to attend to an unknown matter. She returns just minutes later and apologizes casually for the delay. We are all invited back into the other room, instructed to mingle while more drinks are served. I really should limit myself or refrain completely since my head is woozy from the glasses I consumed before dinner.

My curious ears steal bits of random discussions as I trade champagne for bubbly water.

"Where do you think he is?" someone whispers.

"Maybe it's just her tonight," another responds. "I guess we'll see."

I stop listening and visit with a woman from lab class. When our banter starts to dwindle, I glance at my phone and realize that it is already midnight. There are two recent texts from Paul.

Hey babe, how's it going?

Wow, getting kinda late. You okay?

After shooting him a quick message, I stash the phone back inside my clutch. When I look up again, I notice Cheryl slip away from the party again. She glides down that same hallway she first entered from. I glance around at the other students, wondering when people might start leaving.

"Do you know when this thing ends?" I ask the guy in front of me.

"They usually go pretty late." He shrugs. "The first dinner party I went to lasted well into the morning."

Before I can respond, Cheryl returns with someone I have never seen before. They walk in side by side, her arm threaded elegantly through his. The man is wearing a fitted black suit and a crimson tie that matches Cheryl's dress. His slicked-back hair is much darker than hers, and his eyes are a piercing blue. *That must be her husband.*

They make their way around the room, pausing to speak with every student in attendance. Some greetings are short and courteous. Others evolve into long conversations, filled with genuine smiles and infectious laughter. I cannot seem to drag my eyes away from them. Cheryl and her husband look like celebrities—movie stars signing autographs at an after party. I occasionally chime into conversations around me until they finally approach.

"Veronica Kwan, meet my husband, John Lewis."

I am instantly overcome by his striking face. He looks like a Ralph Lauren model.

"Hi there." He offers me a handsome grin. "Nice to meet you."

I extend my hand and feel the color spread to my cheeks.

"Miss Kwan was in my class last year," Cheryl says. "She is quite a promising student."

"Is that right?" John beams at his wife.

She nods, cocking her head at me. "Very smart."

"And how did you like Cheryl's course?" he asks.

"Oh, I loved it," I tell him honestly. "It was the first graduate class I ever took—a great way to jump-start my education."

"Well, as long as she didn't scare you off." John chuckles. "My wife can be pretty intimidating to first years."

Cheryl raises an eyebrow playfully while we share a quiet laugh.

"Well, Miss Kwan," John says before they move on, "it was a pleasure to meet you."

During the next three hours, we divide into small groups to play charades and Monopoly. Such an odd dichotomy—ball gowns and board games. But this is the most fun I have had in a long time.

"Aren't they marvelous?" whispers one of my teammates while I shuffle the deck. "A true power couple. He's just as enchanting she is."

Several students depart after just a few rounds, excusing themselves politely to call cabs. I wonder—albeit briefly—if I should do the same before deciding against it. There are still enough of us here to confirm that I am not imposing. We talk and play games until we inevitably succumb to exhaustion. By the time I step outside to leave, it is already five in the morning.

After giving one last wave, I climb into the taxi. *What a party.* As we drive back to my hotel, cruising down clusters of sleepy city streets, my mind lingers on Cheryl and John. Apart, they are incredible. *Inimitable.* Each of them is brilliant, stunning, and undeniably magnetic. But together, they are unreal.

CHAPTER 34

Cheryl asks me to meet her after class the following week. Of course I oblige. *How could I not?* I wait for my professor patiently while students ask her clarification questions about their newest assignment. She answers each one concisely, pausing only to insert witty remarks that no one else seems to pick up on.

Cheryl turns to me after the last student leaves and sighs quietly. "I'm feeling a bit tired this afternoon."

I blink. Nothing about this woman looks tired, even in the slightest way.

"Care to join me for a coffee?"

I nod, attempting to hide the bundle of nerves and excitement vibrating in my core.

"Follow me." She gives a small grin.

We arrive at Cheryl's office—a roomy space with neatly labeled bins and file boxes lining the walls. The place is bright and warm, with subtle touches of tasteful décor. Cheryl drapes her coat over a dark-velvet chair and switches on the coffee maker. I set my bag down, looking around while the dark roast brews.

Cheryl opens a cabinet then hands me one of the large mugs. "So, how did you enjoy the party?"

"It was lovely. I had a wonderful time. Thanks again for having me. You really didn't have to pay for my hotel stay."

"Oh, nonsense," she says absentmindedly. "It was nothing."

"Well, I really appreciate it. You and Mr. Lewis are very generous."

"Just 'John.'" Cheryl faces the wall while pouring us each a coffee. "He abhors that nonsense as much as I do."

"John," I say, making a mental note.

"Cream and sugar?"

"Black, please."

"A young lady after my own heart."

I relax when I hear the smile in Cheryl's voice.

She turns around to hand me a hot mug. "Here you are."

"Thank you."

"Have a seat." She gestures to a small leather couch. "I'm sure your feet are tired from so much walking."

"A little bit," I say honestly. "The campus is pretty large."

Cheryl takes the chair across from me. "How long until your next class?"

I glance at the wall clock. "I have about an hour."

She nods before bringing the mug to her lips.

"I like your office," I say between sips of coffee. "The design is very chic."

"Oh, you think so?" Cheryl looks around and shrugs. "I was thinking it came out a bit too garish."

"Not at all. My friend Abby would love it. This is exactly her style."

"Is she a mate from New York?"

"Yes—my best friend. We met freshman year at NYU."

"Oh?" Cheryl arches an eyebrow.

"I honestly don't know how I would have gotten through college without her."

"University friendships can be fantastic, can't they?"

"Definitely."

"That is, when they last." I wait for Cheryl to explain, but she takes a long sip instead.

I shift in my seat. "So, where did you go to school?"

"I attended Cambridge back home and completed my studies at Brown."

"That's impressive."

Cheryl cocks her head slightly. "When I first came to the States, I was extremely homesick. I missed my mates from England and..." She shakes her head. "God, it was dreadful."

I find it impossible to imagine Cheryl being insecure.

"But I was determined to make things work—to rise above those feelings. After all, they were ultimately holding me back. So I immersed myself in my studies. I exclusively ate, slept, and breathed psychology for years."

I nod, fascinated by her commitment.

"I encourage you to do the same thing," Cheryl says thoughtfully. "I truly believe that it makes all the difference."

CHERYL'S ADVICE STICKS with me while walking to my next class. She's right. I need to focus more—on my courses, on campus life, and on everything psychology related. Maybe I should join a club, try to conduct some sort of on-campus experiment, or simply devote extra hours to studying. The possibilities are endless. I am going to work harder, impress the hell out of my professors, and ace every exam from here on out.

My coffee chats with Cheryl eventually increase, both in length and frequency. They also become a favorite part of my routine. At the weeks go by, I find myself looking forward to our visits more than any of my actual classes.

"That was an incredible discussion today, don't you think?" she asks.

"It really was." I lean back against her office couch. For the past several days, I have been filling in for Cheryl's teaching assistant, who is currently feeling under the weather.

"What was your favorite part?"

I tap a finger against my lips. "Probably that debate on the validity of personality testing."

Cheryl smiles and hands me a mug. "I thought so too."

"The coffee is exceptional today," I tell her between sips. "Did you do something different?"

"Two pinches of cinnamon." She winks. "An old trick gleaned from my grandmother."

"Genius." I inhale the spicy aroma. It's funny how comfortable I feel around Cheryl now, especially considering that I still find her formidable.

"How are things going with Paul?" she asks.

"Pretty good. We went to the fair last weekend, and he won me a stuffed monkey."

"Chivalry is alive and well, then." She lets out a short laugh.

"Apparently."

"That's sweet, though." Cheryl stares into her mug. "He seems nice."

"He is. Nicer than anyone else I've ever dated."

"Reminds me of John," she says with a glimmer in her eye.

"Oh?" I grin.

"He has always been very stable."

"How did you two meet?"

"I actually met him when I first started at Brown. We lived in nearby dorms and kept running onto each other at on-campus events and parties."

"That's so cute. So you started dating during your first year?"

"Not exactly. John kept asking me out, but I refused to be distracted from my coursework." Cheryl shrugs. "The chemistry was impossible to ignore, though. It was... palpable."

I blush when I remember feeling the same feeling about Paul. "So, what happened?"

"I finally agreed to date him after graduation, and the rest is history."

"Wow. College sweethearts."

Cheryl's nostalgia fades. "The important thing is, I made sure to figure out what I truly wanted before diving into anything."

I nod before finishing my drink.

"That's the secret," she adds. "It's vital to establish your own trajectory first. Everything else comes later."

I set my mug down on the table between us. She has a good point.

Cheryl is quiet for a moment. "Veronica," she says sincerely. "Promise me that you will prioritize yourself. Promise me that you will always protect your ambition."

I meet her gaze as she continues.

"I couldn't bear to watch another young woman lose herself to love. It happens far too often in this world. Oldest story in the whole bloody book."

I nod, wondering exactly what she means. Our discussion shifts to something lighter before I can ask. Soon, we are laughing about this afternoon's mandatory—and boring—presentation on school safety.

"That's pure irony for you." Cheryl chuckles. "The dean's Power-Point put so many students to sleep that it became a legitimate safety hazard."

"I know," I say between giggles. "They were dropping like flies. I counted at least twenty students who fell off their chairs before he finished talking."

"Therein lies the true tragedy of having a monotone voice."

After noting the time, I reluctantly excuse myself. I thank Cheryl for coffee and glance at the clock again, shocked at how quickly another hour flew by. That is the strangest thing about talking to Cheryl—it's effortless. Sure, she is brilliant and intimidating, but I am far too captivated to be deterred by her intelligence. It's inspiring. *She* is inspiring.

CHAPTER 35

I land at San Francisco International Airport a few months later. There is another dinner party tonight—the fourth one I get to attend. Normally, I would have flown in yesterday and stayed over at a nearby hotel. But Paul had a romantic date planned for us last night—a black-and-white movie in the park. It was sweet at first, but our evening devolved shortly after the credits rolled. On the way back to my apartment, we ended up getting into a horrible fight. *About this trip of all things.* Paul wanted me to cancel it, but I refused. I reminded him that it's paramount for me to be here. After all, Cheryl will be a valuable connection once I start looking for residency opportunities.

Paul has not accompanied me to San Francisco during the past few visits. I feel bad leaving without my boyfriend, but Cheryl has never invited him to her house. He probably feels a bit left out, and the thought of asking for an invitation on his behalf has definitely crossed my mind. Still, the last thing I want to do is offend Cheryl or John. *Not after everything they've done for me.*

I change into my gown in the airport bathroom. Tonight's choice is a brand-new Balenciaga—emerald-green and velvet, with the most divine beadwork around its collar. I have been discreetly keeping the tags on these dresses and returning them after each party. Everyone always looks so stylish in elegant attire, and I do not want to disappoint. I would also prefer to keep my bank account intact.

I finish getting ready before hobbling to the taxi line in my strappy heels. It is an expectedly long wait, but I budgeted enough time to ensure I wouldn't be late. When my turn finally arrives, I give the driver Cheryl and John's address.

"Fancy," he says as we pull into their driveway. "You live here?"

"God, no." I laugh. "My professor does."

He shoots me a suspicious look. "What a nice professor you have. Hope he treats you well."

Suppressing an eye roll, I step out of the cab. I know what the driver is thinking, but I don't bother correcting him. This is nothing like that. I do feel guilty taking these trips on the Lewises' dime, though. I have offered to pay my own way—flight and hotel expenses included—but Cheryl insists. She maintains that spending time with her brightest students is what keeps her going. "It helps me look past the failures and fuckups I still have to teach," she joked one evening.

There's a host of new students here tonight. I fail to recognize most if not all of them. *Am I the only person who's been here before?* As usual, Cheryl makes her grand entrance precisely thirty minutes after the party's start time. Her dress is a slinky fuchsia gown that hugs her curves subtly. John walks besides her, looking as handsome as ever.

To my bemusement, Cheryl and John skip their usual round of greetings. There are no introductions or conversations once they arrive.

Instead, my professor makes a cryptic announcement: "The average person has thirteen secrets right now."

This crowd is somehow more hushed than before. Even the waiters stop serving canapés, listening attentively while she speaks.

"Your mission, if you choose to accept it," Cheryl says with an eerie grin, "is to uncover at least three secrets tonight."

A light murmur echoes through the room. Apparently, this is tonight's activity. Cheryl provides a list of three simple rules. First, we must speak to at least ten different people. Second, we can ask each person a maximum ten questions. Third, you can only lie once during the game.

An uneasy air falls over the room as the game begins. One woman hesitantly asks me if I have ever been pregnant. A third-year forensics major wonders how many crimes I have committed. We trade partners every few minutes, asking each other intimate questions that would normally be considered offensive. Nothing is off-limits in this game.

To my surprise, John exits partway through. He has an odd look on his face—most likely the product of agitation—before disappearing down a dark hallway. Cheryl, on the other hand, seems completely unfazed. She continues circling the room while listening to our exchanges.

"There you are!" she greets me enthusiastically. It's been a few weeks since our last visit.

"Hi, Cheryl," I say, forcing a smile. Her little game is making me tense.

She takes a swig of wine. "It's so good to see you."

The students around me scatter slightly, no doubt trying to avoid her prying eyes and ears.

"Are you enjoying yourself?"

"Definitely. This is wonderful."

Cheryl raises a blond eyebrow. "Tsk-tsk, Miss Kwan. You've already used up your lie."

I swallow hard. The ease I normally feel around her fades to an undeniable apprehension.

"I can tell that you're not having fun. The truth is in your body language."

"Sorry," I say. "This game just makes me a little nervous."

Her eyes narrow slightly. "Why is that?"

It suddenly feels like I am back in her class, sweating bullets on the first day of school.

Cheryl shakes her head and takes another sip of wine. "I assure you," she says in a measured tone, "this game can be loads of fun."

I nod and force another smile.

"I'll show you." She matches my expression. "How about you ask me a question?"

"Um, okay. What is your worst childhood memory?"

"Interesting one." A short laugh slips through her lips. "Let's see. Probably when my mother died."

"Oh, God. I am so sorry—"

"Don't be," she says through gritted teeth. "She was a dreadful woman." Her face quickly returns to its normal state. "Go on, then. Ask me another."

"Um... why did you become a professor?"

"Miss Kwan," she says in the same reproachful tone. "You are forgetting the point of this game. You want to find out my dirty secret, don't you?"

Silence is my only response.

"Ask me something deeper. Something darker."

She clearly knows that I'm at a total loss. Ever since we first met, she has been reading me like a book.

She leans in, so close that no one else can hear her. "I'll give you a little hint," she whispers. "Ask me something about my marriage."

My stomach tightens.

"What are you waiting for?" She downs her wine before setting the glass on an end table.

"I'm not exactly sure what you mean. I don't feel comfortable—"

"Oh, Veronica." She shakes her head. "You are such a bore."

Her persistence is frustrating. "Fine. Is your marriage a happy one?"

A glimmer flickers through Cheryl's eyes, and a coy smile replaces her pout. "Now you're getting somewhere. Not *entirely* happy."

Her answer disconcerts me. I always assumed that she and John were made for each other—the perfect couple. I wait for Cheryl to walk away, but it seems that she won't leave until we finish our game.

"Why is that?" *Fourth question.*

She taps a red nail to her mouth. "A lack of... honesty."

This conversation is at once enticing and unnerving. *Why am I talking to my professor about her marriage?*

Her eyes look hungry. "Go on. Ask me more."

"Fifth question. Has your husband ever had an affair?" I regret the inquiry as soon as it departs my lips.

"Well played," she muses, genuinely impressed. "But no. Keep trying."

"Okay, let's see. Has he ever lied to you about—"

"You're moving in the wrong direction." Cheryl leans in and puts a hand on my shoulder. "Remember, every person is a puzzle to solve."

Hearing my own words thrown back at me is chilling, especially in this context.

"Maybe you were onto something before," she whispers.

My heartbeat reverberates in my ears. *Why is she telling me this?*

"Go ahead, Miss Kwan. Ask me."

I pause before biting the bullet. "Have you ever cheated on your husband?"

A devilish grin meets my eyes. "Yes."

CHAPTER 36
SEVEN YEARS AGO

A nother term, another set of classes. I love most of the subjects and professors so far. *Well, some of them.* Despite the nagging feeling in my gut, I finally signed up for Cheryl's lab course. Things ended weirdly between us at the last party I attended. When Cheryl revealed that she had cheated on John, I was left with an odd sense of responsibility to tell him.

It is probably irrational given that I barely know him, but the thought of John getting hurt tugs at my heartstrings. I have since turned down every invitation Cheryl has sent my way, whether it's for a fancy party or a casual coffee chat. Though I've been polite about it, at this point, I'm sure she knows I'm avoiding her.

I am still dating Paul, albeit casually. Our relationship resembles more of an on-again, off-again situation than anything serious. We usually hang out after class, but I would not call him my boyfriend. The latter part is why I don't think he has a right to judge me for making plans this weekend.

I am flying out to San Francisco later today. Cheryl kept pressing, and her persistence knows no bounds. The mere tone of her latest invitation was enough to make me crumble. Something in her voice seemed to threaten negative consequences if I continued to decline.

Honestly, the idea of landing on her bad side is more terrifying than all else. Legitimately offending Cheryl Lewis is a nightmare I refuse to entertain. *An academic death wish.* Murmurs of her vengeful side have circulated around campus, though I have ignored them for the most part. Until now.

Besides, no other professor has shown signs of remotely taking an interest in my work. I need as many positive references as possible in order to obtain my dream residency placement. That's a fact. So essentially, this is a business decision. At least, that's what I am telling myself. The better part of me knows why I am really here.

My flight is delayed, turbulent, and overbooked. I catch a taxi upon landing then stop at a liquor store on the way over. After selecting an expensive bottle of wine, I arrive at Cheryl and John's house. They invited me for the entire weekend. I am already stunned that the couple asked me here by myself, but I only plan on staying for today.

"Thank you so much," Cheryl says when I present the wine. "We'll have to break it open during dinner." She takes my coat and hangs it in the entryway closet.

"Thanks for having me." I follow her down the hall.

"Nonsense. I've been feeling awful about how we left things at that last party." A cheerless expression spreads across her face. "I wanted to apologize. You have always been such a promising student—so loyal."

I look at her cautiously.

"Loyal to your work," she adds. "To your studies. So dedicated." She smiles between clipped sentences. "Anyhow, I wanted to make it up to you."

"Oh—no need." We enter the kitchen, which looks starkly different drenched in daylight. The space is bright and airy, with sunshine rushing in through crystal-clear windowpanes.

"I wanted to let you know that I can only stay tonight," I tell Cheryl. "I have to—"

John enters the room before I finish. "Hello, Miss Kwan."

"Hello, Mr. Lewis." I realize that this is the first time I have seen him in street clothes—a burgundy V-neck sweater and dark jeans.

"Aw, remember," he says with an easy grin, "call me John."

"John," I say, lamenting the budding flush in my cheeks—an inevitable reaction to his casual charm. "Well, then please call me Vonny."

"Of course." John opens the fridge and pours himself a glass of iced coffee.

I notice Cheryl watching us out of the corner of my eye. *Is she worried I might reveal her dirty little secret?*

John walks over and kisses her on the cheek.

"Darling," she says. "I just realized—we're out of rosemary."

His brow tenses briefly as he takes a long sip.

"I need it for the lamb." She gives a subtle pout.

"I think we have some in the cupboard, don't we?"

"No, no. I need *fresh* herbs."

John nods and finishes his coffee. "Want me to pick some up from the market?"

"That would be lovely," she responds melodically. "You read my mind."

They exchange smiles while I stand awkwardly between them. I suddenly feel out of place, an intruder in their happy home.

He rinses out his glass. "Let me just grab my coat."

Cheryl watches him leave the kitchen. "Veronica, you get on well with John. Why don't you go along too?"

I hesitate as she continues.

"He always picks out the wilted herbs. Can you make sure he gets good ones? I want the lamb to taste *divine.*"

"Are you sure you don't need help here?" I gesture to the kitchen. "I can stay and—"

"Positive. I prefer cooking alone anyway."

I follow John out to the car and explain that Cheryl wants me to come along. He does not seem fazed, simply nodding and opening the door of a jet-black Tesla for me.

"Candy?" he asks as we pull out of the driveway.

"Um." I glance around, confused. "What?"

He opens the center compartment to reveal a portable sugar haven. "My secret stash," John says with a wink. "I have no willpower when it comes to drugstore sweets."

I laugh and welcome this surprising new side of him. It's refreshing, down-to-earth, and endearing. An unexpected glimpse beneath the intimidating exterior I have come to associate with all things Lewis.

"Reese's are my enduring favorite." John peels open the orange foil to remove a chocolate cup. "You're not going to make me indulge alone, are you?"

I peer inside the console and examine my options. "Hmm." Another laugh escapes my lips. "This feels like peer pressure."

"Well, I'm flattered to be considered your peer."

The heat returns to my cheeks with a vengeance.

He shrugs. "Makes me feel like less of a working stiff."

My eyes go wide. "Oh, c'mon. You're nothing of the sort."

He considers me as we approach a red light.

"Quite the opposite, in my opinion," I add without thinking.

"Is that so?"

"It's just..." I unwrap a Starburst slowly. "Nothing about you seems remotely boring."

Silence ensues as we turn out of the neighborhood and merge onto a busier city street. I immediately regret my comment, realizing in retrospect how flirtatious it sounds.

"For what it's worth," John says, "nothing about you seems remotely boring either." A sideways grin—fleeting but unmistakable—takes hold of his mouth.

It is in this precise moment that I realize how attracted I am to him. Talking to John is at once calming and stirring, natural yet challenging. *Get a hold of yourself, Vonny. John is off-limits.*

Our drive is much longer than either of us anticipated. Just before the first market locks its doors, we find ourselves stuck in a downtown traffic jam. Despite the circumstances, being with John takes my mind off of any apprehension I previously felt about this trip. For a while, our conversation flows freely, ranging from mundane topics to political ones. I have to remind myself that this man is my professor's husband. It is not until our discussion takes a turn, however, that my anxiety reemerges.

"It's really nice that you flew out here again," he says. "I know Cheryl has missed having you at her student parties."

Memories of her confession come flooding back. "Uh, yeah." My eyes jump to the stalled traffic. "I've just been really busy."

"I was trying to remember when your last visit was."

"Last year. It's been a little while."

He nods while pulling into a crowded parking lot. "Cheryl always speaks so highly of you."

"That's very nice." I force a smile. "She's great."

He chuckles. "Well, she's not everyone's cup of tea."

I feign surprised and wait for him to continue.

"I know that my wife has ruffled a few feathers around campus. That's kind of her specialty—pushing people's buttons. The worst part is that most of them don't even realize it until later." He makes an indistinguishable sound under his breath and keeps his eyes fixed ahead. "So... she's really never upset you?"

I am not exactly sure where this is going. "Why do you ask?"

"Most of the students that come to our house are dying to impress Cheryl. I can tell. They turn sheet-white the second she walks in."

"I know that she can be intimidating."

John clearly has something else to say but is fighting to urge to elaborate.

The silence makes me want to fill in the gaps. "I mean, when I was new at UW—"

"Hey," he says suddenly. "Can I ask you something?"

"Shoot."

He clears his throat. "Well, I heard you guys speaking in the kitchen."

My shoulders stiffen. *Oh, God.*

"What did Cheryl mean when she said that she wanted to make something up to you?" John looks at me intently.

I swallow hard. He's so direct, there really is no way to skirt his question, but I do my best to be vague. "Um, the last time I was here, we played a game. It just... it sort of made me uncomfortable."

"Which one?"

"Something about secrets."

He grimaces. "That's right. I remember her twisted game. I ended up leaving that night. I hate when she experiments on students."

"Experiments?"

"Yeah." John massage his temples. "It's fucked up. Cheryl will do anything for an experiment—literally anything. She's always been overly invested in her work."

I let out a quiet laugh as a wave of relief washes over me. *It was just an experiment.* As bizarre as that game was, everything boiled down to a test. Cheryl never cheated on John. She just wanted to see how I would react.

He must've noticed the tension leave my shoulders, because he looks over at me. "What is it?"

"Oh, nothing."

"Tell me. Please?"

Once again, I fall prey to his question. "Cheryl said something that night, but I understand it now. It was all just—"

"What did she tell you?" John's tone is serious, expression grim.

"About your marriage. But I'm sure it was just part of her experiment."

A knowing expression spreads over his face. "What, exactly?"

I freeze. *What if it wasn't a ruse?*

"*Please* tell me."

"She said..."

His gaze intensifies.

"Cheryl said that she cheated on you."

From what I can tell, John does not appear surprised in the slightest.

"But it was all a lie. That was the game."

"Unbelievable." He exhales. "Sometimes, I don't know why I even bother restraining myself. My wife doesn't even try."

"But it was a lie. She only told me that because of the—"

"No," he says grimly. "It wasn't just for the game."

We sit in stillness for what feels like ten minutes. John stares through the windshield, speechless, as busy shoppers pass the car.

"I shouldn't have said anything." I shake my head. "I'm sorry."

"No." He turns to me. "Please don't feel bad. You do not owe anyone an apology, Vonny. I'm the one who should be sorry."

My breathing returns to normal, shoulders loosening slightly. I look up to meet him.

"It wasn't right of me to put you in that position." John's piercing blue eyes darken.

"Did you know?"

"Uh, I suspected." He sighs softly. "But..."

All I can do is nod.

"I guess I just didn't want to believe it."

"Sorry," I whisper.

"Hey, it's not your fault. I asked you point-blank."

"I know, but I'm sorry you got hurt."

"Thanks, Vonny." My name sounds gentle on his tongue.

I nod again, trapped in his gaze. A charged silence blooms between us before he breaks it suddenly.

"Well, we should probably head inside. Cheryl wants those herbs for dinner."

"Yeah." Blushing, I pry my eyes away. "Let's go."

CHAPTER 37

M y cell phone buzzes before I get to class. I pull it out of my bag
and glance at the screen, but it's an unknown number. I recognize the area code immediately, though—somewhere in Brooklyn.

"Hello?"

"Hi," a familiar voice says. "Is this Vonny?"

I press the phone closer to my ear. "Abby?"

"Yeah, it's me."

My heart stops. *It's really her.*

"Anyway," Abby continues, "I know it's been a long time..."

"Way too long. Totally my fault—I'm sorry."

Abby's laugh is strained. "It's okay. I'm sure you've been busy."

"I have, but it's no excuse. I've been meaning to call you." The
truth is, every new commitment has overshadowed—and nearly
eclipsed—my friendship with Abby. I have been so preoccupied with
work that I've unwittingly dropped the ball in terms of keeping in
touch.

"Yeah, well... the real reason I'm calling is to tell you some good
news." The rise in her tone is hopeful.

"Oh, what kind of news?"

"My parents are throwing me a massive party for my twenty-
fifth! It's not for a while, obviously, but they've already started planning it."

I linger at the edge of campus, a grin spreading across on my lips.

"I've thought about this a lot, and I would really like you to be
there."

Unexpected tears well in my eyes as she tells me the details. It's embarrassing and sappy, but I am absolutely thrilled to hear from her. This call functions as an emotional reality check. It reminds me of how often we used to talk, and it hits home how rarely we do anymore.

"So, it'll be a pretty large group. I can't wait for you to meet everyone."

"Wow." I take a deep breath and steady my voice. "That all sounds awesome!"

"Thanks. So... think you'll be able to make it?"

"Yes—of course! I would love to be there."

"I'm so glad to hear that." Abby exhales softly. "I'll text you once I know more!"

"Perfect."

We spend the next half hour catching up—just like old times. She spares no detail while telling me about her boyfriend, Nick. She explains how they first met through work and recounts the way he asked her out. I hear the smile in Abby's voice as she playfully notes his quirks, admitting that she secretly adores his lack of style.

My heart swells at the sheer happiness in her words. I feel the affection, the love. I have missed Abby more than I realized. Her party is almost a year out, but I am going to book my flight tonight. That is the last thing I tell her before we hang up. I would not miss it for the world.

The blissful nostalgia is fleeting, only to be replaced by unrelenting guilt shortly after the phone call ends. I think about the mass of unanswered texts, missed calls, and unopened emails dwelling in my inbox. Abby did not simply withdraw from our friendship. I am the one who faded, disappeared altogether.

The absence of our regular conversations should have affected me a lot more. *Shouldn't it?* Our friendship used to be paramount—a bond we both believed would endure. I think of Paul, of Cheryl. *Have they replaced Abby entirely?*

The idea leaves me unsettled as I sit through the remainder of my Thursday courses. Despite my best intentions, distraction ultimately proves futile. Abby's sudden invitation forces me to take stock of every relationship I currently have. I spend the next week examining my dwindling social life, realizing that self-imposed stress is the primary culprit.

Working hard and studying nonstop seemed necessary in order to attain academic success. But they created a tunnel vision that blinded me from the truth—my dedication allowed me to justify unhealthy behavior. Case in point, my situation with Paul.

Our on-again, off-again romance has all but stalled out completely. We hardly resemble the bare bones of a real couple, much less a happy one. I know that. He does too. Hearing Abby talk about Nick was illuminating—so much tangible emotion came through my phone.

Paul and I don't have that kind of connection. The reality is, we never did. It's not fair to either of us to continue pretending. I do care about him as a person, though. My honest hope is that we can find a way to salvage our friendship.

"WHAT ARE WE DOING?" Paul asks over pizza a few days later.

His question seems like the perfect segue. "I've actually been wondering that too. We're just not—"

"Vonny, look. This clearly isn't working." He surprises me by taking the words right out of my mouth.

Relief washes over me. If he already feels that way, we should be able to end things amicably. As friends. "I totally agree."

"I think we should be exclusive." He takes my hand. "Only see each other from here on out."

My lips struggle to form words as my thoughts catch up. *Exclusive?*

"What is it?" He threads his fingers through mine.

"I... I think we're on different pages."

Now, Paul is the one in shock.

"I-I thought you felt the same way."

"You want to break up?"

"It's just, we've drifted a lot." I sigh. "Especially lately. Don't you think?"

"Of course I do. That's exactly why I feel like we should be exclusive." He clears his throat. "Now that you finally have some distance from Professor Lewis and those stupid parties."

"Well, I just think that—"

Paul pulls his hand away before I can finish. "I can't believe this." A pained expression spreads over his face.

"I'm sorry."

A stiff silence hangs over us. Our waiter delivers two pizzas that go uneaten, cheese hardening as the minutes pass.

"I wanted to fight for us." His voice is despondent. "But clearly, you've already made up your mind."

"I care about you," I tell him. "I really value our friendship—"

He laughs softly, eyes forlorn. "That's the thing."

"Paul," I protest when he pushes out his chair.

"I don't want to be your friend." His chair scrapes against the floor as he gets up. "I want more than that."

Without another word, he storms out. Part of me wants to chase after Paul, but following will only escalate the heightened tension between us. My gaze eventually lands on our untouched dinner and half-sipped drinks. I stare at the food, zoning out until a voice halts my train of thought.

"Finished?" The same waiter smacks his gum while gesturing to the doorway. "I don't want to rush you, hon, but we're pretty busy."

"Yeah," I say, sitting up straighter. "Sorry."

He returns moments later to present me with a bill and two take-out boxes.

"Have a good night." I pay in cash and grab my coat.

"You too," the waiter says. "Hey, want some advice?"

I look at him expectantly.

"In my opinion, you shouldn't waste tears on that schmuck. He's not worth it. What kind of guy walks out on his date, anyway?"

I don't have the heart to tell him that I'm the schmuck in this situation. Instead, I muster a lousy smile. "Thanks."

CHAPTER 38
SIX YEARS AGO

It is a cold autumn day in Seattle. Fall colors abound, with vibrant orange leaves scattered across the damp pavement. Pulling my scarf tighter around my neck, I hurry across campus. The coffee house is packed with students, so I reroute and head to the library instead. My developmental psychopathology class begins in about an hour. I need to finish our latest assignment—a beast of an essay—and study for my upcoming exams. I haven't yet reached the doorway when I hear my name.

"Veronica!"

I reel to see Cheryl, waving at me from across the lawn.

"Wait up," she calls.

I swallow hard as she strides toward me in sleek heeled boots. Fortunately, our paths have not crossed much since last year. My last visit at the Lewises' house left me reasonably uncomfortable.

"Hello." I attempt a polite tone when Cheryl approaches.

"It's been a while. Wonderful to see you." Blond waves tumble over her slim shoulders as she speaks. My former professor wears a navy peacoat and lilac scarf. Something about her seems off somehow, but I can't put my finger on it.

"I've missed you," she adds sweetly. "Do you have time for a quick chat?"

Glancing around, I consider making an excuse. Stressed-out students clutching books and juggling paper coffee cups buzz by us in droves. With midterms fast approaching, I am just as overwhelmed as they are. Maybe I should simply tell Cheryl the truth. Honestly, though, being back in her presence eases my anxiety. It makes me realize that I miss her too.

She must notice my hesitation. "It's all right. I'm sure you're busy."

"Actually, I would love to catch up."

Her red lips morph into a perky grin. "Excellent! Shall we speak inside? I've got a bit of time before my next section begins."

We travel across campus, discussing the beautiful foliage during this time of year. Our conversation topic strikes me as odd, if not a bit suspicious. Cheryl isn't usually one for pleasantries. She generally abhors small talk of any sort.

"So," she says as we enter a heated lecture hall, "how have you been?"

"Pretty good." I remove my coat and settle into a front row seat. "How about you?"

Cheryl places her purse on a desk and stands near the whiteboard. "Oh, you know..."

I wait for her to continue, but she doesn't. Instead, she levels me with a deadpan expression.

"Uh, what are you teaching this quarter?"

She ignores my question and moves toward the entrance. *Where is she going*? I watch curiously as her hands pull the door shut.

"It's a bit chilly in here." Her gaze is fixed on the handle. "Don't you think?"

"Actually, I'm a little warm."

She turns the lock.

"Um..." I straighten in my seat. "What are you doing?"

She turns around slowly before returning to the front of the room. "I prefer that no one disturbs us. Zero interruptions. After all, we have so much catching up to do."

My breathing quickens. *What does she mean?*

"Why don't I ever see you anymore, Veronica?" She cocks her head and leans against the wall. "Did I do something to upset you?"

"Um, no." I shift in my chair. "I've just been tied up. You know, busy with classes and studying."

"Interesting. I was starting to wonder if your last visit to my home had anything to do with it." She considers her polished nails a moment before looking up at me again. In the next instant, she moves closer. "You were definitely acting peculiar when you came back that afternoon." Cheryl hovers over my desk, tapping her nails against its wooden surface. "After your little errand with my husband."

The room is silent as her eyes burn into me.

"Well, don't be so bloody reticent." She scoffs. "I'm told you can be quite brazen when you want to be."

I hear my own heartbeat, feel it pounding against my chest. This is not what I pictured when Cheryl said "chat."

She paces slowly around the podium. "Loyalty is one of the most important qualities a person can have, Miss Kwan. It's a quality I thought you possessed." She pauses. "For that very reason, I trusted you with my secret."

"Cheryl, if—"

"But I made a mistake." She sweeps her lids shut. "An error that would prove fatal." When she opens her eyes again, they're blazing. "You betrayed me, Veronica."

My throat tightens.

"You told John about the affair."

I want to respond, but my voice is nonexistent. I am powerless as she inches closer.

"You even managed to dismantle my marriage. No easy feat."

"Please," I finally say. "Just let me explain—"

"I'm afraid it's a bit late for that." Her tone is steady, face chilling-ly composed. "The papers are already filed."

"You're getting a divorce?"

She doesn't dignify my question with a response.

"Cheryl, I'm sorry. I-I really didn't mean for any of this to hap-pen. John said that he already knew about the affair—"

At this, she lets out a shrill, unsettling laugh. "Well, my dear. He lied."

My mind goes blank.

"I guess you're *both* liars," she says. "And now you have to find a way to live with yourself."

I grab my coat and stand up. "I-I think I should leave."

"Yes," she says quietly. "You probably should."

I hurry over to the doorway, Cheryl's unwavering gaze fixed on me as I go. My shaky fingers jostle the handle a few times before I re-member that she locked it. I take quick, shallow breaths while turn-ing the lock. Then I race out of her room as fast as I can.

For the rest of the day, I have this unshakeable feeling that Cheryl is behind me. I picture her peering silently over my shoulder. I see her standing at the ready, just waiting to strike. I imagine her whispering, "Miss Kwan," until I actually start to hear her voice. But every time I turn around, Cheryl is nowhere to be found.

CHAPTER 39

I reread the headline for the fifth time this morning. "Beloved University of Washington Professor Found Dead."

No matter how many times my eyes gloss over the article, I can't make sense of it.

Cheryl Lewis, 37, was found dead in her family's British estate last Tuesday. The property was burned to the ground—

I crumple the newspaper into a tight wad then hurl it across the room. Too exhausted to get up and too wired to go to back to sleep, I languish in bed. News of Cheryl's death started spreading a few days ago, and our school paper has been publishing updates ever since. The police in her hometown originally chalked the fire up to an accident. Unfortunately, they are now suspecting arson. *Murder.*

I have not seen Cheryl since she confronted me on campus a few weeks ago. Our last conversation dwells in my head, an uninvited and permanent houseguest. Her accusations play on a ceaseless loop that makes my temples throb. *"You have to find a way to live with yourself."* Cheryl deemed me a liar. *She blamed me for everything.*

Eventually, I manage to peel myself from the warmth of my sheets. Both feet drag as I pad into the kitchen, searching for something to numb the amplifying pain. The thought of food only makes me nauseous. Instead, I pry open the freezer door and pull out an unopened bottle of vodka.

This apartment feels oddly still, somehow frozen in time as I fix myself a drink. *What if Cheryl was right?* I can't help but feel partially responsible for her downfall. If Paul were here, he would probably confirm my biggest fears. He'd reiterate that my idolization of her was unhealthy—toxic. I picture the judgment on his face, his gaze shrouded in disappointment. Then I would see the rage burning in Cheryl's eyes.

The icy liquid scalds my throat but stings less with each swallow. A lengthy sip for my late professor. One more for my bitter ex-boyfriend, then another one. I am vacant—a void that needs filling. My fingers reach for the bottle before pouring a fresh drink. With every gulp, I try to forget everything related to Cheryl Lewis and Paul Bertrand. Heavy memories fade with each mouthful. I empty one cup then another until I lose track.

PHYSICAL AGONY STRIKES before I even have the chance to open my eyes. The feeling is intense—a strong pulsating I have never experienced before. My lids part briefly, only to snap shut again. I bring my damp palms to my face. This is like that awful hangover I had freshman year but about a hundred times more painful.

The living room slowly comes back into focus from my spot on the couch. Daylight floods my tiny apartment with a blinding brightness. I massage each temple and instantly wish the shades were drawn. Then I force myself to sit up, silently cursing the crick in my neck as I go.

My throat runs bone dry while my mouth tastes stale and sour. Both feet drag along the floor as I shuffle toward the kitchen, stubbing my toe on the way. Something hard—a glass bottle—spins across the matted carpet. *The vodka.* Groaning, I bend to pluck it up, and the blood rushes to my brain. I barely remember the majority of last night. *Did I black out?*

My head continues to pound while I fumble around for my phone. The screen is offensively bright, so I squint to make out a series of recent notifications. *Shit.* The realization hits me like a land-mine. *My flight.*

The flood of missed calls, texts, and Facebook messages makes my stomach pitch. Most of them are from Abby. I missed her birth-day party. *How could I let this happen?*

I grip the phone tighter and immediately try to call her. Abby's big party was ruined, and it's all my fault. The call rolls straight to her voice mail. I try again, but she declines. Abby clearly does not want to speak to me. I keep calling, though, because I need to tell her how sorry I am. My stomach does a back flip when I finally hear her voice.

"Vonny."

"Abby! Oh my God, I'm so, so sorry—"

"I bet." Her tone is stiff, measured. "I called and texted you a mil-lion times. I even tried calling the school. Then I finally got in touch with Paul, and—"

"You called Paul?"

"I was worried about you! I thought something terrible might have happened. Like you were injured or kidnapped or something." She scoffs. "But then he told me that you dumped him and—"

"Abby, please. Just let me explain."

She draws in an audible breath. "Go ahead."

"Missing your party was a total accident, okay?" I clear my throat. "Cheryl died."

"Wait... *who*? Who died?"

I soften at her concern. "She was my professor—my favorite pro-fessor."

"Um, I'm sorry to hear that."

"Thanks," I say. "Anyway, I kind of lost it after the news broke. I ended up drinking too much and blacking out last night."

Abby sighs.

"It's no excuse for missing my flight, but—"

"Look. This is about more than the party, you know?"

I wait for her to continue.

"It's about our relationship."

"What do you mean?" The uneasy feeling in my stomach worsens. If I could only explain how much Cheryl means to me—meant to me—but Abby doesn't seem to want to hear it.

"Well, I feel like you basically fell off the face of the earth since I last saw you."

Her words sting. Now Abby is attacking me on top of being apathetic about Cheryl's death. "That's a little extreme, don't you think?"

"Is it?" She meets my question with a question.

"I think so."

She sighs again. "Everything was great between us when I visited you. But ever since then, it's like you've forgotten about our friendship. It's like... like you've forgotten about me."

"Abby," I say gently. "That's not true. You know it's not."

"It is, though. And I think I've made more than enough of an effort."

"Hey. Cut me some slack here."

"Honestly, Vonny. I'm beyond cutting you slack. It's clear that you've moved on and created a new life in Seattle. You have people there who—"

"Oh, okay. So let me get this straight. I'm not allowed to have any relationships beyond ours. No other friends besides you—"

"That's *not* what I'm saying." I know I'm spot on about her jealousy, but she has the gall to sound offended now.

"It is, though, right?"

Abby's shallow breathing is the only sound on the other end.

"I think that's exactly what you mean."

"Wow." She pauses for a moment. "I feel like I don't even know you anymore. You've turned into this—"

Something inside me snaps. "Maybe you don't. Maybe we've both changed, and we just don't know each other anymore."

"And whose fault is that?" Her voice rises.

It's clearly meant as a rhetorical question, but I am fuming inside. "Don't try to blame this all on me!"

"We both know the truth—whether you want to admit it or not."

I wait for her to take it back, but she doesn't.

"I... I can't do this anymore," Abby adds. "It just isn't worth it."

Her words slice through me like blades. "So you're just going to throw our friendship away like it's a piece of garbage?"

"Let's be clear. *I'm* not the one who threw our friendship away. That was all you."

Shock and anger hit me in equal measure. "You're so wrong. You're the one who—"

"Whatever." Her reply is barely a whisper. "I think we should just agree to part ways or something."

I inhale sharply. "Are you serious?"

Abby's lack of response serves as a tacit confirmation.

"I... I can't believe you." My own words sound warped, distant.

Silence descends as reality sets in. Neither of us speaks for the longest time—lamenting alone but together.

"C'mon," I finally say. "This is insane. We're sisters, remember?"

Abby sniffles. "We used to be."

"We st-still are." My voice comes out strained, and I nearly choke on the sob rising in the back of my throat. "We'll always be sisters."

"No, Vonny."

"Why?" I demand.

"I can't count on you. You've proven that to me."

Tears ravage my eyes as her voice fades to a whisper.

"Thing is," Abby adds, "I just don't trust you anymore."

The line goes dead.

CHAPTER 40

Two weeks later, I walk into the lecture hall where I first met Cheryl, room 506. Part of me still cannot believe that she is really gone. One quick glance at the wall clock elicits a smile. Cheryl never arrived on time, whether she was attending a party or showing up to class. It was always fashionably late or bust with her.

The room is empty right now, but I am sure another course will start soon. My feet carry me to the back—right where I sat during our first lecture. I plan on remaining plastered to this chair until someone kicks me out. Paul was sitting beside me then.

The void is a painful reminder that he is no longer part of my life. Whenever we bump into each around campus, he offers nothing more than a brief nod in my general direction. I guess I should just be grateful for any sort of gesture. At least he acknowledges me, which is more than I can say about Abby.

We have not spoken since that awful phone call. I reached out to her a few times via text, but she has yet to respond. She couldn't have meant any of those things she said about me turning into a different person. I hope not anyway.

I had no idea how angry she was. We definitely drifted over the past year or two, but we did not lose touch completely. Not from my perspective. Abby and I were supposed to be forever friends—platonic soul mates through thick and thin. I keep expecting her to come to her senses and return my messages. For now, though, there is only radio silence.

When I look up, I know that I must be imagining things. John Lewis is standing at the front of the room. I rub my eyes, expecting him to disappear in an instant. But there he is, my late professor's husband, silently reading the smudged cognitive behavioral therapy notes covering the white board. Cheryl's handwriting was pristine—a far cry from this leftover word jumble. John continues to stare straight ahead. For the longest time, I continue watching, wondering if he might vanish. Grief can do odd things to people.

Finally, I've had my fill of the vision. It's too painful to watch him frozen there, even if it is just my imagination. "John?"

He turns around and looks as startled as I am.

"Veronica?" Surprise washes over him. "Is that you?"

"Yes." I stand. "Hi."

"What are you—I mean, how?" John runs a hand through his disheveled hair.

I walk to the front of the room, taking in his stark appearance as I go. John is almost unrecognizable. His eyes are sunken in, and he has not shaved in at least a week, maybe longer.

"I'm in town picking up a few of Cheryl's things." He gestures to the large reusable bag in his hand.

I am surprised the university did not offer to ship everything after she passed away.

"The dean said it would be better to retrieve them in person," he says as if reading my mind. "Little did I know that I would be signing a stack of CYA paperwork during my visit."

"Wow, really?"

"Yeah." He rolls his blue eyes and shrugs. "Apparently, there's a whole process for these things."

"Right," I say quietly. "I'm sorry."

"Thanks, Vonny. How are you?"

I glance around the room. "I was just sitting in here because this is where I first met her."

He nods. "I was feeling a bit sentimental myself. One of Cheryl's colleagues told me this is the lecture hall she taught most of her classes in. Thought I would just come here, and..." His chin falls to his chest.

"I understand." Being in this classroom with him—the very place I met his wife—is both uncanny and comforting.

John surveys the empty seats then points to the last row. "That one was yours, I assume?"

"Yep—all the way in the back. I thought it would somehow make things easier. But she called on me anyway."

John releases a quiet laugh. "Cheryl did have a sneaky way of doing things, didn't she?"

We stand here together, careful not to broach the awkward subject of our last encounter.

After a minute, he regards me with an unreadable expression. "Well, I'd better be going. I still have to meet with the president."

"Oh, of course."

"You're welcome to come to the service if you wish," he adds hesitantly. "It's this Saturday."

"Oh?"

"It's mainly close friends and family, but I know Cheryl would want you there."

John must not know about what happened after class that day. *The way she blamed me for everything*. I part my lips to speak, but decide that it's not the right time.

"We're holding her funeral at a church near the house," he adds.

"I'll do my best to be there."

John smiles faintly and waves on his way out. As he leaves, I wonder if he will ever find out that Cheryl died hating me.

DESPITE ANY RESIDUAL hesitation, I keep my word. The flight, which I booked shortly after seeing John, is a turbulent one. We travel through San Francisco's pale-gray skies, landing on a slightly damp runway. The slow descent and stormy weather only serve as symbolic reminders of Cheryl's bitterness rotting in the foreground of my mind.

At the airport, I hurry into the nearest bathroom and take the first open stall. Inside, I exchange my travel outfit for an all-black ensemble. Frigid air shoots through an overhead vent as I slip into my shift dress, realizing that this look is less chic than I initially imagined. *Cotton on goose bumps.* Cheryl would hardly approve.

It's pitiful how much I still care about her opinion. I remind myself for the hundredth time that she is gone, but that does not work. Cheryl's presence was far too strong to be snuffed out. It looms large even after her untimely death. A living, breathing entity.

I manage to pull on a pair of stockings without snagging the sheer fabric. After sliding into a pair of dark flats, I make my way outside and enter a crowded taxi line. The wait is longer than expected. I glance anxiously at my phone, silently praying that I will make it across the city before Cheryl's service begins.

Finally, I climb into a cab before providing the address John gave me. A nonnegotiable stop at the florist delays my arrival a bit, but I breathe a heavy sigh of relief after securing Cheryl's favorite flowers. As we pull up to a grand church, my hands wrap around the sprawling bouquet of Himalayan poppies. The blue buds mingle with delphiniums, hovering over my fingertips in a delicate arrangement.

Sharp wind currents greet me as soon as I step out of the car, and I clutch the bouquet tighter to my chest. My flats, however, are a lost cause. Neither ankle is spared from the sodden, overgrown grass leading up to the entrance. When I reach an elaborate doorway, the golden glow of candles meets a sweet ceremonial hum that draws me closer.

Despite the warmth emanating from inside, I am shocked to see a near-vacant church. My phone confirms that the service should start any minute now. *Where is everyone?* Cheryl was always surrounded by a mass of people, from enamored students to esteemed colleagues. I figured that every person in her orbit would be present today.

While the empty pews certainly give me pause, I sit and shift my focus to the front row, which is filled with who I assume to be Cheryl's family members. A familiar shade of bright-blond hair buoys my supposition. I glance around but am careful to avoid the closed casket lying nearby.

A flash of movement catches my eye, and John enters from a side door before joining the others. His appearance is a far cry from what I witnessed last week. Today, he is clean-shaven and sharp. *Handsome as hell.* He looks like the man I met at that first Lewis party so many moons ago. John smooths his jet-black suit and sits next to an elderly woman in front.

The music intensifies, heightening briefly before fading out. Silence magnifies each shuffle, sniff, and cough once the service begins. Hushed cries echo around the arched space as loved ones eulogize Cheryl.

"She was kind."

"A gentle soul."

"Just the sweetest."

The words fade in and out, painting a skewed picture of the woman I called Professor. By the time the ceremony concludes, I envision Cheryl as a veritable chameleon. A different person in the eyes of every beholder. *Was her shape shifting intentional?* I have a feeling she knew exactly what she was doing.

Several pallbearers join John to carry Cheryl's casket down the aisle. Each man stares straight ahead until they reach the church's sizeable exit. Despite her gruesome death, I imagine her resting soundly inside, body still and pristinely preserved. I picture a smile on Cheryl's red lips as they lower her into the broken ground.

People say that funerals are for the living. Honestly, I have to agree. Cheryl would be appalled by this entire service. I hear her haughty laugh, her dismissive sigh, her pointed commentary. I see Cheryl leaning casually against the wall with a disapproving stare. *What a ghastly show,* she says while folding her slim arms. *A complete bore.*

CHAPTER 41

Conflicting emotions take hold as I follow a string of guests to
the reception. We walk down a narrow hallway, filing through
two narrower entrances to arrive at a dimly lit room. Portraits are
displayed on tall mahogany tables in every corner. One in particular
reminds me of the *Mona Lisa*, with Cheryl's unmistakable gaze taking center stage. Her eyes seem permanently plastered to me. They
follow my every movement, my every thought.

Some of these images are from the Lewis household. John probably chose them himself. Our tiny crowd travels as a unit, examining
each frame intently before ultimately dispersing. Small talk sounds
quietly as some people head to the refreshment table. In line, I catch
glimpses of food, noting the abundance of charcuterie. Olives and
salted nuts surround heaps of dried fruit and cured meat slices.

Despite the generous amount I've piled on my plate, I find that I
am not actually hungry at all. My appetite wanes the more I think of
Cheryl. In this room full of strangers, I begin to imagine exactly how
depressing my own funeral might be. *Who would even attend?*

No Abby. No Paul. No true friends. No Cheryl. Gone, too, are
her coffee chats and extravagant parties. I feel my chest tighten as the
realization washes over me.

"Vonny," says a familiar voice.

I turn around and see John standing by the makeshift bar.

"Thanks so much for coming." He takes a step toward me, drink
in hand.

"Of course."

The intermingled scents of rum and spicy cologne greet me as we inch closer.

"To be completely honest, I'm not sure if Cheryl would have really wanted me here."

"Nonsense." He waves off my concern. "She'd definitely want you here."

"So... how are you doing with everything?"

"Oh, you know." He pauses. "It's all very surreal."

I set my plate down on the table's edge. "That makes sense."

Just then, a portly gentleman hits John playfully on the back. "Johnny Boy!"

"Ah." John winces briefly before turning to shake the man's hand. "Uncle Milton."

Milton reaches between us to grab a fistful of olives from the tiered tray. "How are you holding up, then?" he asks before popping them into his open mouth.

John rattles off something standard before turning to introduce us. "By the way, uncle, this is Veronica Kwan, Cheryl's star student by a landslide."

Milton coughs violently before extending an olive-stained hand.

"Nice to meet you." I shake it tentatively. "I'm sorry for your loss."

Drink service increases, and conversations multiply around us. Eventually, Milton bumbles off to chase down a server.

"Sorry about that." John offers me a half smile. "He's quite a character."

"No worries. Cheryl's uncle?"

"Cousin, actually."

My eyebrows furrow.

"It's the strangest thing," he whispers. "Milton insists that everyone address him as 'Uncle.' It's been that way for as long as I can remember. Honestly, I'm not even sure if Milton is his given name."

We share a laugh before John introduces me to a few more family members.

"Can I give you a lift back to the airport?" he asks once the reception starts to wind down.

"It's okay. I'll take a taxi."

"I really don't mind." John smiles politely. "It'll give me an excuse to duck out of here early."

I glance around the emptying room and notice Uncle Milton return to the charcuterie platter.

John follows my gaze then brings a hand to his forehead. "He's probably gearing up to tell his classic fishing expedition story." In his finest British accent, he continues, "'Did you know that I once caught a catfish twice my size?'"

I hear another violent cough before Milton turns to one of the pallbearers. "Have I ever told you about my trip to the Mississippi, son?"

"Right on cue." John winks.

I laugh again, relishing the welcome bit of comedic relief.

"Are you sure I can't take you? You'd actually be doing me a huge favor," he says.

"All right." I finally relent. *After all, he insisted.*

THE RAIN STARTS AGAIN shortly after we climb into his car, pelting the windshield like a series of watery bullets.

"How are your classes going this term?" he asks.

"They're okay. I'm a little preoccupied with residency applications, though."

"I'm sure. Where are you applying?"

"My top choice is UCSF, but I'm considering other options since the process is so competitive." As we round a corner, my stomach grumbles. I blush, wishing I had forced myself to eat more after the service. "Hey, John? Do you still have that secret stash of—"

"Of course." He grins, sliding open the middle console without looking. "Help yourself."

I open a pack of Starbursts then unwrap one of the red chews.

"Any of the lemon flavor in there?"

"Ew." I wrinkle my nose. "Who likes the lemon ones?"

"Hey, don't hate on lemon Starbursts. They're the best."

"Suit yourself." I shrug. "You can have my rejects."

Another easy laugh with John Lewis. We pull up to the airport as I am telling him about my career goals.

"Thanks again for coming today."

"Of course," I say, gathering my coat. "Thanks for the lift."

"Don't mention it."

"Um..." I try to come up with more to say. Some part of me doesn't want to leave him. "It was really good to see you again."

John smiles warmly. "It was good to see you too. Don't be a stranger, okay?"

I match his expression before opening my door. "Deal."

"Take care, Vonny."

I wave while walking toward the airport. My flight departs on time, wheels leaving the wet runway before ascending into another gray sky. It has been an unexpected day to say the least. My unnerving morning preceded a bizarre afternoon, with Cheryl's funeral placing me on edge. This evening, however, was something else entirely.

Seeing John meant more to me than I could have ever predicted. It was a genuine bright spot amidst this otherwise dark period. At forty thousand feet in the air, I admit something to myself for the first time. *I miss him.*

CHAPTER 42
FIVE YEARS AGO

I'm in line at a new café in Seattle when I see him.

"Vonny?" John sounds as surprised as I am. "Hi."

"No way." This is the fifth time we have run into each other recently.

"I would say what a coincidence, but I think that phrase loses its effect after the third time around."

"Seriously," I agree. "It's like we're inadvertently stalking each other."

John's laugh brightens his blue eyes. He looks even better than the last time I saw him.

"Power lunch?" I gesture to the café entrance.

"Another client meeting. They chose the place today."

I nod. He mentioned having a lot of new business in Seattle.

"I'm definitely still getting used to the area."

"Has commuting here been tough?" I ask.

"A little tiring at times, but I'm racking up frequent flyer miles like crazy."

"Silver linings, at least."

"Exactly." John's dimples deepen as he smiles.

I grin back. For a while, I was drawn to him because of his obvious connection to Cheryl. But I have seen him in an entirely new light ever since the memorial service.

As the line inches forward, he asks, "How are you?"

"Hanging in there. A bit stressed with school, but what else is new?"

"You're probably just being hard on yourself."

"Here's hoping it'll pay off." I shrug. "We'll see."

Before I know it, we've already made it to the counter. Our conversations are always like this, flying by before we realize how much time has elapsed. I secretly love these serendipitous meetings with John. They make me feel lighter, somehow—completely at ease. I have come to value his company in ways I cannot possibly explain.

John collects his order. "I better head back to the office."

"Oh, right. Sorry I kept you for so long."

"Not at all. I always enjoy talking with you." He draws in a quiet breath. "Um, this may be weird, but would you want to meet for coffee later? I have some time after my next meeting, and I—"

"Yes. I'd love to."

"THIS IS REALLY STARTING to grow on me." John takes another sip of the caffeinated drink I urged him to order.

"I told you that I take coffee enlightenment *very* seriously."

He shrugs. "Well, I believe you now."

"Especially when it comes to sugary overpriced beverages." I smirk.

"With hard-to-pronounce names," he adds.

"Obviously. That part is nonnegotiable."

We laugh as people waft in and out of the place. Our banter makes me relaxed enough at this point that I feel comfortable broaching a difficult subject. *Cheryl.* The unnecessary guilt I was hauling around has lessened significantly, and it's time to tell John about my last conversation with her.

He notices my expression shift. "What is it?"

"It's just... I've been thinking about the last time I saw Cheryl."

While I ramble on about what happened that day, he listens intently.

"Anyway," I say, finally coming up for air, "I wanted to tell you because—"

He holds up a hand. "Look, what she did was horrible."

"I want to think that there was no basis to anything Cheryl said, but she was just so adamant."

John sighs. "Our marriage had already deteriorated well before she met you. We were... unsustainable. Don't let her accusations get in your head. You didn't do anything wrong. Trust me."

Seattle's sky darkens before we leave the coffee house. John and I walk along the waterfront, conversation evolving as we go. Vibrant shades of neon illuminate the pier while we wander. Eventually, we make our way back to where we began the evening.

"Thanks again for meeting me," John says. "I'm really glad we did this." He lingers for a moment, withholding unknown words.

"Me too." My lips curl into a gentle grin. "I like spending time with you."

"I do too, Vonny."

Before we part ways, John wraps me in a quick hug. An unmistakable rush courses through me at his touch. The pull is charged—magnetic. I wonder if he feels it, too, or even a fraction. There is no way to know for sure.

"Well," I say, pulling away slightly. "I'm that way."

"Right." He takes a step back.

My every impulse is to lean in again—to hold on tightly and not let go. I want to follow it, but I fight the urge.

"Good night."

"Bye, John." I head toward my bus stop while working up the courage to add one more thing. After a few steps, I turn around and meet his gaze. "Until next time."

He smiles. "Until next time."

CHAPTER 43
FOUR YEARS AGO

After I finish packing up the last box, I pause briefly to glance around my apartment. *I did it.* I survived grad school and even managed to matriculate with honors. I chuck an empty tape roll into my trash bin—the last item standing—and smile to myself. *San Francisco, here I come.*

My previous visits to California seem so foreign now. They were always for one of Cheryl's exclusive, mysterious parties. Quick weekend jaunts with luxury accommodations. This time, though, I am not just visiting. I am moving to San Francisco permanently. UCSF was my top choice for residencies, and I received an acceptance three months ago.

I OFFICIALLY COMPLETE my first month of clinic work and sign out for the night. My co-workers, who became fast friends, are taking me out to celebrate at a nearby restaurant.

"Meet you there?" Maria asks from across the hall.

"Yeah," I say. "Just have to log a few more notes. I'll catch up with you guys!"

I shut down the computer and grab my coat from the rack. Every day is a long one, but my work here is so rewarding. I honestly cannot imagine doing anything else. Right after I exit the hospital, someone calls my name.

"V-Veronica?" says a deep, staggered voice.

I turn around to see a familiar face. *It's him.*

"Is that really you?" John asks, incredulous.

I have not seen him in about a year, maybe longer. We stopped running into each other after that night in Seattle.

"Hi," is all I can manage as the shock wears off.

"What are you doing here? It's been a while."

"Work... and you?"

"I just had dinner with some friends and was about to head home." John regards me for a moment. "Buy you a cup of coffee?"

"I've got plans," I tell him. "We're celebrating tonight."

John's face falls slightly. "What's the occasion?"

"Survival." I smirk. "Actually, we're celebrating one month of clinic work. I'm doing my residency at UCSF."

"Congratulations!" John beams. "You got it after all."

"Thanks." I smile back. "Yeah, I'm really happy that it worked out."

Although ample time has passed, I feel the same chemistry I did before.

A knowing look crosses his face. "Can I take you out some other time?"

"I would love that."

"Perfect." John sighs softly. "It's really good to see you, Vonny."

"You too." Inside, I'm soaring.

CHAPTER 44
THREE YEARS AGO

It takes a few dinners before John and I articulate our mutual feel-ings. We have been together for about a year, "casually dating." But the truth is, there's nothing casual about my attraction to him.

As we grow closer, he starts to divulge more details about his re-lationship with Cheryl. I begin asking more questions, too, which feels less strange than I anticipated. Their marriage deteriorated over the years, dwindling until it became a shell of its former self— mercly a façade that Cheryl lorded over the rest of her image-obsessed social circle.

"Was any of it true?" I ask him one night over sushi. "When she told me that you were planning to leave her?"

"Yeah." John grimaces. "Yeah, it was."

I take a lengthy sip of sake.

"I was tired of her games. All the fancy parties and shallow dis-cussions." He shrugs. "You know how rocky things were between us."

I nod, remembering how stunned I was when he first told me.

"I just couldn't take it anymore."

"What was the last straw?" I ask him.

"Easy." He leans in. "Her experiments."

"What do you mean?"

He lowers his voice a bit. "Cheryl used to run these experiments on everyone we knew. Friends, co-workers, and even family. She al-ways had people eating from the palm of her hand."

"What kind of experiments?"

"Well, I don't have to tell *you*." He gestures toward me. "Students were always her bread and butter. She'd laud them until they became her biggest fans—until they'd do basically anything for her."

I swallow hard. "Like what?"

"Oh, you name it. Anything and everything. I didn't realize at the time, but now I'm sure of it. There was this grad student several years ago, Michael. He was her star pupil. Couldn't do anything wrong. He's actually the reason she started hosting dinner parties in the first place."

I feel myself hanging onto John's every word. He has my undivided attention.

"Well, little did I know, she started sleeping with Michael the second after he graduated from UW."

"Are you serious?" The shock hits me in waves.

"Dead serious. I found Cheryl's secret notebooks after she passed away. They were locked in her desk at home. She had recorded these specific observations about every one of her favorite students—their habits, quirks, and thought patterns. Creepy stuff."

"No one knows about this?" I ask. "I mean, she could have potentially been fired."

"I know," he says grimly. "I thought about telling people. I really did." John's gaze sinks to the floor. "This may sound twisted, but part of me didn't want to mar her memory."

I open my mouth to protest, but I actually know what he means. "So she was sleeping with her ex-students?"

"Just Michael," he clarifies. "At least, that's what the journals say."

"Is that who...?"

He knows what I mean. "Sadly, no." John shakes his head. "She also cheated on me with one of our friends."

I reach across the table and take his hand. "I'm sorry."

"Thanks, Vonny." He laces his fingers through mine. "At the end of the day, psychology was her truest love." John sounds withdrawn, almost desensitized. I remind myself that he had time to come to terms with Cheryl's infidelity.

"You loved her, though, didn't you?"

"Yes." His eyes take on a somber look. "I did at one point. To be honest, I mourned Cheryl heavily right after I got the news. Took me months to go back to work—to start taking care of myself again. I think that part of me believed she could still be alive, you know?"

The thought alone makes my chest tighten.

John shakes his head. "I actually entertained that idea. Part of me wondered if it was all just some big ruse—faking her own death." His eyes darken. "It would have been Cheryl's grandest experiment yet."

I listen, rapt, as he tells me more. After tonight, I view my late professor through a starkly different lens. It feels as if the blinders I wore for so long have permanently been removed. In my mind, Cheryl is no longer a role model, but a master manipulator.

CHAPTER 45
TWO YEARS AGO

"It really is the ideal residency for me." I squeeze John's hand across the table at our favorite restaurant—an Italian place near my office. "Better than I could have imagined."

Neither of us intended to fall so deeply, but here we are. *John and me.* In a way, I think we helped each other heal. He understands me in a way that no one has in quite a while. And although I denied it for the longest time, I can be honest about my feelings now. I am in love with John Lewis.

"They're lucky to have you." He smiles back then loosens his tie.

I was always under the impression that John worked in sales or marketing, but he is actually a private wealth advisor at one of the largest firms downtown. He manages finances for a few high-profile clients, some of whom we wine and dine regularly.

"Are you free for an engagement next week? The Smith Gallery opening is on Thursday night."

"Of course." I stab a rogue noodle from my carbonara and swirl it through the creamy sauce.

"Albert can pick you up after work," he tells me.

"Sounds good," I say before taking another bite.

"Thanks for always going to those things with me."

"I actually enjoy it." If it's with John, I'd go almost anywhere.

"Every one of my clients adores you." He tilts his head and gazes at me. "You've been so amazing through all of this—balancing work with obligatory events."

I blush, but the past several months truly have been a whirlwind. I was once a grad student, struggling to finish my thesis on time, and now I am a psychiatry resident participating in a world-class program. When I look up from my wineglass, John is staring at me with an unreadable expression.

"What is it?" I ask him.

His blue eyes twinkle underneath the restaurant's chandeliers. "I was going to wait for the perfect moment." John pushes his chair back then pauses to reach into his coat pocket before taking a knee.

My breathing becomes shallow.

"Veronica Kwan," he says, taking my left hand. "I have never met anyone with a bigger heart. You are beautiful, compassionate, funny, and brilliant. You've brought light and love back into my life."

John's words overwhelm me. *I can't believe this is happening.* My heart beats even faster when he opens the box.

"Will you marry me?"

"Yes!" I can't help but shout as we embrace. "I love you."

John slides the ring onto my finger. "I love you, Vonny."

We leave the restaurant—fiancé and fiancée for the first time. In the car, Albert congratulates John and me, eyes crinkling in the rearview mirror as he regales us with sentimental stories about his forty-five-year marriage. He even insists on treating us to ice cream on the way home. The gesture is sweet and unexpected, much like John's thoughtful proposal.

We decide not to tell anyone else about our engagement just yet. Still, part of me wants to call Abby and catch her up on everything—all of the good and bad from these past few years. But she made it clear that our friendship is over. *Sisters no more.* The thought leaves an awful stabbing feeling in my gut. How strange that the happiest moment of my life is tinged with such sadness.

CHAPTER 46

I stare at myself in the floor-length mirror and take a deep breath. My wedding gown is lace, with embroidered accents on the sleeves and tiny pearls around the neckline. The dress is a bit old-fashioned, but I kept seeing it in a boutique window and eventually fell in love with it. *Kind of like the way I fell for John.* I notice him coming in the reflection and quickly try to hide myself, but it's no use. He's already here.

"Hi baby," he says.

"Hey, you." I reach up and give him a quick kiss, careful not to smudge my lipstick.

John reads me instantly. "You're nervous."

"Not about you and me," I tell him honestly. "It's..."

"I know." He takes my shaky hand and holds it between his palms.

"I just—I mean, are we doing this too soon?"

John is quiet for a moment. "You know I'll wait for as long as you like. We can ditch this whole ceremony—order pizza and drive to the beach."

I have to laugh as I imagine the two of us in wedding attire, sitting on the sand while we wolf down our slices. "Yeah, right."

"I'm serious, Vonny. I just want to spend my life with you. I don't care how we do it."

I search his blue eyes until I find my answer. *I want to marry him right now.*

Just then, John's mother steps into the bridal suite. "What are you doing, Johnny? Get out of here!"

He opens his mouth to protest, but she shoves him out of the room before winking at me.

"I'm not really a superstitious person," Carol Ann says after he leaves. "But I wanted to steal a moment alone with my future daughter-in-law."

I soften as she moves closer. We have only met a few times, but Carol Ann has always treated me with generosity and respect.

"How are you feeling, dear?"

"A little overwhelmed, I guess."

"That's understandable." She takes my hand delicately in hers while she speaks. "Wedding days can be daunting, can't they?"

I nod and exhale a heavy breath. There are so many people I envisioned being part of my wedding day. But the past is the past, and I can't just wish them here. Abby. My parents. Even Cheryl. *As if Cheryl would give us her blessing.* But I wouldn't be here in San Francisco, marrying the man I love, without her—or any of them.

"I hope you don't mind me saying this," Carol Ann continues, "but I believe that your parents would be very happy for you today."

It's like she sensed that I needed to hear those words. My bottom lip trembles. "Thank you," I whisper. "I really appreciate that."

Carol Ann gestures to my veil. "May I?"

"Please," I say before turning back to face the mirror.

My soon to be mother-in-law sweeps her fingers gently through my hair before securing the veil to the crown of my head. We talk some more before the ceremony begins, and I feel my nerves ease considerably in the process. Although my own mom can't be here today, I find solace in Carol Ann's unmatched kindness.

JOHN AND I ENTER THE reception hall to jovial cheers and whistles. After fretting over our guest list for months on end, we opt-ed to keep the wedding on the smaller side. My preference would have been an intimate gathering of our closest friends and family. John's circle is much larger than mine, though, so we accommodated accordingly. Seeing the smiling faces surrounding us, I am actually quite pleased with the way everything turned out.

Toward the end of the evening, a few guests approach us to say goodbye. We make plans to meet up with some of John's friends af-ter we return from our honeymoon. The crowd dwindles as people take off for the night. John's advisor and friend, Wesley, appears with a pristinely wrapped gift in tow.

"Congratulations, madam." He extends a hand. "I am absolutely thrilled for you and Mr. Lewis."

"Why, thank you." I offer a coy smile. Perhaps it's the spirit of the day or the toll of too much celebratory champagne, but something causes me to pull him in for a long hug.

Wesley stiffens slightly before returning the gesture.

"Call me Vonny," I remind him for the umpteenth time.

He nods briefly, though I doubt he'll ever oblige. Ever since we first met, Wesley has displayed nothing but extreme etiquette and decorum. When he first called me "madam," I thought it was an act, but psychoanalyzing someone John trusts implicitly is not a bound-ary I'm willing to cross.

John laughs at my ruffling Wesley's feathers, clearly amused at our little exchange. "Thanks for coming, Wes."

They chat while I excuse myself to fetch another glass. The more I get to know the people in my new husband's life, the more deeply I fall in love with him. Everyone is so courteous and respectful. De-spite our quick engagement, John's family and friends seem to have accepted my presence at his side. Any residual anxiety about infringing on Cheryl's memory lessens with each social interaction. As far as I can tell, my long-held fear is unfounded.

CHAPTER 47
ONE YEAR AGO

A glance at the wall clock tells me that it's nearly midnight. John is working late again, and I am too tired to wait up. We have slowly been redecorating the house ever since I moved in. Although each room is already in impeccable shape, professionally furnished by Cheryl's interior designer, I want it to feel like home. *Our* home.

My latest project is to create a giant gallery wall along the staircase. I sit cross-legged on the carpet, still in my work clothes, sorting through a host of old photographs. My fingers sweep them into a neat pile before placing the pictures into a labeled box. Standing, I hoist up my materials then head down the hall.

Our basement door is shut, so I reach out with my free hand, jiggling the knob until it finally turns. The floorboards creak shrilly as I take the first step into the dark stairwell. As I fumble around for a light switch, something steals my attention—an undeniable sound. It's coming from behind me.

A brief but unmistakable movement in my peripheral vision confirms my suspicion. *Someone is here.* Every limb freezes in response before I can turn around. Paralyzing, all-encompassing fear takes hold as a pair of hands approaches my back.

No sooner do I realize than the attacker shoves me forward. My body tumbles headfirst into an opaque void, trembling as it pounds against the uneven steps. My own scream is all I hear until the darkness swallows me.

"VONNY!" JOHN'S PANICKED voice calls from somewhere above. "Are you okay?"

I don't know how long I've been unconscious, but when I try to look up, pain radiates from my core.

"Baby!" His frantic tone intensifies. "My God—hold on."

Sudden light floods the basement, and I wince. John races down toward me, feet pounding against each step as he goes.

"Vonny!" he repeats when he reaches me. "What happened?"

"Someone was here... in the house."

"What—when?"

I struggle to sit up as the memory comes back.

John's entire expression changes as he takes in the sight of me—it must be bad.

"Someone p-pushed me," I say, teeth chattering. There's blood, and my arms are covered in bruises. "It all happened so fast..."

"Oh, baby. Come here."

When John tries to hug me, I flinch.

"I know it hurts, but we need to get you upstairs." His brow creases. "I'm going to take you to the hospital."

"No—I'm okay."

"You're *not* okay."

I swallow back tears and nod. I should be checked by a doctor just in case.

"I'll go slowly." He scoops me into his arms as gently as possible before carrying me up the staircase. "Almost there."

As we near the top, the floorboards creak again. I nearly jump out of his arms, but John doesn't let me fall.

"It's okay," he says. "Just hold on."

"What if they're still here?" I ask in a hushed whisper.

We make it down the hallway, then John lays me down on the couch and considers my concern. "I'm going to look around for a few minutes, okay? Don't worry—I'll be right back."

"Please be careful."

"I will."

From the moment he disappears back down the hall, my anxiety heightens. Each second is riddled with terror. At one point, I hear a few scurrying sounds that make my skin crawl. *Is he okay?* I strain my neck to get a better view of the vicinity.

"John?"

Nothing.

"John, are you okay?"

The house goes eerily quiet.

"Babe?" I shout.

The faint sound of footsteps simultaneously startles and relieves me.

"I'm back," John says. "No sign of anyone."

"Okay—good."

He places his hand gently on my shoulder.

"Should we—"

I stop when John's expression shifts dramatically.

"What is it?"

He strides over to the corner. "Do you smell that?"

"Smell what?"

A disturbed look mars his beautiful face. "That scent... I'd know it anywhere."

"John? You're not making sense."

"Stay right here. I'm going to check downstairs."

"In the basement? *Why*? We were just down there."

But he is already walking away.

"Careful!"

He nods absentmindedly and leaves the room.

The sharp pain in my legs eventually evolves into a dull, widespread ache. Everything feels heavy. Both arms are weak, with a stinging sensation emanating from every scratch and cut. Each minute feels eternal as I struggle to move my position. I try to listen for signs of my husband, but all I hear is silence.

Then his footsteps echo back down the hall as he rushes to my side "Vonny," he says, breathing ragged.

"Is everything all right? What happened?"

"We need to leave. Now." The urgency in his words sends chills down my spine. I have never seen him like this before.

Whatever has caused this change in him, I'm sure there will be no going back. *We aren't safe here.*

CHAPTER 48

We leave the urgent care building and amble back toward our car. After diagnosing me with a concussion and examining my head extensively, a physician prescribed some medication and large quantities of rest. He eyed John suspiciously during the entire visit before ultimately asking him to step out of the room. I assured the doctor that I did, in fact, fall down the stairs. Then he took a few notes and sent me to the pharmacy.

"Here we go," John says while he helps me climb into the passenger seat.

"Thanks."

He closes my door then walks around to the other side, never taking his worried eyes off me. Back in the car, he digs a white bottle of out of the bag. "Do you want some medicine now?"

I nod stiffly.

"I know you're exhausted," he says after I've downed two pills, "but can you tell me what happened one more time?"

I lean my head back. "Okay." I recount everything I remember—opening the basement door, hearing the sound behind me, then being pushed down the stairs.

"God." He takes my hand. The warmth from his palm is soothing. "I should have been here, baby. I'm so sorry that you—"

"No." I squeeze his fingers. "This isn't your fault."

My husband is quiet while I think back to those last few moments at our house. *Did he find something in the basement?*

"Okay, John. You need to tell me what's going on."

He stares into the empty hospital parking lot, gaze unwavering. "John. Tell me."

After another minute of silence, he speaks. "It was her."

"Who?"

"*Cheryl.*"

"What are you talking about? She's dead." My throat closes around the last word.

John turns to face me. "I know. She died. Or that's what we all thought. It was in the papers, on the news..."

"Baby, you're still not making sense."

"When I went down to the basement... my gun was gone."

"*What* gun?" I raise my voice. "We don't have a gun."

"I do," he says quietly. "I'm sorry—I should have told you. I always kept it for protection. And now, well, the irony is not lost on me." His eye line sinks even lower.

"I don't see how this related to Cheryl."

"She was the only one who knew about it—she knew where I kept it."

"But—"

"There was a code on the lock box." His voice breaks. "Cheryl knew the code."

My stomach drops.

"She's alive, Vonny."

Heavy rain pounds against the windshield as my professor haunts my memories. Her sharp tongue. Her experiments on students like me. Her unexpected death. Despite all the cruel ways she toyed with our emotions, John and I still keep her picture, hanging above the main staircase. It serves as a reminder of sorts—my strange way of acknowledging Cheryl's former presence. After all, she is the reason we met.

As we drive to a hotel to stay for the night, I am more fixated on my bruises than what John said. It is not until we turn off the lights that reality hits me. *She's still out there.* I wonder why Cheryl would come back into our orbit after all these years. The thought of where she has been and what her motives might be are enough to rob me of sleep.

Only one thing is certain right now—whoever broke into the house was clearly trying to hurt me. After John falls asleep, I actually begin to fear for my life.

CHAPTER 49

S hortly after the incident, John and I go to our local police station. They file a report but shrug off any concerns about Cheryl being alive.

"They didn't even hear us out," I say.

"Of course not." John looks at me with clouded eyes. "We sound crazy. They have no reason to believe us. I smell my late wife's perfume one night, and suddenly, she's alive? Yeah, right."

"I know." Cheryl's death was documented about five years ago, but we know it can't be anyone else.

"Don't worry. We'll figure this out."

Despite his reassurances, uncertainty dwells in my husband's dismal stare. *Even he needs convincing.*

Once we return home, Wesley helps us install an expensive security system that monitors every inch of the house's perimeter. Its primary function is to put our minds at ease, but unfortunately, neither of us feels safe.

THE MONTHS BLUR TOGETHER like inkblots on a page. Mysterious late-night phone calls plague our landline. John or I always answer on the first few rings, only to hear total silence on the other end. We are unable to trace them. One evening, I hear a muffled voice just before the caller hangs up.

My residency work inevitably takes a backseat to my vicious, all-consuming paranoia. In desperation, I start seeing a psychiatrist.

We discuss my deep-rooted fears, embarrassing secrets, and darkest thoughts.

Any progress I begin to make is stymied by vivid memories of my attack. The sudden onset of violent nightmares renders me hopeless, frantic, and defeated. My doctor prescribes daily medication and a host of sleeping pills. The combination's efficacy is promising at first, but residual side effects leave me in a more fragile state than before.

John notices my anxiety intensifying. "I think you should get away for a little while. I'll take care of the arrangements, but we need to get you out of San Francisco."

"She'll come for me, John. I know she will."

His face falls. "Baby, *I'm* the one who betrayed her. I married you after my 'loving wife' supposedly died. In Cheryl's mind, I'm the one at fault here."

I think about the affairs and shoot him a skeptical look.

"I know." John sighs. "She had a twisted concept of loyalty."

"But she hurt me that night. She was targeting *me*, not you."

"She was trying to send me a message." He puts a hand on mine. "Trust me. Ten years with Cheryl was enough to get inside her head, even just a little bit. The second you leave home, she'll surface. She wants to confront me alone."

I consider his proposition.

"Please, Vonny. I need to end this. Once and for all."

I obsess over the potential outcomes of John's crazy plan every waking day and sleepless night. On one hand, I am terrified of being alone. Especially during a time like this. But on the other, we have to draw Cheryl out somehow. John and I have no clue where she might be hiding or what she wants from us. There is no way to contact her, so this is our only option.

Finally, we decide to move forward. I learn the plan inside and out. John and I talk through hundreds of different scenarios just in case something goes awry. We buy a used car with cash and register it under a different name. I have a burner phone in my purse, along with an unregistered handgun that John taught me to use. Taking these precautions makes me feel like I am stuck inside a twisty thriller. But instead of action and adventure, there is only panic and dread.

⁂

ALMOST A YEAR AFTER the attack, John helps me pack up my car. I spent the previous night watching him sleep, remembering how pleasant our shared life was before Cheryl reappeared and ruined everything. The memories ultimately make my decision easier. If we can settle things with her, I'll get my life back and more. John and I deserve a bright future together.

My husband stands at the front of our garage, lingering before I leave. Everything is in place. He closes the gap between us, pressing his lips to my forehead and holding me tight.

"I love you, Vonny," he whispers. "Everything is going to be okay. I promise."

Tears prick my eyes once I drive away. Both hands clutch the wheel steadily, resisting every urge to turn my car around. I suck in deep breaths and remind myself why this is happening. I am going to Nevada because our lives literally depend on it. This is for us—for John and me.

CHAPTER 50
PRESENT DAY

The tinny sound of the cell door shutting behind me is a soothing one. I've been hoping for the sweet release of that clink ever since I got here, but I'm leaving the jail with far more than I walked in with—my memories. *I am myself again.*

It feels strange to suddenly recall every detail about John, from his gaze to the tone of his voice. I remember just how in love we were. And how much I miss him. Cheryl would probably say that I am in the early stages of grief.

The last thought stops me dead in my tracks. *Cheryl.* She is still out there.

"Something wrong?" the guard asks. I'm grateful that the shift change relieved me of the smug watchdog who only worsened my paranoia.

I shake my head slowly and keep following the new guard. Before long, I'm collecting my possessions in some kind of lobby. I still have no idea why I am being released. Either Wesley worked his magic, or there was not enough evidence to keep me locked up anymore. Maybe it was a combination of both factors.

"Hey," I call after the guard before he leaves. "Do you know why they're letting me go?"

An amused expression flickers across his otherwise grim face. "I heard them talking last night. Apparently the chief of police ordered them to release you. Something about evidence. Lee didn't look very happy when he hung up the phone."

"Huh," I mumble. *Definitely Wesley. But how?*

"Look, just be happy you're free." The guard chuckles and walks away.

I am almost hoping to run into Lee and Ryan on my way out. I consider telling them everything, especially since they have no choice but to believe me now. I can recount the past decade without missing a beat. But I still don't have sufficient evidence that Cheryl murdered John, and I've no desire to go back into the interrogation room after the way the detectives treated me. Part of me wants to flash them an unforgettable look or say something punchy and sarcastic. "Thank you for the visits, gentlemen. I will truly miss our time together." I look over my shoulder in one last attempt to catch a glimpse of them. Unsurprisingly, the detectives are nowhere to be found.

Stark rays blind me momentarily as my eyes readjust to outdoor lighting. Luckily, our dark Rolls Royce is parked right in front of the building. I force a smile and wave while approaching the car. I try to take comfort in the fact that I am going home.

Albert steps out on cue then walks over to open the passenger door for me. "Hello, madam. Pleased to meet you under better circumstances."

I am so thrilled to see a familiar face that I pull him in for a quick hug. "Albert! It's so good to see you."

Although we make small talk during the drive, my mind is somewhere else entirely. I assume that Wesley must have played a central part in my release. For some reason, though, I doubt that I will ever get a full explanation from him.

"Well, look where we are," Albert chimes suddenly. "Gorgeous Pacific Heights. You're nearly home, madam."

I TURN MY KEY AND WALK through the same doorway I have entered a thousand times. This moment should be no different than the rest, and yet it is entirely foreign. The midmorning sun pours into the foyer as I take it all in—the beautiful floor vases, grand spiral staircase, and the photographs of my life with John on display.

I drift through the house, struck by an abundance of memories. Big moments like birthday parties and our first wedding anniversary. Small ones, too, like making s'mores and camping out in the backyard. The moment when we first met so many years ago.

Floating from room to room, I notice little details I previously ignored. Each precious inch of our home is bathed in a sentimental glow. The sight of his favorite picture—an orange sunset from our trip to Italy—sparks unexpected tears. I have known about John's death for weeks, but its impact is fresh and sobering. It feels like the news is just hitting me now. I remember everything about John, and I miss it all.

The landline rings, so I hurry back into the kitchen to answer it.

"Hello?"

"Oh, Vonny." Carol Ann sounds relieved. "Thank God. I've been trying to reach you."

"Hi!" I smile into the phone. Now that I have my memories back, I remember how sweet she always was to me. "I just got home."

"How are you, dear?"

"I finally remember. It sort of happened while I was in jail." I begin to recount events from the past few days, sparing no important detail. It feels comforting, even cathartic, to talk to her again. Carol Ann is as shocked as I was about my arrest. I tell her that the case is stalled, but she does not seem upset.

"I don't even care who did it anymore. My heart is broken. There's no room for spite or revenge."

I know exactly what she means—revenge won't bring John back. But that doesn't mean I'm ready to give up on catching his killer.

Cheryl is still out there, though I don't need to further involve my grieving mother-in-law. *I'll figure this out on my own.*

"I just miss him so much," she whispers.

"I do too."

After we shed some tears together, she says, "Please come visit sometime soon, Vonny. I'd really like to see you."

"I will. I promise."

After our call, I make my way upstairs in hopes of taking a long, hot shower. I want to stand under near-scalding water and wash away memories from the past few days. I kick off my shoes, unbutton my coat, then toss it onto the bed. Then something catches my eye. I freeze. There is a tiny pale paper scroll near my pillow.

My first instinct is to scream, but I settle for looking over my shoulder instead. No one is here—just me. After a few unnerving seconds, I tiptoe over to my side of the bed. I extend my arm slowly as if reaching into the flames of a fire. Then I pick up the scroll and unwrap it.

Clutching the paper between shaky fingers, I read the short message inside. Printed in serif typeface is a San Francisco address.

On the surface, it looks like a simple location. But the address makes my stomach tighten. It's the spot where John proposed to Cheryl so many moons ago—a cliff overlooking the beach. If memory serves, she used to endearingly refer to it as the place where "the ocean meets the sky."

Further examination reveals tiny font near the bottom. I hold the paper closer to my face until I make out the message: *5 a.m. tomorrow. Come alone.*

I hold the note in my hands, weighing my options. Cheryl obviously does not want me to call the police or contact the detectives, but I would be stupid not to loop someone else in.

Lee is the last person I want to talk to, so I dial Ryan's number and leave him a message. My hope is that he receives it with enough time to provide backup tomorrow. All things considered, I know what I need to do. I have to meet Cheryl where the ocean meets the sky.

CHAPTER 51

Early morning arrives before I have fully come to terms with the gravity of my circumstances. Neither detective has called me back, and I am beginning to lose my resolve. I dial Wesley shortly before leaving the house. He has been with me almost every step of the way. Surely, he will know what to do.

"Wesley," I say when reaching his voice mail, "call me back. It's urgent."

Just in case, I text him so he knows exactly where I am headed. Between notifying him and the detectives, I have to believe I won't be alone today. A glance at the clock confirms that I need to leave immediately.

For the first time in months, I drive myself. Our neighborhood is still asleep, leaving me to silently ponder the confrontation looming ahead. *What does Cheryl want with me?* By taking John away, she's already shattered my sense of happiness. She may want to destroy me as well, but I need to hear her confess. More than the evidence of her crimes, I need to understand why. If I cannot face her now, I will always be haunted by strange noises in the dark and mysterious hands at my back.

THE BEACH IS LIFELESS and grayer than cement. The sky is so overcast that I can barely see the figure up ahead. A blurry outline atop the cliff, Cheryl sits squarely on a bench overlooking the ocean, her back to me. I have the growing sense that she knows I am here.

After parking several yards downhill, I reach across the center console for my weapon of choice—a small chef's knife, secured in a protective case. After I stick the sheath in my back pocket and take a deep breath, I dig Cheryl's note out of my purse. Then I open my door tentatively, staring up at the cliff ahead. Cheryl's silhouette is crisp against a mound of clouds.

The starkness of this landscape is nothing but ominous. A dark sky smudging into darker water. I trudge up the hill, trying to steady my breathing as I go. Cheryl remains completely still while I approach. There is no sign of how she got here—no car or bicycle in tow. I did not notice any bus stops nearby, and I doubt she would take a taxi.

Brandishing the scroll, I step close behind her. "Hello, Cheryl."

She does not even look at me.

"I remember everything," I begin. "Every single thing. And I know exactly what you did."

Still, there is no response.

"Are you really going to ignore me?" My voice cuts over the wind.

When she does not react, I walk around the bench to face her. Then I scream. Cheryl sits lifeless, blood trickling down her scalp and a vacancy in her eyes.

"Cheryl?" I whisper, knowing full well that she is dead. I muster the strength to check for a pulse anyway. *Nothing.* The sight of the body is sickening, but I cannot peel my eyes away.

I haven't seen her since the investigation ramped up—since she fled my house in the middle of our conversation. Despite what the detectives believe, I'm certain now that I did not imagine her being there. The woman in my house that day was no vision or ghost. That's when I realize it—smack in the middle of studying her flawless, bloodstained face. This woman is not Cheryl Lewis.

The resemblance is uncanny. They could almost be twins, but with my memories intact, the disparity is clear as day. *Who is she?*

My shock has not even started to wear off when I hear someone approaching. I whip around to see a familiar figure walking toward me.

RELIEF FLOODS ME. "WESLEY! You got my message?"

"Hello, madam." The composure in his voice makes me realize how fast my heart is beating.

"I-I don't know what's going on. I came here to meet Cheryl, and—"

"I see you received my message."

When a blank look crosses my face, he gestures to the paper scroll in my hand.

"I don't understand," I tell him. "What do you—"

He lets out a haughty laugh. "Oh, Veronica."

Wesley laughing at all is odd enough, but him using my first name is entirely unnerving.

"You left the note? Why? What are you doing?"

"Tying up a few loose ends. *You've* been a particularly exhausting one."

His words hit me like tiny bullets. *He's not here to help me.* The cavalier way he eyes the bloodied corpse beside us freezes me in place. "But Cheryl... she was..."

"You'll be disappointed to know that Cheryl Lewis is long dead. She was killed in a fire six years ago."

"But she... Cheryl came to my house, and—" Then I remember that the woman that day wasn't my professor at all. I haven't felt this much brain fog since I woke up in that Nevada hospital. *Cheryl really is dead.* My head swivels between Wesley and the impersonator's body propped on the bench. "What do you know? Who is she?"

Wesley chuckles. "Local talent. It's amazing what you can find on Craigslist. Two thousand dollars for the whole job."

My throat goes dry. "You hired her? Why?"

Wesley takes a small step toward me. "Don't you understand? I needed to make you look insane."

I look at him through lost eyes. *Why is he doing this?*

"Let's go back a bit, shall we?" He paces near the bench, looking smug as ever. "You'd never guess it now, but I come from the other side of the tracks. A far cry from the posh life you and John have." He pauses for a moment. "Well, *had.*"

"So it's all about money." A sour taste fills my mouth.

He merely shrugs.

"All these years..." It takes a moment, but I find my voice again. "You were just taking advantage of John—exploiting him."

"Actually, John made most of his money once he married Cheryl." He emphasizes her name with a wave of his hand. "Now *she* was my golden ticket. Cheryl had a small fortune before they got married. I worried briefly about a prenup, but she was as blindly in love with John as he was with her."

"So you stole from them?" I ask, fighting back the urge to scream.

A knowing look flickers across Wesley's face. "Something like that." He unfastens his watch then places it in his coat pocket.

"And then Cheryl died."

Wesley eyes me with a cryptic expression. "No. And then *you* came into the picture. You caused quite the divide between John and Cheryl." His stare seems to burn straight through me. "The affairs were one thing, but there was something about you that she just couldn't get past. It was her tragic undoing."

Memories of my last conversation with Cheryl race through my mind. Though Wesley's confession relieves me of some of the guilt I feel over her death, her anger with me was apparently very real. My heart aches. *I never wanted this.*

"They decided to separate because of you. But I couldn't let them get divorced. Cheryl would have taken half of everything, and John was noble enough to give her every asset she brought to the table in the first place."

I have to strain to hear him over the wind roaring in my ears. A thunderclap threatens to rip open the darkening clouds as he continues.

"So I killed her." Wesley says it so matter-of-factly that it takes a minute for the realization to hit me.

"*You* killed Cheryl?"

"Such a pity. I always liked her," he says with a far-off look in his eyes. "But there were just too many assets involved." Wesley removes his coat and folds it neatly in half. Then he drapes it over the bench, pausing only to ruffle the corpse's blond hair.

My stomach pitches. An hour ago, I thought of this man as a genuine friend. But it doesn't take long for me to see Wesley for what he really is—a money-hungry, murderous criminal. He even seems to delight in revealing his true colors.

"John inherited everything once she died, and all was right in the world," he says crisply. "That is, until he married you. Even *I* didn't see that coming. The whole thing was so unlike him."

John's voice, his blue eyes, and his gentle touch fill my senses. "We loved each other."

"Sure, John was enamored, but *I* saw things clearly. Somebody had to." He scoffs. "I knew that his fortune would immediately become your private pool to dip into whenever you so pleased."

"John trusted you. *We* trusted you."

"Well, I didn't trust *you*. And that, my dear, was an issue. I couldn't have you going around sticking your nose into John's finances. After all, you might have noticed a few discrepancies and reported me to your clueless husband."

My shock begins to dissolve, giving way to anger.

"I eventually realized that there was no point in killing you. John would just remarry again and again and again." He rolls his eyes. "So I discovered a brilliant little loophole."

The rain starts, but Wesley shows no signs of stopping his diatribe.

"I just needed to make you believe that Cheryl was still alive. Messing with you both was simple enough. There was one night when you were alone—"

My stomach drops. It all starts to make sense. "You were the one who pushed me down the stairs."

"So you *do* remember?" He sounds surprised.

"I do now. What about the perfume?"

"Easy enough to procure." He shrugs. "I knew John would recognize his late wife's signature scent. He was so hung up on thinking Cheryl was still alive—more than you ever knew."

"You're lying."

"Am I?" he asks, taken aback. "John had me hire a private investigator to look into the fire. Even years later, he wouldn't give up on his crazy theory. Part of him still couldn't accept her death. That woman really did a number on him, didn't she?"

I glare at Wesley through damp lashes.

"John was already suspicious enough on his own. So with just a few clever sprays of perfume—plus the stolen gun, of course—he had no choice but to believe Cheryl was still alive."

My reality shatters even further.

"I knew John well enough to realize that he would want you out of harm's way. Again with the steadfast nobility."

"You wanted to get him alone."

Wesley nods. "With John out of the picture, everything would go to you. I knew that you would be a wreck after he died, flailing about with no idea what to do. Naturally, you would keep me on as your trustworthy advisor." He releases an eerie laugh. "And I would be able to continue siphoning off funds in peace."

"How could you?" I ask as tears prick my eyes. "John thought of you as a friend."

"A *friend*? I was glorified help." Wesley's voice rises.

"You're wrong!"

"No," he says through gritted teeth. "John was no more to me than a benevolent master."

"So you did kill him, then?" The words leave my mouth as a half question, half statement. "You killed John."

Wesley nods again. "Obviously."

Somehow, hearing him say it makes the truth pack a harder punch. I choke on quiet sobs as the pit in my stomach deepens.

"Unfortunately, my plan to make John's death look accidental proved difficult. I ended up shooting him with his own weapon."

Another creepy laugh makes me jump.

"So I had to adjust my plan a bit. The next step was getting you convicted for his murder." A glimmer flits across his face. "I came up with it so quickly. You had amnesia and couldn't remember anything. I realized that I could plant evidence and make you look guilty." Wesley pauses to roll up his shirtsleeves. "You would be out of my way—neatly tied up in prison. Then I, as your principal financial advisor, would have had no issue moving assets around."

I scan through the last several weeks, wondering exactly what else he did. "Did you orchestrate the lawsuit with Marshall?"

"Heavens, no." Wesley scoffs. "That pathetic attempt was *his* and his alone." He sighs. "I did get rather lucky on that front, though, didn't I? Gaining your trust and all."

My mind continues scrutinizing the recent past. One unanswered mystery comes screaming to the forefront. "The laptop."

Wesley nods. "You should really get those locks checked, madam."

The blood drains from my face.

"It was so funny to watch when you found it again in that very same drawer. Your reaction was priceless—catnip for any skeptical detective."

"You... you were watching me then?" The thought makes me cringe.

"Constantly. I've had cameras in the place for ages."

So much for our state-of-the-art security system.

"The pills were a nice touch, don't you think?" His eyes light up. "You had all this medication in your little cabinet, just waiting to be played with."

"You drugged me?"

Wesley gasps, feigning alarm. "Oh, madam. All I did was provide the means for you to drug yourself. All I did was mix in a little of this and a little of that."

Another pang of anger strikes. *He really did make me look insane.* The actress, the laptop, and the pills. It was all Wesley's doing.

He relishes my reaction. "Those detectives really started to doubt you, didn't they? Especially Lee. He was just perfect. Suspicious of you from the very beginning. My kind of officer. Which brings me to her," he says, pointing to the dead woman on the bench. "Since you somehow managed to get out of jail, I've been forced to think up yet another plan."

I meet Wesley's smug stare. "I'm not giving you another penny, you bastard."

"Well, well, look who's finally woken up." He looks at me expectantly.

"Whatever you're planning, it won't work." I roll my shoulders back as I speak, trying to project an air of confidence.

"I think I liked you better without your memories. You were much more pleasant." He cocks his head and takes a menacing step toward me. "Here's the plan: First, I toss this corpse over the cliff. Then I do the same to you."

The rain pricks my lids while Wesley talks. I swipe away droplets and attempt to calm my breathing. I never viewed Wesley as a physical threat, but the person standing in front of me is stronger and taller than I remember.

"I-I already called the police!" My voice strains against the wind. "I told them everything."

"Oh, madam." He waves my statement off like an afterthought. "I think we both know that you've lost your credibility with the authorities. Besides—" He gestures to the remote landscape. "If someone was really coming, they would certainly be here already."

"You won't get away with this!" The waves crash beneath us. "They'll figure it out."

"But that's the brilliant thing! There's nothing to figure out. You jumped, remember?"

The wind burns my ears, and his words cut into me like blades.

"The pressure got to you," he continues. "The guilt. Your husband's murder. And you just couldn't take it anymore, could you?"

My heart thuds against my rib cage as Wesley takes another step closer. I inch backward, nearly losing my footing. I must be getting dangerously close to the cliff's edge. I don't dare look, though. My attention is completely fixed on the man across from me.

Wesley comes within two feet of me, and my whole body stiffens.

"It was so generous of you to divide up your assets the way you did. Some will go to your in-laws, of course, but who are we kidding? You have no family or friends of your own—nobody to look after. Most of the money will go to me."

"That's n-not true!" I shout through chattering teeth. My clothes are sopping wet, and my hair is plastered to the sides of my face. Rain continues to pelt my icy skin.

"Oh, but it is, my dear." He flashes an indulgent smile. "It's all right there in your will."

He is going to kill me. I maintain eye contact, reminding myself of the weapon in my back pocket. Wesley remains quiet, no doubt sizing me up. The rain and waves boom in my ears as my heartbeat picks up speed. Each sound amplifies until I cannot distinguish one from the next.

I have to keep my head—distract him until I can get the knife ready. "Why are you telling me all this?"

He straightens a little. "Hmm. I might have wasted my breath explaining all of this to you, but I've always fancied myself a bit of a showman."

My hand is almost to my back pocket when Wesley's body coils again.

"Besides," he says, "it's been a true pleasure watching your demise." Then he lunges.

All I can do is react. I hurl myself to the side on pure instinct before he can push me over the cliff. Backpedaling, I try to reach for the knife again, but Wesley is coming at me with too much speed. I am able to evade him once again, but then he charges forward again, his dark eyes nothing but rage and frenzy. In that split second, I see the blade is already in my hand. I plunge it into his body.

He cries out, trying to grab hold of me. I stab him again. It feels like someone else is gripping the knife, turning its bloody blade while I watch. Adrenaline courses through me as I put more distance between us, but the damage from the knife is not enough to stop him.

The next time he comes at me, I can't get the blade up quickly enough. Instead, I dive headfirst in the other direction.

What happens next does not occur in slow motion like I have been led to believe. Nothing dramatic or drawn out. It all happens relatively fast. I do not even see Wesley go over the edge. But I do hear his unmistakably haunting scream. The wind swallows it up, and in the next instant, the sea drowns it out.

LEE AND RYAN TAKE MY statement in full before sending me home for the night. This time, I am able to provide my entire story, including the last nine years. It won't take them long to find the tangible evidence of Wesley's crimes once I give them John's financial records.

To my surprise, Lee musters up an apology in the eleventh hour. Though lackluster and a bit contrived, his words are appreciated. I shake his hand before turning to Ryan.

"You've been through quite an ordeal, Mrs. Lewis," the young detective says. "Please take good care of yourself."

"I will," I assure him before heading out. "Thank you."

I should feel safe now. The house is undisturbed. Wesley is gone, and no one is going to hurt me anymore. I am alive. Still, it is difficult to reconcile the fact that it was never Cheryl coming after me. It has just been her ghost this entire time.

CHAPTER 52

I am nothing short of distracted while boarding my evening flight. It has been two weeks since that fatal confrontation, but I am no longer considered a person of interest after Lee and Ryan uncovered Wesley's paper trail. Though I am a free woman, the cliff incident lives at the forefront of my mind, bleeding into every thought and dream. Wesley lives there too. Honestly, it's as if he never died.

"The average person has thirteen secrets right now." I remember Cheryl's words while making my way through the stuffy A320 parked at San Francisco International Airport. A flight attendant pastes a sweet smile onto her pink lips, but the exhausted look in her eyes belies some hidden worry.

From his padded seat in the fourth row, an older man sips a mixed drink and stares out the window. I can only guess who he's thinking about as his wife hunches over a dog-eared paperback novel, nursing her tiny glass of what I assume is spiked orange juice.

Unlike its upscale counterpart, the economy section has neither predeparture alcoholic drinks nor hints of tranquility. I count at least two crying babies—make it three—before even approaching the first exit row. I am hesitant to make eye contact with anyone as I continue moving slowly down the aisle.

When the line comes to a standstill, I check my cell. No messages. No missed calls. A fleeting wave of relief runs through me after sticking my phone away. I glance up when the line still hasn't moved. A preteen boy is trying to hurl his carry-on into an overhead bin, which is several feet above his head. The woman in front of him turns around to help, and I feel my entire body brace when I see the perfect blond waves of her hair. I relax slightly when my brain registers that I have never seen her face before. Somehow, though, her features are all too familiar—rosy lips, deep-blue eyes, and sharp cheekbones.

When I finally reach the back of the plane, I am grateful to find three empty seats. I cram my purse under the seat in front of me while praying that I will have the row entirely to myself. There is medication in my purse, but even with that, I am not sure that I can handle any type of conversation until more time passes. Light banter still seems too risky. It might lead to subjects that I wouldn't want broached—topics I simply cannot discuss.

This plane is filled with strangers. Unfortunately, I am now seated beside two of them. My gaze remains plastered to the blank TV screen ahead while they buckle their seat belts. As curious as I am, any urge to introduce myself pales in comparison to my heightened anxiety. I conjure up an image of each seatmate instead. My imagination runs wild, creating personalities, identities, and hypothetical histories.

My own history is as twisted as they come. I fell prey to my professor's manipulative tactics, only to gain perspective shortly before she was murdered. I eventually married her husband. These events set into motion a series that none of us could have predicted.

Even though I survived, my fear did not die with Wesley. Instead, it morphed into an obsession about what happened on the cliff. About what led me to that exact moment. It is the precise reason I crave the anonymity of an economy seat over the personalized experience of first class.

"The average person has thirteen secrets right now." Cheryl's voice runs through my head again as the flight attendants perform their safety briefing. "Safe" is such a subjective term—entirely open to interpretation. I have not felt safe for as long as I can remember.

When we taxi to the runway, my paranoia swells, intensifies. I try desperately to steady my breathing.

As we ascend into the shadowy night sky, I wonder if any other passengers are harboring secrets as dark as mine. I tell myself that this concern is mostly irrational. That does little to mitigate the fear entrenched in my core. The revelation that Wesley was hiding in plain sight leaves me irrevocably paranoid. He stole for years, spied on John and me, then went after us one by one. And I trusted him until the very end.

In search of a distraction, I begin scrolling through photos on my phone. The digital images are crisp and saturated. I see mundane and monumental moments—snapshots of John and me during our short time together. I miss my husband.

I look at a few more pictures, reminiscing, before opening my messaging app. A recent text from Abby brings a welcome smile to my face. After the memories came flooding back, I finally understood everything that happened between us. Then I apologized properly. We spoke for hours—nostalgic and teary-eyed—before agreeing on a visit.

I am headed to New York right now. This trip—and this trip alone—is important enough to draw me out of any self-imposed isolation. Abby and I will catch up and return to our old stomping grounds. I will finally get to meet her husband, Nick. Things definitely won't be the same. Honestly, though, I am okay with that. My hope is that our relationship will eventually supersede what it once was.

I close my eyes and draw in a deep breath. The engine vibrates under my feet, humming rhythmically while an overhead vent streams air across my face. I cannot rewrite the past, nor would I want to. So many awful events occurred during the past nine years. Despite all the loss, though, there is a great deal I have gained.

I graduated with honors, earned my PhD, moved to two new cities, and became a licensed psychiatrist. I got back my best friend—someone who always felt like family. Though I lost John, I have a home filled with beloved memories of the man I loved deeply. Once I return from New York, my plan is to start working again. I vow to focus on the bright spots—the stars amidst darkness. Much like this airplane I am traveling in, all I can do now is keep moving forward. In the end, that's all any of us can do.

Acknowledgments

Although writing is often a solitary act, producing quality books requires a skilled team. I am fortunate enough to work with a phenomenal group of steadfast and talented people. Without them, this novel would simply not be possible.

I want to thank my friends and family for supporting me on this wild ride. To my husband, Chris, my first and forever beta reader—I adore you. To my parents, Suzanne and Derrick, who always buoyed my loftiest ambitions with love and encouragement—your unwavering faith in me means more than I can properly express. To Sami, who cheers me on with an unrivaled enthusiasm that only a sister can muster—making you proud is priceless.

To my agent, Liza Fleissig, who championed this story from the very beginning—your dedication, positivity, and sheer hard work helped find *Last Liar Standing* the most incredible home. Thank you for believing in my manuscript so staunchly.

To Lynn McNamee, the owner of Red Adept Publishing—thank you for taking a chance on *Last Liar Standing* and this young author. Your experience, passion, and wit truly set Red Adept apart. It has been a joy to work with such a remarkable editing team: Sara N. Gardiner, Marirose Smith, Lynne Cantwell, and Irene Steiger were all instrumental in bringing *Last Liar Standing* to fruition. You four are legitimate rock stars. Thank you for doing this story justice.

To the folks at Streetlight Graphics, who dreamed up an enviable cover, thank you for your creativity and precision.

Finally, thank you to the marvelous network of authors I have gotten to know along the way. I count myself lucky just to be part of this literary community.

About the Author

Danielle M. Wong has never met an adventure she did not love. She began traveling at a young age, developed a permanent case of wanderlust, and never looked back. Each place possessed a singular kind of thrill and sparked a unique feeling—a sentiment she aspired to immortalize through her writing. An extended visit to England inspired Danielle's debut novel, *Swearing Off Stars*. The book was published to critical acclaim, winning an Independent Press Award, a Benjamin Franklin Award, and an International Book Award, among others.

Author by day and reader by night, she enjoys creating and consuming all forms of media. Danielle's work has appeared in *Harper's Bazaar*, *The Huffington Post*, *PopSugar*, and *Writer's Digest*. She has multiple short stories published in the Be the Star You Are! series and is currently writing her next novel.

Read more at https://daniellemwong.com/.

About the Publisher

Dear Reader,

We hope you enjoyed this book. Please consider leaving a review on your favorite book site.

Visit https://RedAdeptPublishing.com to see our entire catalogue.

Don't forget to subscribe to our monthly newsletter to be notified of future releases and special sales.

CPSIA information can be obtained
at www.ICGtesting.com
Printed in the USA
LVHW111605140622
721231LV00004B/128

9 781948 051965